Second Coming

D. B. BORTON

Copyright © 2017 Lynette Carpenter

Published by Boomerang Books

This book is a work of fiction. The names, characters, businesses, places, events, and incidents are either the products of the author's imagination or used in a fictitious manner. Any resemblance to actual persons, living or dead, or actual events is purely coincidental.

All rights reserved. No part of this book may be used or reproduced in any form whatsoever without written permission from the author.

Print ISBN: 978-0-692-83514-2
E-book ISBN: 978-0-692-86339-8

DEDICATION

To Rob, for his big heart,
and in loving memory of
M.J., B., and C.,
who showed me the way to go home

CONTENTS

ACKNOWLEDGMENTS

I'd like to thank my research assistant and D.C. tour guide, Carol Blum. I'd also like to thank Robert Flanagan for his editorial comments.

CHAPTER ONE

I wasn't kidnapped by aliens. That line sells tabloids, but it wasn't true.

No, I went with the aliens of my own free will.

The night it happened I was drinking in this bar I go to sometimes. The place was too far from downtown to be popular with college students, and that's why I go there, especially when I'm feeling low. My dissertation, a semiotic study of package labeling in the United States (1946 to 1959), was bogged down in the third chapter, and I'd been avoiding my dissertation director, who also happened to be sleeping with my ex-girlfriend Anita. Spring Break would be over in one short week, which meant I'd soon be facing a roomful of freshly tanned freshmen, bored, hung over, or buzzed, who would write me papers that began, "Their are many problem's in todays American society."

Before me on the bar, the rings of water left by my beer mug arranged themselves into patterns, and as time passed, these patterns seemed to take on a profundity of their own. I had tuned out the drama of March Madness, 2007 edition, hung suspended from the ceiling nearby, the clink of glasses, and the drone of the crowd behind me, even when it rose to a roar in response to something happening on the screen. I was repressing, for the moment, my anxieties about world peace, the wars in Iraq and Afghanistan, global warming, the state of the economy, the nuclear weapons Korea might be developing, the nuclear weapons we had already developed, the genocide in Sudan, the proliferation of natural disasters, the threat of terrorism, and the prospect of new weapons of mass destruction. I was indulging in self-pity, luxuriating in it like a heavy fur coat.

The guy next to me leaned over an empty stool and spoke.

"Forgive me," he said.

I looked up at him. I took in the Bud Light on the bar, the cell phone he held pressed to his ear. I could hear a voice in it, chirping. Beneath the heavy odor of cigarette smoke and beer, I caught a whiff of something, soft as a whisper yet so powerfully evocative that I was momentarily knocked loose from ordinary time. Pipe tobacco, yes, and something else—an elusive scent of aftershave, familiar to me as my own heartbeat and yet, I couldn't place it. I almost missed what he said next.

"Pardon me," he said. The cell phone chirped again.

"Excuse me," he said.

You probably think that his eyes glowed with x-ray vision or something, but he looked like a normal guy. Actually, he looked a lot like Alec Guinness—the young Alec Guiness, with a face open and expressionless as wallpaper paste.

"Yeah?" I said.

The crowd thundered its disapproval of something, and his eyes shifted, then returned to my face. He was wearing a gray suit and narrow dark tie in a place that ran to work shirts, bowling shirts and Hoosier apparel. On the bar in front of him sat a gray fedora. I was wearing dirty jeans, a hooded sweatshirt, and sneakers. Tonight, the eve of St. Patrick's Day, the bar was awash in red, not green; I.U. was playing U.C.L.A. in the second round of the West Regionals. My neighbor outclassed everything in the joint, including the scotch.

"Could you tell me, please, what state we're in?" He spoke pleasantly with a refined but restrained accent, possibly British, that went well with the suit. I could see now that he wasn't that young, but he had the kind of face that was hard to pin down. Forties, maybe?

"I don't know about you, man," I said, "but I'm in a state of depression, in transit to a state of intoxication." Bars bring out the worst in me, and depression wasn't helping. I was a walking cliché.

He studied me a minute. "Excuse me," he said. "I was speaking geographically."

"Oh, geographically." It had been two beers, maybe three, since I'd had the occasion to speak to anybody and I noticed that my tongue was getting in the way. "Let me give you a hint. See that TV set up there? The one that everybody in this place is watching except you and me?"

He glanced at the television and nodded.

"What game are they playing on that TV?" I asked. With the freshmen gone, it had been a while since I'd instigated a Socratic dialogue, and I thought I might have more success with an adult, anyway. Socrates had never faced a twenty-first-century eighteen-year-old, or he would have taken the hemlock sooner.

"It appears to be basketball," he said, cautious.

"Very good," I said. "Therefore, we must be in the state of —?"

He looked at me in some consternation, then muttered something into his cell phone. The phone twittered briefly and fell silent.

"That's okay," I said. "I'm just being a prick. You're English, aren't you? Look, we're in the state of Indiana."

Enlightenment smoothed his brow. "Ah, Indiana! Home of the Indianapolis Five Hundred. The Crossroads of America." He nodded soberly. "Indiana."

"Yeah, that's right," I said encouragingly. "Except the Five Hundred takes place in May, and this is March. That means it's playoff time. Sweet Sixteen time. NCAA Championships. March Madness."

"Championships," he repeated. "I see. Could you tell me, please, how far we are from the state of D.C.?"

I shook my head. "D.C., man, that's a state of mind. A whole different ballgame. Out here in the sticks, we're light years away from D.C."

He stared at me, then something shifted in his face and he said, "You're making a joke, is that right?"

"Yeah, that's right," I said. "I'm a real comedian tonight. Sorry."

He smiled indulgently. "Not at all," he said.

The bartender drifted over and picked up my empty mug. I nodded at him.

"Listen, can I ask you a personal question?" I leaned closer to the Englishman. When he didn't back away, I continued. "How can you stand to drink that light beer crap? I mean, I know you're probably used to drinking it warm, being from England and all, but that stuff is crap."

He frowned at his bottle and glass. "I didn't know what to order. You see, I haven't drunk a beer in a very long time."

The bartender set my mug down. "Bring another draft for my friend here," I said to him. I slid over to the stool next to the Brit, and spoke to him confidentially. "We should really be drinking a German bock or a microbrew, or even a Killian's, seeing as how it's Saint Paddy's day. But they don't have any of that here. You could get it in town, but then you'd have to put up with the students."

The bartender set a mug in front of him. I watched him take a tentative sip. "It's very tasty," he said. He plucked a napkin from a nearby dispenser and dabbed at his upper lip.

"You bet it is," I said, and slapped him on the back.

He took another swig and smiled at me. "Now, about D.C.," he said. "How would one get there from here? To Washington, specifically?"

"You want to go to Washington?" I asked. "You a protester?"

He frowned. "I'm not at liberty—," he began.

I flapped a hand at him. "Never mind, you want to go there," I said. "What you want to do is take I-70 east to Breezewood—."

"Breezewood," he echoed.

"Town of Motels," I said. "In Breezewood, you catch I-95 south, and it takes you right to the Beltway."

"The Beltway," he repeated with some uncertainty.

"That's the freeway around D.C.," I explained.

"Would that be the Circumferential Highway?"

I shook my head. "The Beltway." I put down my coaster in front of him, then drew a circle around it with condensation from my mug. "It's kind of like a semi-permeable barrier, you know, like a, like a—a cell wall. You know about cells, right? Building blocks of life?"

"Yes." He smiled as if the question amused him a little.

"Right, well, the Beltway is like a cell wall. It keeps a lot of stuff from getting into the city where the government is."

"You mean, I won't be able to enter the city?"

"No, no, you'll get in all right," I said. "Paying customers are welcome, especially if you're in the market for tee-shirts, Washington Monument thermometers, miniature Smithsonian reproductions of eighteenth-century chamber pots, shit like that. It's ideas and opinions they want to keep out. Objections to the way they're running the show. You don't have any of those, do you?"

"Yes, I do," he said.

"So you are a protester," I said.

You'll say I should have considered the other option. You'll say that in these days of vigilance against terrorism, I should have notified the FBI immediately. It never crossed my mind that he could be a terrorist. I'd read that the 9/11 guys had caroused a lot before their mission, and talked about the bevy of babes they expected to encounter in heaven. This guy looked more like a middle manager at a company that made widgets—a guy whose heaven would not be overpopulated with babes. Plus, he had a British accent, and the Brits are supposed to be our allies. But what did I know?

"Well, more power to you," I said. I was feeling light-headed. I'd been keeping to myself, avoiding my friends. And after all that solitude, I was warming to the company of this British stranger.

"It's not power I want," he said.

"Just an expression," I said. "Anyway, don't listen to me. Just get on the Beltway and follow the signs into the city."

"Oh," he said. "And this I-70 and I-95, those are interstate highways?"

"Yep." I picked up the salt shaker and made a long line of salt on the bar in front of us. "We're here," I said, tapping the bar with my fingertip below the line, "and Indianapolis is here." I touched the line of salt. "You follow that all the way through Ohio and West Virginia and Pennsylvania." I made another line of salt perpendicular to the first line.

"Breezewood?" he asked, pointing to the intersection.

I nodded.

He followed the new line of salt to the end. "Washington?"

I beamed at him. How I'd missed intelligent adult conversation!

"I am extremely grateful to you," he said, licking the salt off his finger. "I hope I haven't bothered you."

"Nah." I waved away his gratitude. "I was just sitting here, drowning my problems."

"You have problems?" he said.

I signaled the bartender for another round and told him. He hadn't finished the last round, so maybe I was buying his time. He was a good listener. Some of his questions were pretty basic, but others were truly sensitive and profound—or at least, they seemed so at the time. He wanted to know what a dissertation was, and a dissertation director, and once we got that squared away, he asked if it was customary to have sex with one's dissertation director, since my dissertation director also happened to be Anita's as well. That was a hard question to answer; it took a lot of explaining.

"Perhaps that is why you're having difficulty with your dissertation," he ventured. "When you work on your dissertation, you are reminded of your former girlfriend, and you become angry and sad. Then you have difficulty concentrating."

I know now that the reason I got stuck on my dissertation was that I'd picked a lame topic, but in the alcoholic haze of my melancholy that night, what the Englishman said struck me like an epiphany. I barely noticed that his consonants were starting to liquefy from the beer he was floating them in. The guy was definitely not a hardened drinker.

"Jesus!" I said. "I bet you're right!"

Then he asked me to explain what my dissertation was about, and I started in on that, but I hadn't gotten far when he asked me to explain what semiotics was. So I blathered on about signs and representation and meaning, and did a few semiotic interpretations of the labels on the whiskey bottles lined up behind the bar, and the bottle of ketchup on the bar in front of us.

"It's rather like mathematics, isn't it?" he said. "But—well, more amusing and less practical."

"I wouldn't call it impractical," I said, but I hadn't taken offense. If he'd pressed me, I would have admitted that the primary use of semiotics, as far as I could see, was to provide me with a dissertation topic and afterward, if I was very lucky, a university teaching job in an American Studies department, preferably west of Dubai. But in the interest of demonstrating its practicality, I turned on my stool to look around for something else to interpret. That's when I spotted the new arrival.

He was the tallest human being I'd ever seen, on or off a basketball court, but broad-shouldered, like an offensive lineman. He had just walked in, and stood with his back to me, so I could see only his silhouette. He stood with his legs apart, scanning the room, and the pose seemed familiar to me somehow. Then he turned in my direction. He was wearing a sport coat that looked like it had been cut from a charcoal plaid tablecloth, an open-necked gray textured shirt, and black pants. Wavy dark hair combed back from his forehead gleamed under the artificial light. He wore long sideburns. Deep-set eyes drooped sleepily under long lashes, until he saw us, and then they opened wide. He smiled, the left side of his upper lip lifting like a lopsided stage curtain over a nice set of teeth and a full lower lip. Semiotics would be wasted on him. The King had returned as Bigfoot.

I rapped the Englishman on the elbow with my knuckles. "Hey, man," I said, watching the tall man advance toward us. "You got a friend? Tall dude looks like Elvis Presley on growth hormones?"

CHAPTER TWO

The tall guy reached us as the Englishman turned around. The Englishman didn't seem all that happy to see his buddy, which dimmed the wattage on the tall guy's smile. Now that he was close, he didn't look all that much like Elvis Presley. Or rather, he looked more like an Elvis impersonator than like the King himself. His crooked smile pushed his cheeks up under his eyes and gave him kind of a goofy look.

"I've been waiting a long time," he said to the Englishman, a little reproachfully, I thought. "I came to find you."

"That's my fault," I said. "He was letting me bend his ear. Tell you the truth, we're both a little bit soused."

The tall one's smile wavered, and he glanced at the Englishman's ear.

"My traveling companion," the Englishman said with a gesture in the tall man's direction.

"Elvis," the tall man supplied and shook my hand. He had to bend over, like a gorilla greeting a flea. "I'm real pleased to meet you."

He had an odd accent, too. His words were stretched out in a drawl and then snipped off at the ends, like sausage links. I began to wonder if these guys were from some former British colony—New Zealand, maybe, or Newfoundland or the Falklands—someplace with its own quirky dialect and accent.

"Henry," I said. "Go by Hank." I offered my hand to the other stranger as well, and he took it, though he almost missed the opportunity because he was glaring at Elvis.

"My name's Smith," he said. "Lawrence."

"Mr. Henry," Elvis repeated.

I shook my head. "Just Henry. Hank."

"Like Henry Wadsworth Longfellow," Elvis said. "'By the shores of Gitchee Gumee—,'" he recited. "And Henry Ford! And the bald boy in the funny papers—the funniest living American."

"Plenty of Henrys," I agreed. "Plenty of Lawrences. But not many Elvises."

"I know," he agreed happily. He slid onto the barstool next to me, tucking his long legs under the bar by bending his knees. "What are we drinking, cats?"

I ordered him a draft.

"Did you tell Lawrence how to find D.C.?" he asked.

"'S all right here," I said, and tapped my fingertip on the bar. But the lines weren't as straight as they had been, and Lawrence's elbow was white. "Hey!" I pointed at his elbow. "You've wiped out Breezewood. You can't get there without going through Breezewood! You can't get anywhere without going through Breezewood."

Lawrence squinted at the bar. "And where, I might ask, did Indianapolis go?"

He had a hard time with "Indianapolis," but that was understandable under the circumstances. There were a few syllables left over when he finally got it out.

"Aww, Indianapolis isn't worth bothering about," I said. "Best thing is to go around it." I saw his syllables and raised him two. I leaned down and blew away the remains of Indianapolis, then traced the quarter-circle of I 465 in pepper.

Elvis took a sip of beer. "Very delicious," he said. "It appears to contain a great deal of air." He looked down the bar. "Do they have Cracker Jacks?" he asked hopefully.

There was a commotion all around us. Lawrence, who, from his expression after two beers, showed all the signs of sliding into depression as well, didn't even look up. Elvis did, and noticed the television screen suspended above the bar to our left.

"Basketball!" he said. "I love this game. Bill Spivey is swell." He produced the last word like a parlor trick.

A short, stubble-studded dark-haired man sitting at the bar on our right made a noise. "Bill Spivey was arrested for point-shaving," he said to the fly-specked mirror behind the bar. "Him and his pals cost the Wildcats their next season."

"No!" Elvis turned to look at him. "When did this happen?"

The man regarded him with amusement. "Couple years before you tried on your first blue-suede shoes, Sonny," he said. "Nineteen fifty-one."

"I find this difficult to believe!" Elvis declared. "What is this 'point-shaving'?" he asked me.

Down the bar to our left, a youngish guy wearing a bowling shirt and a blond ponytail said, "Spivey was framed, man. He wasn't even convicted. Fuckin' shame he never made it to the N.B.A."

I started to explain, but I couldn't be heard now above the din of Hoosiermania.

"Who's playing in this game?" Elvis shouted in my ear.

"Hoosiers and Bruins," I said. Then, recalling how clueless his sidekick was, I added, "Indiana and U.C.L.A."

But he surprised me. "John Wooden's team," he said, nodding. "He is a swell coach."

Indiana's Stemler hit a three-pointer and the room was on its feet.

"Your friend doesn't seem much interested in basketball," I said to Elvis.

He leaned down again to shout in my ear. "He's missing his family. He hasn't seen them in millennia. He's always like this when he drinks alcohol. He forgets to remember to forget." He turned his attention back to the television. "But why did that team get three points for that basket?"

I explained about the three-point line, rather pleased to be asked a question I could answer. Inspired by the stranger's interest, I was finally beginning to catch some of the enthusiasm around me. Indiana was trailing, but the game was close, with less than two minutes to the final buzzer.

U.C.L.A.'s Afflalo hit two free throws. Amid the groans and the curses, one voice with a Southern drawl was heard to say, "Oh, he made both of them! That was swell!"

A few heads near us turned, but with thirty-eight seconds to go now, most eyes were glued to the television. In front of the Indiana bench, Stemler was struggling to get the ball in-bounds, when U.C.L.A.'s Collison got a hand on it and stole it, drawing a desperation foul from Calloway.

"Oh, look!" Elvis had risen from his bar stool in excitement. His height seemed to give added volume to his voice. "A steal! Wow!" In the silence that dropped like a guillotine, he was the only one clapping.

I took one look at the faces turned in our direction, and got a grip on the big man's elbow. "Come on," I said. "Time to go."

"But the game isn't over, Hank," he protested.

"It is over," I said. "Trust me."

With my free hand, I set Lawrence's hat on his head and took hold of his sleeve. "Time to go, Larry," I said.

I nearly lost my balance as Lawrence slid off his stool and crashed into me. I got an arm around his waist and hoisted him, still tugging on Elvis. The silence had yielded to a menacing rumble, and I was counting off the seconds in my head like an in-bounder on the sideline. Elvis's size would discourage any sober man, but this mob wasn't sober. They were disappointed and angry, and they were looking for someone to take it out on. The blond ponytail on our left had picked up his beer and edged away from us.

A burly six-footer in a green work shirt with "Duffy" stitched over his heart looked the type to throw the first punch. "Whatta you?" he bawled. "A fuckin' Bruin? You look like you could be a fuckin' Bruin."

"Don't have a cow, man," the big guy protested. He made a placating motion with his hands, except that his palms were turned toward him.

Lawrence was more or less on his feet now, and appeared to have taken in the situation. He spoke sharply—something that sounded like "Yarp!" Then he said something else I didn't catch.

To me, Elvis said, "Hank, I am only exercising my First Amendment right to free speech, isn't that right?"

"Not the best time to be doing that, big guy."

There was another exchange between Lawrence and Elvis as I dragged Lawrence toward the door. Elvis, a giant redwood to my sapling, wasn't draggable. The language they used wasn't a language I spoke or recognized. Turkish? Icelandic? Duffy moved in and gave Elvis a belligerent shove. It was a challenge to get in the big man's face, but Duffy was trying, dancing on his toes.

"You a fuckin' Bruin *and* a fuckin' foreigner?" he growled. "Or is that the way they talk out there in Los Angeleez?" His buddies were closing in behind him.

Elvis turned in apparent bewilderment. "Hank, why is he so frosted?"

Lawrence spoke again and I said, "Come on, before you start a riot."

Elvis turned then and headed for the door. That was when Duffy lowered his shoulder and charged. It must have been like trying to tackle a bridge pylon. Duffy slammed into Elvis and crumpled, which did nothing to endear Elvis to the home crowd.

I hit the parking lot running. Lawrence, to my relief, was keeping pace with me. Elvis brought up the rear, still protesting in that peculiar language. A cream-and-crimson mob of drunken Hoosier boosters was close on our heels. Luckily, we'd gained some time when they'd all stumbled over Duffy in their rush for the door.

I was headed for my vintage Escort, but Lawrence said, "This way." His tone of command reached my feet first, and they veered off to follow him as he cleared the gravel and plunged into a thicket. I was gasping for air, but neither of my companions seemed the least bit winded. Elvis quickly outpaced us with his long strides. Behind us, the boosters were baying for blood.

We were in the woods now, feet pounding on ground softened by leaf mold and spring rain. Twigs crackled underfoot, branches snapped as we plowed through them. A startled owl added to the ruckus. Blinded by the dark, I couldn't see anything when I felt Lawrence's hand on my arm. "In here," he said.

I heard a rustle, and then a faint whirring sound. A powerful paw lifted me into the air and set me down. Underneath me, the ground sloped up. At the top of the rise Lawrence plunged through a lit doorway, and I followed. When I turned around, Elvis was gazing back into the darkness from which we'd emerged, a glint in his eyes which must have been a reflection off the interior lighting. He stood with his feet apart, grasped his lapels and flexed his shoulders.

"Yarp," Lawrence said, in that commanding voice of his. Then he said something that sounded like, "Deglet orosco."

Elvis turned back to us with a grin, and blinked at me in such a meaningful way that it could have been meant as a wink. The glint was gone. He put a hand on my shoulder and guided me down a hallway.

I thought that my panic must have been causing me to hallucinate, because we seemed to be inside a submarine of some kind. What I saw was seamless metallic walls curving into a ceiling—

kind of like a stretched Airstream camper. It was lit by a glow from a source I couldn't spot. I followed Lawrence until we came to a large semicircular room that appeared to be a control room of some kind—all gleaming metal and instruments and screens. Not a submarine, then, but some kind of experimental military aircraft. Maybe Lawrence and Elvis were engineers, because they didn't seem like military types. I could still hear a hum, and feel a faint vibration through the soles of my sneakers. The air in the room faintly held Lawrence's own bouquet of pipe tobacco and aftershave, and, fainter still, a fruity scent I couldn't place.

"Welcome to our pad, Hank," said Elvis.

"Sit here," Lawrence instructed, and I did.

Before I could figure out how to fasten my buckle-less seatbelt, though, I heard a whoosh and we were airborne. Elvis was bracing himself with one hand on the back of my seat, but he swayed ominously as we rose. If he falls on me, I remember thinking, he'll flatten me. But he held his balance, still grinning at me. On one screen in front of me, I saw a receding image of angry Hoosiers crashing around in the underbrush; they were curiously outlined in red light, as if through night-vision lenses.

"This heap can really burn rubber," Elvis said.

The odd thing about our ascent, apart from its suddenness, was its verticality. This realization confirmed my suspicions that I was in some kind of experimental craft, since I'd read about an air force jet that could rise vertically and even hover above the ground and fly backwards. But I couldn't believe how big the cockpit was. It had to accommodate Elvis, of course, but this place could have accommodated a regional gathering of Elvis impersonators.

"Can we drop you off somewhere, Hank?" Lawrence asked politely.

To my relief, he didn't appear drunk, but I was pretty sure he was above the legal limit for piloting an aircraft. I hoped this thing had an autopilot.

"Why don't you come to Washington, D.C., with us?" Elvis said. He had removed a comb from his pocket and was combing his hair. He gave me his lopsided smile. "It will be fun. Like Jack Kerouac and Neal Cassady."

"I'm still on Spring Break," I admitted. I thought of my apartment, conspicuously empty now that all Anita's stuff was gone, forlorn. I thought of the freshman research papers piled on my desk, full of feigned and grammatically suspect outrage over such transgressions as steroid use and music piracy. I thought of the barricade of dissertation books between me and my bed, and my laptop open accusingly on the kitchen table.

"To Breezewood, then?" Lawrence said, passing his hand over the panel in front of him.

"To Breezewood," I said.

I was feeling lightheaded and overheated. I'd left a jacket in the bar, I now realized. "I don't suppose they serve alcoholic beverages and peanuts on this flight?" I said.

"We can pick some up on the way," said Elvis.

CHAPTER THREE

Elvis wanted to know how far we were from Memphis, Tennessee.

"Not too far by plane," I said, "but we're headed in the wrong direction. We're too far north."

"Is there a highway that goes there?" he asked. "Our map is broken." He gestured toward a darkened screen.

"The best thing, in that case, would be to follow the rivers," I said. "If we fly south, we'll intersect the Ohio River. The Ohio meets the Mississippi at Cairo, and you can follow the Mississippi down to Memphis."

Elvis turned to Lawrence, and a debate ensued. I reached a tentative hand out to touch the glowing gray metal of the instrument panel, which was smooth and cool to the touch. There was writing etched on it, but I didn't recognize the symbols. There was also an old-fashioned paddle ball resting on top—one of the ones made out of wood, with a little rubber ball attached by a rubber band. The ball barely vibrated as the plane moved through space. Finally, Lawrence heaved a sigh, passed his hand over the panel again, and I felt the craft turn and reverse directions. Elvis sat down in the seat next to me, smiling happily.

"I get my wish," he said. "Do you think that we will be able to see Graceland from the air?"

"It's probably lit up like a Christmas tree," I said.

Elvis leaned forward, held a hand over a circular light on the panel, and two wide doors parted in front of us like an eye opening.

They slid back to expose a panoramic view of the night sky.

"Wow," I said. "That's some sunroof."

"Hank," Elvis said. "Do you think he is there right now? Do you think that we might get to see the King?"

Well, that stymied me. How was I going to break the news? It was beginning to sink in that these two, in spite of their high-tech aircraft, were considerably behind the times. Where had they been for the past fifty years? In the lab? Did they come from some remote civilization that had been cut off from the rest of the world but was advancing much more rapidly? A civilization founded by marooned beatniks and Elvis fanatics?

"Elvis," I said gently, "you're not going to see the King, man. The King's dead. I'm sorry."

"Oh," he said, and that one syllable let all the air out of him. I watched him deflate until he was just a limp pair of slacks and a loud jacket in a ducktail. Even Lawrence threw him a sympathetic glance. Then he said, "Are you sure? When did he die?"

"I don't know, man," I said. "Maybe forty years ago. Something like that. But his house is still there. That's where he died. It's a historic landmark. You can even take a tour and visit his grave."

Lawrence gave me a warning look, but I could see that Elvis wasn't ready to digest this last piece of information.

I began to look around for the facilities. I didn't want to seem crass and insensitive, but after all the beer I'd drunk, I needed to take a leak.

"You got a lavatory on this plane, Lawrence?" I asked.

"A lavatory?"

"Yeah—you know, a toilet."

"Oh." He looked around. He got up and studied one of the long, curved walls of the cabin, looking exactly like a man who has misplaced something. He passed his hand over the wall, and a door flew open. Several long metal poles came clattering down and a multicolored ball rolled out. "Sports equipment," he explained. "But I know we have one," he said, as he wrestled the poles back into the closet and the door slammed shut. He tried a few more doors, then announced, "Here it is."

Sure enough, it looked like most of the airplane lavatories I'd ever seen, down to the petite bar of Cashmere Bouquet soap gracing the metal counter.

"Say, where are you guys from, anyway?" I asked when I resumed my seat. "Not from around here, obviously."

"Oh, we're from a place far, far away," Lawrence said.

"Yes," Elvis said, rousing himself a little. "You won't have heard of it."

"Try me," I suggested.

"Try you?" Lawrence echoed. He frowned at the cell phone, which he'd placed in a holder mounted to the instrument panel. He reached up to his ear, and I glimpsed something metallic inside it, like a hearing aid, which he repositioned. Then he reached out and dealt the cell phone a single blow with his fist. "Oh, you mean, tell you the name of our country and you'll see if you recognize it."

"Bingo."

I saw him mouthing "bingo," but he didn't follow up on that one. Instead, he said, "Suppose I told you that we were from Kyrzygstan."

"Former Soviet republic?" I said. "Must be somewhere near Kazakhstan and Uzbekistan and those other stans. Is that where you're from?"

"No, Hank," Elvis said. "He's just pushing your leg. He knows that most Americans do not know much about the geography of your world."

"So where, then?"

Lawrence cleared his throat.

I waited. "Come on," I said finally. "Let's hear it."

"That's it," Lawrence said, and cleared his throat again.

"That's it?" I said. "That's the name of your country?"

"Actually," Elvis said, "it's the name of his planet." He leaned forward, waved a hand over another light, and a brightly lit bird's-eye view of the Ohio River spread out across the windshield.

"You mustn't feel bad that you haven't heard of it," Lawrence said. "It isn't even in your galaxy."

"That explains it," I said. "I'm pretty well up on my geography."

"Then perhaps you should be down, Hank," Elvis said, and laughed at his own joke.

That was okay. I was glad to see him perking up a little.

"Did you understand my joke, Hank?" he asked.

"Yeah, I got it," I said. "You're a real comedian."

Elvis sighed. "I don't want to be a comedian," he said. "I want to be a rock and roll star."

"Also an admirable career goal," I said.

"I want to play the guitar and sing and wivel my hips like the real

Elvis."

"One wivel on national TV," I said, "and you'd be headed for megastardom. Let's get you on *American Idol.*"

"Okay," he said. "I would dig that. What do we do?"

"First things first," I said. "How is it you know so much about American culture, but everything you know is half a century out of date?"

Lawrence and Elvis exchanged glances.

"Our television is broken," Elvis said.

"Ask him how it broke," Lawrence said.

"It wasn't my fault," Elvis said, giving us the full benefit of the prominent lower lip.

"He tried to plug an RCA Victor record player into our infoscan unit, and disrupted the power source. The unit can't be fixed until we get home. That was in Earth year 1957, shortly after we left."

"Left?" I said. "You were here before?" A leaf fluttered in the pages of my memory. I got up and retraced my steps to the lavatory. I stopped at a section of wall where three black-and-white photographs with crenulated edges had been Scotch-taped to the smooth surface. I pointed at them. "You were here before."

"Yes, yes, Hank, that's us!" Elvis beat his fingertips against his chest in what was apparently a gesture of excitement.

I studied the photographs. One showed two men, ordinary in every way except that one was extremely tall. Both men wore suits and ties. They sat in folding lawn chairs on a small strip of cement that might have been a patio outside of a nondescript place showing a door and window. The door had a number, 101, on it. A motel room?

The second photograph showed the same two men in the same suits, sitting on bleachers, surrounded by smiling boys. The boys all wore jeans and team tee shirts and ball caps that said "Lobos." A few of them had baseball gloves in their laps. The tall man also wore a Lobos cap. He didn't look remotely like Elvis Presley. But there was something familiar about the broad grin.

In the third photograph, the tall man, wearing the same suit and the Lobos ball cap, stood in front of something resembling a flying saucer. He had one arm draped around the shoulder of a kid wearing a Cub Scout uniform. Both were smiling for the camera.

I glanced around the cockpit. Round room, check. Windows on top, check. Ergo, this was the flying saucer in the photograph. My

Spring Break was looking up.

"Who's the kid?" I asked.

"That's our friend Robbie Donovan," Elvis said. He reached out as if he would caress the Cub Scout. "He was a very good friend. His parents owned the Siesta Motor Court, where Lawrence stayed. Have you heard of it, Hank?"

I shook my head. "Where was this?"

"In Española, New Mexico," Elvis said. He was squinting at the photographs. "That suit is Nowheresville. I look squared."

You'll say I should have reacted with alarm to the flying saucer, or to the mention of New Mexico, or to the two things together. But I was transfixed by the Elvis transformation.

"Lawrence looks just the same," I observed. "But you—." I turned to Elvis. "What happened to you?"

"I redesigned myself," he said, and opened his arms wide. "Do you dig the threads?"

Lawrence made a noise I took to signal exasperation. "He's just told you that you've modeled yourself on a dead man. I told you you were taking a chance."

Elvis was crestfallen. "It's not fashionable?"

"I didn't say that," I said. "In some neighborhoods, it's very fashionable. Some guys earn big bucks imitating the King. In Vegas, they have Elvis impersonator conventions and—."

"We're picking up a radio transmission," Lawrence cut in. "I think this may be Memphis coming up."

As we approached, Elvis bounced a little in his seat like a kid, and I was relieved to note that the ship we were in—a spaceship, I guessed I'd have to call it now—was well-equipped with stabilizers that took his weight into account.

If we'd been riding in an ordinary plane at night, I would have had to just pick out any old Classical mansion and label it "Graceland" to satisfy my companions, but because the image on the screen was brightly lit and clearly focused through some bit of extraterrestrial sleight of hand, I could actually make out the Corinthian columns guarded by lions, the kidney-shaped pool, and the semi-circular wall beyond. I'd seen the place up close and personal twice in my life, once as a kid, and once, the year before, with Anita, my ex.

So we hung there in the air a while, our running lights off, while I gave them a virtual tour of Graceland, doing my best to conjure up the jungle room, the trophy room, the *Lisa Marie*, the TV room, the dining room.

"Many famous Earth people have eaten in that room, I suppose," said Elvis.

"Yeah, Anita says——." I stopped, surprised by a bubble of emotion in my throat.

"Who is Anita, Hank?" Elvis asked.

Lawrence frowned and shook his head. "She's his ex-girlfriend," he said to Elvis. "She is having sex with his dissertation director."

"She was cruel to a heart that's true," Elvis said, with sympathy. He laid a hand on my shoulder. "Don't worry, Hank. I bet there are lots of dolls in Washington, D.C. We will find a baby for you."

When Elvis had finally seen everything that could be seen of Graceland from the air, we changed course for D.C. Lawrence was yanking at his tie.

"Only a primitive people would tie a rope around their neck and call it a fashion," he grumbled. "No offense, Hank."

I grinned at him. "You don't see me wearing one, do you, Lar?" With Lawrence's movement, that strangely familiar scent wafted my way and enveloped me. I sniffed. "What's that cologne you're wearing?"

"English Leather. Isn't it fashionable anymore?"

I smiled reminiscently. "My grandfather used to wear English Leather. I've been wondering why I was feeling such a strong compulsion to sit in your lap and search your pockets for candy."

Lawrence shifted uncomfortably. "In that case, perhaps you could make an alternative recommendation."

"And the pipe tobacco?"

He reached into an inner pocket and pulled out a pipe. He handled it awkwardly, as if uncertain which end was up. "It came with the suit," he said.

Elvis was looking thoughtful. "Hank, tell me about the Elvis impersonators in Vegas," he said.

Lawrence groaned. "Not tonight. Hank's tired, and I'm tired."

"Maybe Hank wants to watch the movie," Elvis offered. He turned to me politely, "Would you like to see our movie, Hank? We only have one, but it's a very good one, with James Stewart and Jean Arthur."

"That would be *Mr. Smith Goes to Washington*?"

"Yes. Have you seen it?"

"Not recently. But it is a good one." I thought to myself that it would have encouraged an appropriately cynical attitude toward Washington politics, but at the same time fostered too much optimism about ultimate outcomes.

"It's too late to watch a movie tonight," Lawrence said. "I think we should slip into another dimension, put the craft on hover, and sleep."

"No, wait," I said. "You never told me why you came to Earth in the first place, or why you came back."

Lawrence sighed. "It's a long story."

"No, it's not, Lawrence," Elvis said. "We failed."

CHAPTER FOUR

"Elvis is right," Lawrence said over breakfast. "We came to warn your leaders about the consequences of deploying nuclear weapons in outer space. We went to New Mexico to investigate—to see how much progress they'd made."

We were sitting in a diner somewhere off the Pennsylvania Turnpike. I was feeling surprisingly rested after seven hours on some kind of bubble bed that moved like a water bed. If I hadn't drunk so much beer the night before, I would've felt downright swell. I could use a more extended vacation in the seventh dimension some time.

"You know about the laboratory at Los Alamos, right, Hank?" Elvis said.

I nodded.

"The weapons were very primitive, of course," Lawrence continued. "We learned that much. But before we could begin the diplomatic stage of our mission, we aroused some unfortunate hostility in the neighborhood."

"Lawrence got shot," Elvis put in.

"We were forced to retreat," Lawrence said. "We intended to return and complete our mission in Washington, D.C., but our organization experienced some changes in leadership, and the new leaders were not very interested in saving Earth."

Elvis was studying the small pegboard with golf cues that had been provided for our entertainment. If he'd asked me whether it was a game or an artwork, I couldn't have told him. "Politics," he said soberly. "They are jived in our galaxy just like in yours."

"When the leadership changed again," Lawrence said, "we were able to persuade the new leaders that Earth was worth saving, so we came back. It was fortunate that Earth had not sent weapons into space in the interim."

"That's only because they haven't figured out how," Elvis said. "Remember Star Wars? And they didn't even sign the Outer Space Treaty until 1967. Only three countries signed it."

"Two eggs, sunnyside up, biscuits, gravy, and hash browns?" said the waitress. She balanced four plates and a bread basket on muscular arms.

"That's mine," said Elvis and reached to help her unload, but I put a hand on his arm to stop him from interfering with her performance.

"Two Egg Beaters, scrambled, fruit, and banana bread?"

I raised my hand. I wasn't sure my stomach was up to this.

She set down a stack of pancakes in front of Lawrence. "There's your syrup, hon," she said, pointing.

"Thank you very much, ma'am," Elvis drawled. He curled his lip at her. "My mouth is watered." He picked up a small plastic honey bear by its feet and upended it over his biscuits and gravy.

"Anyway, Hank, one of the original signatories of the Outer Space Treaty, the Soviet Union, doesn't even exist anymore," Elvis said. "There are plenty of top-secret defense initiatives to militarize space. Would you like a biscuit? You are not eating very much. Don't you know that breakfast is the most important meal of the day?"

I shook my head. "Can we back up to the part where Lawrence got shot? How did that happen?"

A look passed between them. Lawrence said, "A fight broke out at a Little League Game. We—we intervened."

"All of our new friends played Little League baseball," Elvis said. "Did you play Little League baseball, Hank?"

"Some," I said. "How did Larry get shot?"

"That was my fault," Lawrence said ruefully. "I didn't appreciate how much mistrust and suspicion we had aroused among the locals. We were strangers in a place where very few strangers ever stopped. We were not far from Los Alamos. And, as Elvis says, we spent a lot of time with Robbie and the other children. The parents—well, the fathers especially—they decided that we were Russian spies—you know, Communist infiltrators."

"It was my fault, Lawrence," Elvis said. "I was the one who transported the bat to the fifth dimension." He looked at me. "In front of all of the Little League moms and dads," he added soberly.

"The boys tried to warn us," he went on, "but they were not allowed out of the back yard, and they had failed to teach us about smoke signals." He sighed. "We did not receive the message."

Lawrence's smile showed a trace of genuine amusement. "It was rather like the incident in Indiana last night."

"But Ralph, Robbie's father, had a shotgun," Elvis said.

I didn't interrupt to speculate on the kind of firepower the irate Hoosiers might have produced if given half a chance.

"Fortunately, Lawrence revived," Elvis said, brightening. "And here we are again. You do not have a suspicious father that we have not met yet, do you, Hank?"

My father, last I heard, was living la vida loca in Puerto Vallarte with his third wife, so the less said about him, the better. "I have another question for you," I said. "How is it that you know so much about recent political developments, but you don't know that Elvis is dead?"

"Our infoscan is broken, Hank, but we can still communicate with our superiors," Lawrence said. "Otherwise, we wouldn't have come back so soon."

"Unfortunately, they only tell us what they believe it is important for us to know," Elvis said, "and they are serious-minded political individuals. We no longer have access to communications from your planet. No television," he added sadly, "except for the shows we recorded before our set broke. *I Love Lucy* is our favorite."

"I see. And you came back now because—?"

"We don't trust your governments," Lawrence said. He was sopping up syrup with a wedge of soggy pancake. "I'm sorry, Hank. The stupidity of your Earth governments—."

"It beetles Lawrence," Elvis put in. "Your leaders really battled his cage."

"Hey, no skin off my butt," I said. "I don't trust them, either. And before you inspect my butt," I added, catching Elvis's eye, "it's just an expression. It means I don't care, I'm not offended, it's no problem for me."

Lawrence went on. "Of course, there was a big debate about whether we should come at all. There are certain extremists with a purely pragmatic agenda who want to destroy Earth to build an intergalactic superhighway through this part of the universe. But they are not taken seriously by many."

A piece of melon stuck in my throat. "Good to know," I said.

"And then, others argue that you will burn up your planet long before you can develop the technology to put viable nuclear weapons into space. You call this 'global warming,' I believe."

"How seriously are they taken?"

"Oh, very seriously. But we can't run the risk that your best scientists will develop a nuclear weapon and launch it into space, you see, before that happens. The populace of the planet Zarko are very concerned, and very vocal. They have powerful friends in the government."

"Zarko?" I echoed.

"You wouldn't know it," Elvis said. "It is two galaxies away. They are always obsessing about asteroids." He was using a corner of toast to guide bright yellow egg onto his fork.

"So what are you planning to do?"

"Want me to warm that up, hon?" The waitress stood next to our booth, coffee pot poised over Elvis's cup.

"You bet," he said, and held it up to her.

When she had gone, Lawrence spoke in a low voice. "We don't know yet. Since we didn't succeed very well last time, we're open to suggestions."

"We are all eyes," Elvis said.

"Well, since it's been so long since you've visited Earth, maybe you should lay low awhile, get to know the place," I said. "Things have changed a lot in fifty years, you know. I mean, not the general stupidity of our leaders, that hasn't changed, but other things have."

"How do we do that? Lay low?" Elvis said.

"Sorry," I said. "Another figure of speech. I mean, well, find a place to hide the ship, and just hang out for a while, like you did last time." Catching Elvis's puzzled frown, I amended my suggestion. "You know, remain inconspicuous and meet people and observe the culture."

"We do not know many figures of speech," Elvis said, "only ones we learned the last time we were here, and from television and radio before our infoscan broke. Our translator does not recognize many of them."

"I think you're right, Hank," Lawrence said. "I've always felt that if only I could have stayed longer in Española, I would have understood better how to approach Earth people, and I would have made fewer mistakes."

"Our boss wants us to appear threatening and powerful," Elvis said. His chin was streaked with honey. "But he does not have to deal with the consequences. Larry is a diplomat—a very good diplomat. He is very diplomatic." He took another bite of biscuit. "And now that Larry has been reading Mr. Overstreet's book, he understands Earth people better."

"Which book is that?" I felt a twinge of apprehension.

"You don't know Mr. Overstreet's book, Hank? It was a bestseller. Larry found it in his room at the Siesta. It is called *The Mature Mind*."

"Yeah? What does it say about Earth people and their resistance to disarmament?"

He dipped a forkful of hash browns into a small puddle of ketchup, and frowned thoughtfully. "It says, 'all childish minds are dangerous, but particularly when those minds are housed in adult bodies; for then they have the power to put their immaturities fully and disastrously into effect.'"[1]

I raised my eyebrows. "Sounds like he has our number." When Elvis looked up, I amended, "Sounds like he knows our leaders pretty well."

"I was Mr. Smith before," Lawrence told me. "For our present purposes, can I still be Mr. Smith, do you think?" Lawrence asked.

"Sure," I said. "But people are a little less formal these days."

"So I should introduce myself as 'Lawrence'?"

"'Larry' would be better," I said. "It sounds friendlier."

"Like 'Hank' for 'Henry,'" Elvis said. He had cleaned his plate and was reaching for his comb.

Lawrence and I looked at him. Call me arrogant, but for once I knew just what this highly evolved alien was thinking because I was thinking the same thing.

"You said 'inconspicuous'?" Lawrence said.

Elvis paused. "What's wrong?"

"First, we go shopping," I said.

Elvis brightened. "New threads?"

I left my last buck on the table. My pocket held a diamond, but I

---

[1] See H.A. Overstreet, *The Mature Mind* (New York: W.W. Norton, 1949).

didn't have a finger to put it on. I was ready to check into the Heartbreak Hotel.

CHAPTER FIVE

How I came to be in charge of the logistics, I don't know. It just happened. I was busy as a campaign manager on the eve of the Iowa caucuses.

Take money. Lawrence and Elvis had eleven dollars and twenty-three cents between them, plus a stash of diamonds that could send the world diamond market through the cellar. Diamonds may be a girl's best friend, but they can't help you at the automat—they don't fit into those little slots. I didn't have much cash left after breakfast, and the credit of a graduate student wouldn't buy us a Variety Bucket of KFC. Lawrence—Larry—had discovered on his previous visit that the quality of his diamonds would raise eyebrows at any neighborhood jewelry store. And I had no connections on the black market, not in Indiana and not here.

"Got anything else we can sell or hock?" I asked.

"Just some sports equipment," Elvis offered. "We have some very fine boogleball sticks and frip-frip racquets."

So it went.

"I don't suppose either of you has a credit card lying about, do you?" I asked.

"What does it look like?" Elvis asked.

I held up my overextended Visa, dull with use. Elvis examined it and they held a brief conversation.

"We could clone it," he said.

"Yeah, but the company wouldn't approve its use," I objected.

"The account number and security code would have to be legitimate. And you can't use my numbers. I'm over my limit already. And as for my bank account, forget it. The balance is so low it's beneath contempt. If you guys leave me in the lurch, I'll have to thumb my way back to Indiana."

"Why would we leave you there, Hank?" Elvis asked. He looked at my thumbs.

"Hitchhike," I amended. "If you abandon me, I'll have to hitchhike home."

"By 'money,'" Larry said, "do you mean coins or gold or what? I thought that all of your banking was electronic now."

"That's right."

"Then there is no sweat, man," Elvis said. "We are hip to that."

"We can create a new account electronically," Larry said. "That's what he means."

Then there was the housing question.

"Will we find a motor court?" Elvis asked. "I only got to visit last time," he said wistfully. "I had to stay with the ship."

"We should probably check into a hotel, for the sake of convenience, but we won't have any luggage, unless we go shopping first. And we can't go shopping without a car, because we can't just set this thing down in a mall parking lot." I gestured vaguely at the spaceship around us, which was humming along—invisible, or so they assured me, inside its security shield. "We could rent a car, but only if we can get close enough to some place we can catch a cab."

"I'm sure you'll think of something, Hank," Elvis said.

From the beginning, it seemed, he'd placed entirely too much confidence in me. They both had. Who was I, after all? Just another overeducated Gen X outcast with no practical skills, unless you count diagramming a sentence a practical skill. It wouldn't save the planet. In fact, in terms of planet-saving capabilities, I had zip. When Homeland Security hauled me off to Guantanamo and introduced me to the waterboard, I'd have nothing to offer them. In my spare time, I should start inventing a life.

As it turned out, when we arrived in the D.C. metro area, parking, for once, was not a problem. We set down on stilts in Rock Creek Park, not far from the National Zoo, our landing cushioned by an air pocket created by the ship and the trees mostly undisturbed by our vertical maneuver.

An hour later, we emerged with a new Visa card that Larry

assured me would work. Elvis and I had passed the hour playing a card game with an unpronounceable name, while I explained his new identity. I walked down the ramp, turned to wave at Elvis, and saw nothing there. The invisibility shield was down, Larry explained.

A disembodied voice drawled, "Later, gator."

"Do you think he'll stay put?" I asked Larry, as we began hiking.

"Not for long," Larry said.

The air was chilly, and I missed my jacket, but Larry seemed unaffected.

"You can't blame him, though," I said. "You two have been cooped up in that ship together for a long time."

"Oh, I don't blame him," Larry said. "Not at all. He's an extremely gregarious fellow. But I worry about what would happen if he appeared prematurely."

We emerged at the north end of the zoo. I stopped to study the map. "This way to Connecticut," I said, pointing. "We can follow the fence." I paused. "Tell me something. Where does he come from? A really big planet populated by tall people?"

"He comes from a planet in the Roan Galaxy," he said, distracted by his first sight of the city. "They are famous for their laboratories and design studios. He's one of their best."

I was confused. "Best what?"

"Best models," Larry said. "You know, like—." He looked around for inspiration and spotted the traffic in the distance. "Like a Mercedes, isn't that right? One of your best cars? He's like that."

I stopped, stunned. "He's a robot?"

"A robot?"

"Yeah—you know. Not a life form, but a machine. An android. You don't mean that, right? He has so much personality."

Larry said, "I'm sorry. I expressed it badly. Elvis is a manufactured life form, but he's not a machine in the way that a refrigerator or an automobile is a machine on your planet. On Earth, you tend to classify beings by race or origin because that is a category of significance to you. But in our world, the division between manufactured life forms and nonmanufactured life forms is not absolute, so the distinction isn't very important to us. Yarp—Elvis— is a member of the race of peacemakers—intergalactic police officers."

"But when you created them, the peacemakers, you gave them personalities?" I tried to picture some alien sitting at a high-tech computer console millions of space-miles away, deciding to have some fun with the personality programming. I hadn't seen much evidence that Larry had a sense of fun, of course, but that didn't mean anything. Then it occurred to me to wonder whether Elvis, in all his charming eccentricity, his warmth, sensitivity, and candor, was perhaps typical of those beings who had created him.

"Well, *I* didn't," he said patiently. "I'm not that kind of engineer. But if you're using 'you' in the generic sense, yes. They were given emotions, but it would be an overstatement to say that they were given personalities. Where I come from, we believe that peacemakers should be able to identify with those whom they're policing, so of course, they had to have emotions. But—how can I put it? The structuring of the self into a personality—that is up to the individual."

"Elvis is his own robot."

"You might say that. It can create problems, though."

"If Elvis decides he just has to get out and meet and greet, for example?"

"Yes." Larry sighed. "He has a very good heart and a very good mind. He won't deliberately do anything to jeopardize our mission, but—."

"He's only human."

Larry smiled. He didn't respond, but he didn't have to. Clearly, he believed that Elvis was better than human. I didn't take offense. If I wasn't going to defend neckties, I sure wasn't going to defend the human race.

He started at a blast of music rushing past us on roller blades. "Fashions certainly have changed, haven't they?" he said. "Is that a new mode of transport or is it a form of recreation?"

"Both," I said.

"It looks rather like roller skates," he said.

"Just redesigned," I said, "like Elvis."

I caught Larry's elbow as he stepped off the curb and into the path of a messenger on a bike. "Everything seems to have accelerated," he observed. "But of course, the pace of life will always be faster in a capital city than in the countryside, I suppose. I like to walk, though. You can get to know a planet more intimately if your body makes contact with its surface."

As he continued to take things in, he had plenty of questions. If the devices people were holding to their ears were telephones, not translators, why was everyone talking on them? Did Earth people talk face-to-face anymore, or was that only in bars? Did people not mind the noise and pollution of the gasoline-powered vehicles—the automobiles and the motorcycles and the mopeds? Why were all the cars so big if they carried only one person at a time? Why were there so many stores everywhere? Did people really purchase enough goods to keep all these stores in business? Were there no motor courts in the capital city?

Hanging around spacemen really does something to your head, I can tell you. For example, I was just about to write, "In spite of the chill, the sun was out," when I stopped to consider that, astronomically speaking, of course, the sun was always out. But if I made that observation to Larry and Elvis, they might get that anxious look they wore whenever they had bad news for me. They might change the subject—Larry's usual strategy—or they might inform me, with sorrowful expressions, that, regrettably, the sun would not always be out. Some time in the distant future, the sun would burn itself up, and the human species would need to relocate, assuming that we were still around at that point, which, as a betting proposition, was a total nonstarter. Elvis had told me that there was a planet in our dimension in the Pinwheel Galaxy where the bookies gave thirty-to-one odds against human survival for another millennium. Elvis, though sensitive and sympathetic, was big on candor.

We checked in at the Marriott Wardman Park, where the plastic card Larry had somehow produced back on the ship was cheerfully accepted. We left a vague impression of lost luggage in our wake and went out to cruise the streets of Adams Morgan to see what kinds of men's wear was available in XXL. Half an hour later, having rejected yoga pants, camouflage, Rastafarian caps, dashikis, and embroidered Mexican shirts, we stumbled across a building like a big warehouse, the Columbia Road Discount Center, which advertised, in English and Spanish, "the best prices in town." When we left the store, Larry was wearing khaki slacks, a sports shirt, a sports jacket, and a digital watch, and I was wearing a new pair of chinos, a knit pullover, and a leather jacket.

"I don't miss the tie," he said, "but I rather miss the hat."

We were carrying our old clothes and our other purchases in a pair of carry-on bags we'd bought. We'd again left behind the impression that we were victims of incompetence in baggage claim.

Also inside the bags was the longest pair of Big and Tall sweatpants they had and the largest Hoyas sweatshirt.

"He will be very pleased," Larry said.

I'd decided that Elvis would be a Georgetown basketball recruit from the rural South, and Larry would be his agent. I doubted that there was any place left in the rural South where people would be as clueless as Elvis, but prejudices die hard, particularly inside the Beltway. I didn't think anybody would question his story.

We also picked up a couple of cell phones while we were out, though it took some convincing on my part to persuade Larry that such primitive technology might come in handy. Elvis's phone, in Hoya blue, played the Hoya fight song for its ring tone.

Larry's energy flagged quickly. He was not a shopper. He kept glancing up at the sun.

I tapped him on the arm. "If you want to blend in with Earthlings, look at your watch, not the sun. Younger people look at their cell phones. Just a suggestion."

He smiled sheepishly and gave his watch a conspicuous inspection.

"It's okay," I said. "We'll take a cab back to base, and you can stay home while I take Elvis shopping. You'll need another jacket and dress pants, but that can wait."

We stopped at a cash machine, which gave up its cash without a murmur, and then hailed a cab.

Elvis was still in the ship, playing some kind of video game, and he brightened when he saw his new outfit. Everything was a little short on him, but he didn't know it.

"It's just the beginning, kid," I told him. "Let's go shopping."

"Will we eat something, too? Can we go to a Big Boy restaurant? Or maybe a Howard Johnson's? I never went there before. Or—." His eyes brightened. "How about an automat? Can we go to an automat, Hank?"

"Things have changed since you last visited the planet, big guy, but sure, we can eat."

"And after we get our car, can we go to a drive-in restaurant, Hank? I would like to see the car jumps on roller skates, and also those—." He frowned. "You know, those—." He formed his hands into cees and pointed them down.

"The trays that clip onto the car window?"

"Yes! The car window clip-on trays."

"I don't know about the car jumps on roller skates," I said. "We'll have to look around. But in the meantime, remember, the Hoyas coach is John Thompson. We're going to need a team roster for you to study, so in the meantime, just smile knowingly."

He curled his lip at me. It was a knowing smile, all right, but it was the wrong kind. It was the kind that the King gave his adoring female fans.

"Close enough," I said.

CHAPTER SIX

Fortunately, the smile worked just fine on the server at McDonald's, the salesperson at the Columbia Road Discount Center, the clerk at CVS, and the associate at the car rental agency, all of whom were female. The cab driver, a Sikh who played loud salsa music, could take it or leave it, apparently.

Elvis kept trying to catch sight of his new shades in the rearview mirror as we discussed cars in the cab on the way to the car rental agency.

"What do you drive, Hank?" he asked.

"An Escort."

He frowned. "I never heard of that one."

"Wasn't around when you were here last."

"We should get a Mercury."

"Why a Mercury?"

"Because it has power, roadability, styling, and extra value."

"Roadability? Who says that?"

"Mr. Stevens."

"Never heard of him. What's he do?"

"You never heard of Mr. Stevens, Hank?"

"Nope."

"He's a big star on *The Ed Sullivan Show*. He knows a lot about cars."

"I bet."

"Every week he talks about Mercuries and Lincolns. He knows

all about the important auto races, and who won. Mercuries always win."

"I bet."

"So can we get a Mercury?"

"We'll see."

"There are lots of black cars in Washington, aren't there, Hank? And those funny-looking long cars."

"Stretch limousines. Some of those are Lincolns." He opened his mouth to speak, but I cut him off. "No, we can't get a limousine. We want something sensible and inconspicuous."

He was pouting just a little when we drove off the lot in a pale green Saturn half an hour later. His hair brushed the ceiling and his knees were bent to accommodate his legs.

"You didn't even ask about roadability, Hank," he said, and he was right.

He was a walking encyclopedia of 1950s advertising. In the toothpaste aisle at CVS, he had begun singing the Ipana jingle. In the hair care aisle, he'd added some Brylcreem to our basket. "A little dab'll do you, Hank," he'd said. Then he'd asked, studying my beard and moustache, "Do you shave at all, Hank? You should get some Old Spice. Even the toughest whiskers become weak and willing." As we'd passed the soap, he'd reached for a bar of Dial. "Do we need some more soap, Hank? People who like people use Dial."

I'd steered him toward the checkout. "Plenty of Cashmere Bouquet left, big guy."

"Why don't you call Larry on your cell phone and let him know we're on our way?" I said in the car.

"I can use my communicator," he said, raising his new wristwatch to his mouth. Then he looked sheepish. "Oh, I forgot. It's in my pocket now."

"Humor me. Use your new cell phone."

"Okay." He flipped it open, and I talked him through the business of making a call. He could have been Alexander Graham Bell, he was so excited. "I can hear you!" he kept saying. "Can you hear me?"

We drove to Rock Creek, battened down the hatches on the ship, and then moved into our room at the Wardman Park—just three normal guys in town to see the sights and harass the government. The tough part was separating Elvis from the television set when we were ready to go to dinner.

"Do you know how many channels they have, Hank?" he asked.

"Surely you have some kind of broadcast entertainment where you're from," I said.

"We have some broadcast dramas that tell stories, yes," Larry said.

"But they are all boring," Elvis said. "Nowheresville."

For once, Larry agreed with him. "They are a bit tedious. They are mostly moral stories."

"About how you should love everybody, and put others first, and keep your space clean, and trust the ones who are smarter than you, and be careful not to cut off anyone's power supply, or help yourself to someone else's gnersh before they invite you." He said this in a singsong voice.

"Helping yourself to someone else's gnersh sounds serious," I observed.

"It's a felony in two countries on the planet Pfishe," Elvis affirmed, pronouncing it with a plosive before the eff. "But they are very small countries. Also, you must be happy for others when they win at games, even if they have beaten you, and even if they cheated."

"I'll bear it in mind."

"You have a bear in your mind?" he asked, smirking. "Is it a U.C.L.A. Bruin?"

"Very funny."

"Just think, Hank. If that man in the bar hadn't gotten so frosted, you would never have come with us to Washington. So everything works out the way the Almighty Spirit intends it to." He made a sound like a sneeze, and so did Larry, so I assumed that it was kind of like "amen" or "praise God."

We had a relatively quiet dinner at Legal Seafood, drove around the city, and made an early night of it. Fortunately, it was a Sunday night, so there wasn't much nightlife to crook a wicked finger at Elvis and draw him in. I wasn't quite ready to unleash him on an unsuspecting populace.

In my own room, I finally checked my cell phone for messages. I had three text messages and four voice messages, one of them from my mother. They all said the same thing: where are you? None of them was from my ex or my dissertation director. I texted everyone but my mother to say that I'd decided to leave town for a few days.

I put off calling my mother.

Later, I would come to appreciate just how quiet that first night was.

By breakfast the next day, with less than twelve hours of exposure to the boob tube, Elvis was lobbying for a computer.

"Everyone on television has one," he said. "Even Scooby-Do."

It was no good pointing out that the ship was loaded with the most powerful and sophisticated computers in the universe.

"You can't e-mail anybody on them," he grumbled. "You can't surf the Web."

"What do you think?" Larry asked over the *Washington Post*.

"I guess it could come in handy," I said. "And I could check my own e-mail."

I didn't want to sound greedy, to tell you the truth. Our financial status was still a little vague to me. And I was accustomed to life below the poverty line.

"I could learn more about the Georgetown Hoyas," Elvis suggested. "My team."

Larry went back to his paper. "Well, if you think it would be useful, I don't object."

"I want a Mac," Elvis said, "with the Leopard operating system. If we go to the Apple store, Hank, a Mac genie will help us."

When he left the room to put his shoes on, I said to Larry, "Can I ask you something? I understand that you guys have trouble with idiomatic expressions, but how does it happen that with all your sophisticated translation capabilities, he sometimes gets ordinary words wrong?"

"He prides himself on his language skills," Larry said. "He often shuts down his translator. He prefers to—how do you express it?— wing it. Well, we both do. You've probably noticed I haven't been using my translator much. As long as you're with us, Hank, you're our translator."

So Elvis got his computer, with the help of the Mac genie, and I—God help me—I showed him how to set up e-mail (Elvis789@yahoo.com), how to navigate the Web, and how to download cool desktop graphics. Larry was out when we got back, and when I left Elvis to take a walk, he was poring over images of Graceland.

I was completely unprepared for his announcement at dinner: "I've been friended!"

I glanced at Larry, who continued to wrap his spaghetti, unperturbed—unaware of the implications of that particular verb. We were sitting in a crowded neighborhood Italian restaurant where the tables were too close together for my peace of mind. I did not want to have this conversation at the top of my lungs while sitting knee-to-knee with a bespectacled government-employed yuppie who probably did data entry for the State Department. It wasn't as if Elvis hadn't already attracted the eye of every diner in the place when he'd bumped his head on the grape arbor just inside the door and reduced it to a jumble of grape vines, leaves, and hard plastic grapes that had escaped and rolled to the far reaches of the restaurant.

"Really?" I said, my own fork suspended. "By whom?"

"By lots of people. They are very nice people, too. And they are all fans of the King. Although Dr. Bebop likes Bill Haley better." He sighed. "Thank you for the computer, Hank. I am on Cloud 10."

I stared at him.

He bit off a string of cheese from his pizza. When he'd swallowed, he said to Larry, "I can take cool pics with my new cell and post them on *Facebook*."

"How did you meet these new friends?" I asked.

"In a chat room. You would be surprised, Hank, how many working Americans are actually typing about rock and roll on a Monday afternoon."

"I'm sure I would."

Larry had finally begun to get the picture, and he looked at me, as if trying to assess the damage.

"Did you know that the hound dog song was originally recorded by Big Mama Thornton, Hank?"

"No, I didn't know that. Elvis, how many new friends do you have?"

"Twenty-one."

"And they all know you as 'Elvis 789'? Is that all they know about you—your name?"

He thought. "They know that I am a basketball player. They know that I love basketball, but my soul belongs to rock and roll."

Larry and I exchanged looks, and then he changed the subject, and asked me about the National Cherry Blossom Festival. "They say it is very beautiful in the city at that time."

After dinner, Elvis said, "Hank, can we visit the Lincoln

Memorial? That is where Mr. Smith goes in the movie about Washington, and it is very inspirational. I would like to go there."

"You mean now?" I said.

"If it would be all right," he said. "Larry is also Mr. Smith, and so maybe he would be inspired if he went there."

Larry offered no objection, so we took the Metro downtown and went for a walk. The night air was a little warmer here than it had been back in Indiana, and I was comfortable in my new jacket. Larry gazed up at the brooding Lincoln as birds twittered softly in the trees and moths danced in the artificial light. Elvis went to read the Gettysburg Address.

"I have read about your President Lincoln," Larry said. "He was a great man, and an original thinker."

"Yeah, I know," I said. "Trouble is, we Earthlings hardly ever put thinkers in charge of our governments."

"So whom should I talk to?" Larry said. "Is there not a Lincoln alive today in some country on the planet? Who has the power to mobilize all the people of the Earth for change? To whom would they listen?"

I shook my head. "Hell, I don't know, Larry. Princess Di is dead, and Brittany Spears is not known for her political consciousness. You missed the Academy Awards, and you're too early for the World Cup. But maybe we could get you on *Oprah*."

"What is *Oprah*?"

"A television show. A talk show."

"So is it more serious than *The Ed Sullivan Show*? That one's a variety show, I believe."

"Well, don't be misled by the name. People can talk foolishly just as easily as they can talk wisely, and there's plenty of foolish talk on *Oprah*. Some talk shows are downright stupid."

"Will all the people of the world be able to watch?"

"That I doubt. Closest you might come would be to have the United Nations devote a special session to it, but I can't see them suspending their regular business to watch *Oprah*."

"Then what would you suggest?"

I sighed. Since when had I been designated the savior of the planet? If I got it wrong, Earth could end up just another memorial service plaza on the intergalactic turnpike.

"I don't know, Larry," I said. "Maybe we should make our own YouTube video. Let me think about it some more."

But events overtook us. We had come up from the Metro station and had turned down Calvert and crossed the bridge to stroll through Adams Morgan. We were just on the fringes of the neighborhood when Elvis spun around and bolted down a side street. I was still standing there with my mouth open when Larry tapped my arm as he passed me.

"Trouble," he said. "Come on, Hank."

I'd barely accelerated into a lope when Elvis plunged into a service alley, and by the time I reached the alley, I could hear sounds of a scuffle, and then a gunshot. A woman screamed. A man cried out. I smelled the acrid scent of cordite. In the yellow light of a dim single bulb I saw a body sailing through the air in my direction.

"Hold him, Hank," Elvis called out. "He's under arrest."

The man landed at my feet with a thud and a grunt. He was wearing jeans, a denim jacket, a knit cap, and sneakers. He lay on his stomach, inert. I planted a foot in the middle of his back. That was the sum of my contribution to the night's proceedings.

"Is anybody hurt?" I heard Larry say.

"Are y'all all right?" Elvis drawled.

A woman in a fake-fur jacket was sobbing against the chest of a man whose glasses glinted in the yellow light. As my eyes grew more accustomed to the dimness, I spotted a mammoth handbag on the ground and, nearby, what appeared to be a camcorder. "He just came out of nowhere," the man said, sounding dazed, and I recognized some kind of Midwestern accent.

"He had a gun," his wife said. She was making an effort to swallow her sobs now. "We just kept saying, 'Just don't hurt us. Just take the camcorder and our money and go on.'"

"Anybody shot?" I asked. Everybody on our team was still standing, which I took to be a good sign, but I was too far away to see clearly and I couldn't leave my post. "If not, I could use some help over here, Larry."

I heard hurried footsteps and made out several figures moving toward us down the alley.

Larry came over and gazed down at our captive. "We've got to get out of here," I said in a low voice. "We've got to get *him* out of here, before the cops show up and start asking questions."

"We must call the police, Hank," Elvis said. "How do we do that?"

"What's going on here?" called a deep voice.

"Ask the guy to use his cell phone to call nine-one-one," I said. I didn't want the call to be traced to Elvis's phone. I wanted to buy some time. I wanted to get out of there.

Larry, who didn't strike me as the handy type, was nevertheless using the shoulder strap from the camcorder to tie the hands of our mugger and making a creditable job of it. "Nine-one-one?" he echoed.

"I thought maybe you were the cops," the woman said. "You know, like plainclothes. Though now that I get a look at you, you're more like some kind of superhero." She was feeling the force of Elvis's magnetic personality, and smiling up at him. "The way you came rushing in, it was just like Superman or something. If you hadn't done that, we might have been killed."

A figure approached her and patted her shoulder. "Honey, are you okay?" it said, a woman's voice.

A group of men, backlit so that I couldn't make out their expressions, now formed a small circle around me. At least one of them smelled like tobacco and beer. "What's going on?" one of them said. "A mugging?"

The male victim was talking on his cell phone.

"Yeah," I said. "Keep an eye on him, will you?"

"No problem," one said, the deeper voice this time. Now that they'd been given a job, they focused on the man on the ground.

I seized Larry by the elbow, waved Elvis over, and met him halfway.

"If you folks are sure you're okay," I said, and raised a hand to them, "we'll head out. Just wait here till the cops get here. This guy shouldn't give you any more trouble."

The man looked up in surprise, but he was still engaged in conversation with the dispatcher.

"Wait!" the woman said. "You shouldn't just rush off like that. The police will want to talk to you, I'm sure. They'll probably give him a medal, and put him on T.V."

My worst fear.

"Have a nice evening," I said, smiling, walking backward in the direction of the street.

Larry and Elvis were nowhere in sight.

I turned and fled. When I spotted Elvis and Larry watching for me, half a block up, I waved at them. "Run!" I shouted. "Beat it!"

We could hear sirens as I led them past the main entrance to the hotel, around the corner, and into the parking garage.

As I caught my breath by the elevators, one hand on the wall, I listened to Larry and Elvis argue. Out of deference to me, I suppose, they were arguing in English.

"I'm a police officer, Larry," Elvis said. "I'm not supposed to split like that. If Sergeant Friday were here, he'd tell you the same thing."

"All right," Larry said. "And what would you tell them when they couldn't find the gun?"

Silence.

"Just out of curiosity," I put in, "what did happen to the gun?"

"I de-commissioned it," Elvis said. "I de-activated it."

"You vaporized it?"

"I transported it."

"Somewhere in the twelfth dimension of the Pixor Galaxy," Larry said, "it's raining antique Earth weapons." That was astonishingly witty for Larry, even if it was true.

"Dude," I said to Elvis, "remind me never to piss you off."

CHAPTER SEVEN

The incident didn't make the ten o'clock news an hour later. I went to bed relieved but apprehensive. I'd left Elvis and Larry watching *Blue Hawaii*, one of the movies I'd rented for them while I'd been out walking around earlier.

Elvis had been delighted. "Where did you get these, Hank? At a video store?"

When I'd nodded, he'd said, "It's very thoughtful of you, Hank, but after this, you won't need to go to a video store. I got Netflix."

You might think that with all I had on my mind, I shouldn't have been able to sleep, but I collapsed on the bed and sleep fell on me like a lead blanket. I was still groggy as I brushed my teeth next morning, when it occurred to me to open my door and look for the newspaper. Toothbrush in one hand, I padded to the door and peeked out. I picked up the paper and unfolded it. Clearly, *USA Today* had bigger fish to fry than a foiled mugging in the nation's capital. My sigh of relief was cut short by the sight of a large floral display, discreet as a politician in Iowa, parked in the hall outside the boys' door. I checked the card. It said coyly, "In appreciation," and was signed, "The Management."

I swore under my breath, and, still carrying the toothbrush and newspaper, turned on the television. On the *Today* show, Meredith Vieira was sitting next to two middle-aged people.

"And how did you feel, Pat, when this giant of a man burst onto the scene and rescued you?" Meredith said.

"Well, how would *you* feel, Meredith?" the woman said. I gave her points for answering a stupid question with the obvious answer. She looked different under the television lights than she had last night, but her voice sounded familiar. She was wearing bright pink pants and a flowered pink-and-red blouse that must have given the make-up person fits. The man wore dark green slacks and a pink polo shirt. Together, they were accelerating spring by a good month.

I barely stopped to wonder how word had gotten out so quickly. It must have been a slow news night for some poor AP or UPI stringer, bored with Congressional shenanigans. There had been a time when no respectable newspaper would have been interested in a story like this. It would have been no more than a tabloid headline looming over the conveyor belt at the IGA: "D.C. Couple Saved by 8' Elvis Impersonator!" But now that tabloid journalism had infected the whole industry, the news media at large would do anything to sell papers—probably even run a "kidnapped by aliens" story.

Meredith changed tacks. "So tell us the part about Elvis Presley again. You say he looked like Elvis, only taller. More than seven feet, I think you said?"

Pat backed down. "That could have been a slight exaggeration. There wasn't much light, there where we were. But he was a very tall man, wasn't he, Ed? Like a famous basketball player or something."

Ed nodded agreement, apparently unruffled by his debut on national television. "He was tall, all right. I remember thinking, if he knocks that light fixture down, we'll be in a pickle."

"But he looked like Elvis Presley?" Meredith wants to know.

"Just like him," Pat says.

"In his younger days—you know," Ed says.

"Of course, we weren't Elvis fans in those days," Pat says. "We were too young. And later we were Deadheads." She says this casually, as if clarifying a recipe ingredient: no, it was corn oil we used to use, not canola.

"What Pat means is that we aren't experts on the young Elvis," Ed says. "And of course the light was bad."

"That's true," Pat says, before Meredith can jump in, as she obviously wants to do. "If you put that guy in a line-up with five other seven-and-a-half-foot Elvis impersonators, I might not be able to pick him out." She says this with a straight face.

"When we come back," Meredith says to the camera, "who is this mysterious superhero, and where is he now?"

We were living on borrowed time: that much was clear.

There was a knock on the door.

"Have you been watching television, Hank?" Elvis said. If you'd seen him, you wouldn't have asked whether androids had emotions or not; they were waging battle on his face as he tried to read my expression. He was pleased with his notoriety, but he was also anxious, and prepared to be worried if I was.

Larry was trailing behind. "I'm concerned," he said, "that our mission might already have been compromised. I think we'd better send him back to the ship and move to another location ourselves. Perhaps people will think he's left town."

"I can't go back to the ship," Elvis protested. "I'm going salsa dancing tonight with Pedro and George."

Larry frowned. "Who are Pedro and George?"

A useless question, in my book. The big guy collected buddies the way dark fabric collects cat hair.

He was surprised in turn. "You don't know Pedro and George? Yes, you do know them, Larry. They work at the concierge desk, one to nine. Pedro is the funny one, and George—."

"I don't think it matters," I said. "I don't even know how we'd smuggle him out of the hotel."

"That's true," Elvis said. "I'm too big to keep over wraps."

"Anyway, I'm surprised we haven't heard from the press already."

The phone rang. A female voice, speaking in a conspiratorial whisper, said that a reporter and photographer were standing in front of the reception desk, and did we want to see them.

"Give us a few minutes," I said. "We'll let you know."

"It's all my fault," Larry was saying as I hung up the phone. "I should have made him stay with the ship. But he's—well, he's just not made for solitary confinement. Is that what you call it?"

"Lighten up," I said. I tried smiling, as if taking my own advice. "You haven't failed yet." I walked to the window and looked out. I couldn't see the front of the hotel from where I was standing, but I did catch sight of a van sporting a satellite dish, speeding through the intersection below. I didn't know how good hotel security was, but if we didn't meet the press now, they'd find somebody to bribe and camp out on our doorstep or take the room across the hall.

There was a knock on the door.

Through the peephole, I saw a distinguished-looking dark-haired man in a business suit. I asked him to identify himself.

"Mr. Jones, it's Alex Otaryan, the hotel manager. I want to know if I can be of assistance."

Now, I know what you're thinking, but "Jones" happens to be my real name. I'll admit that I'd considered an alias when I checked in, but discarded it when I thought of the credit card they were likely to ask me for. I found myself hoping I could reach my mother before she saw my picture on television.

I opened the door. "I expect you've had some experience in handling situations like this," I said, and waved him in. "We're open to suggestions."

I could see now that he wore a beautifully tailored suit. He was rather a slight man, with olive skin and black wavy hair. He told us he went by "Alex O.," and invited us to call him "Alex."

He smiled reassuringly and shook hands all around. "I do have some experience, yes—more than I would if I were managing a hotel in Chicago, say, or San Francisco. May I begin by saying that the Marriott is proud to have you, Mr. Preston, as our guest?"

We hadn't let Elvis go all the way to "Presley"; at the time I'd still been under the misapprehension that we could exercise some control over him. Now his surname sounded idiotic.

"So," Alex said, rubbing his palms together, "let us deal first with the immediate situation. Are you willing to meet the press, Mr. Preston?"

Larry and Elvis looked at me. "What choice do we have?" I said.

"Practically speaking, Mr. Jones, none," the manager said. "The Washington press corps is notoriously energetic and persistent, even the ones covering local news, and you haven't, I think, the experience necessary to outrun or outwit them. Forgive me if I'm blunt, but we are in a crisis situation here, and a certain directness is necessary."

"Sure," I said.

"We can dig that, Alex," Elvis said. "Don't sit on ceremony."

"But please do have a seat," I said.

Alex sat, crossed his legs, adjusted the crease in his trousers, placed his elbows on the armrest and tented his fingers. He was reassuringly calm.

"May I suggest that you call a press conference for noon? I can take care of that, if you like. We won't have a meeting room available until then, but it will give you some time to prepare."

He looked like a man who knew that preparation was in order.

"Okay," I said.

"Our business facilities are at your disposal," he said, "should you need a computer, printer, or copier. I suggest that you write a statement covering the basics—whatever you wish to reveal—and make copies to hand out. You may, of course, decide whether you want to entertain questions."

"Okay," I said.

"I warn you that the questions will likely be very direct and, you may think, entirely too personal," he said. "I don't want to frighten you. The press will be, for the most part, civil, I believe. But I want to prepare you."

"Okay," I said. I'd noticed that the prediction of the reporters' civility required more qualifiers than anything else he'd said so far.

"And, of course, they will take photographs and film you."

I didn't say anything. I saw my mother or my sister turning on the television and spotting a grinning blond bearded guy who looked suspiciously like a near relation. Maybe I wouldn't have to appear on camera.

"Always assuming, of course, that no congressional sex scandal or political brouhaha breaks out between now and noon." He gave a small sigh. "That, however, is probably too much to hope for. There's never a good scandal around when you need one."

Something else wormed its way into my consciousness. I looked at Larry. Elvis didn't look much like the communist spy who had visited Española, New Mexico, in 1951. But Larry looked exactly the same. What if somebody recognized him? It was an outside chance, at best; he had an entirely forgettable face, and in any case, nobody would expect him to look the same age he had looked in 1951. But what if some nutcase assumed that all commie spies looked the same, like Agent Smiths in *The Matrix*? And that they all came with seven-foot bodyguards?

"Is there a hair salon in the hotel?" I asked. He couldn't grow a beard in three hours, but maybe we could do something to disguise him.

"Certainly," Alex said, "and we'd be happy to accommodate you in what we might regard as an emergency situation."

"It's just that—well, Larry here shouldn't be recognized on television," I said, "by, um, his business competitors. They don't know he's in town."

I was making it up as I went along, and it sounded lame to me, but Alex smiled at Larry and said, "I understand completely." And by the glint in his eye, I thought he probably did. Not all of it, of course, but some of it.

"If I may, I'd also like to suggest that you move to a suite on one of our secure floors," he continued. "Frankly, our staff is probably susceptible to bribes where information is concerned, but access to key cards is limited, and I don't believe they'd go so far as to provide one to a reporter. We would charge you the same as we're charging for your current rooms to show our appreciation for your cooperation. We would be better able to guarantee your security, you see."

"Okay," I said.

"Well, if you're agreeable, I'll leave you to make arrangements for the noon press conference," Alex said, and stood up. He adjusted his cuffs, which might have been his equivalent of rolling up his sleeves. "Shall I send you one of our stylists?"

The phone rang. It was the front desk again, for Alex.

"The police have arrived," he told us. "They're on their way up, so we'll delay the stylist for a while, shall we? They'll want your statements about last night. My advice is to keep things simple and truthful, but of course, you'll follow your own inclinations."

In the brief time we had, I devised a new back-story for Larry and Elvis. They were businessmen from the Solomon Islands who represented a conglomerate of foreign investors wanting to market a highly competitive product to the United States.

Elvis frowned. "What product?"

As we talked, I was Googling Solomon Islands addresses.

"Uh, I don't know—a special device that improves the stability of fighter jets at high altitudes."

"All right," Larry said. "We can do that."

"I can't be a Georgetown recruit anymore?" Elvis asked.

"Too risky," I said. "The Hoyas never heard of you." I scribbled an address on a note pad. "I'm showing you around as a favor to my cousin, uh, my cousin Mary. Memorize this address. You know where the Solomons are, don't you?"

"Near New Guinea," Larry said. "Northeast of Australia."

"They export palm oil and copra," Elvis said. "And they fish."

"Good. We're going to hope they know less about the place than you do. And remember—we don't know what happened to the gun."

There were two D.C. detectives—a pony-tailed brunette named Murphy and an older bald man named Shoenfeld. They expressed a desire to interview us all separately, and asked if I could wait in the hall for a few minutes. Murphy took Larry back to his room, and Shoenfeld settled in my room with Elvis. When it was my turn, they excused Larry and Elvis to their room, and the two detectives settled down in the two available armchairs in my room, leaving me to sit on the unmade bed.

They asked me politely for my name, address, and occupation, and then asked about my relationship to Larry and Elvis. I gave them my line about Cousin Mary, and Shoenfeld made a note without comment. They asked me to tell them what had happened the night before, and I said that I'd arrived on the scene last, and couldn't see very well in the dim light. I gave them a streamlined version of what I'd seen. They asked me if I'd seen a gun. I said that I'd heard a gun, but hadn't actually seen one. That part was certainly true. They asked if I knew what had happened to the gun, and I said that I didn't. They asked me why we'd left the scene, and I said that Larry had some concerns about being identified either by his competitors or by agents of another government that might want to obtain this technology for themselves. I hoped that Larry and Elvis had explained stabilizers in a sufficiently arcane and confusing way to ward off further questions.

"These stabilizers," the woman detective said, "you understand what they are?"

"Not me," I said. "I'm just a grad student in American studies. My field is semiotics."

They chose not to pursue that, and invited me down to the station some time in the next forty-eight hours to make an official statement and sign it.

"The guy we captured," I said, "does he have a record?"

"Oh, yeah," the male detective said. "We know him well. My guess is he'll plea-bargain, and we won't need your testimony. But it's always a possibility. We won't drag your friends back here from the Solomons unless we need to."

"That's a relief," I said, and we all shook hands.

When they'd gone, Larry and Elvis rejoined me.

"We think they believed our story, Hank," Larry said.

I grinned at him and raised a hand in his direction, but he didn't know what to do with it. "Raise your hand, palm out," I told him.

He did, and I slapped it. "That's known as a 'high five.' It's, like, a celebratory gesture. Like a congratulations. You might see basketball players and other athletes use it after one of them makes a really good move—sinks a basket or blocks a shot. Somebody might say to you, 'Give me five,' and then you slap their hand."

"Give me five," Elvis said to Larry, and held up his hand. When Larry reciprocated, he gave it a whack that made Larry wince.

"Not quite so hard, big guy," I said.

"I'm sorry," he said, contrite.

"Now, bring me the laptop and call down to the desk to let them know we're ready for the stylist."

"But why do we need a stylist, Hank? Are you going to get a haircut, too?"

"We need to change Larry's appearance, so that nobody who knew him in New Mexico will recognize him."

"He is going to get a makeover?" he asked, clearly thrilled. "Will it be an extreme makeover? We could use a queer eye, couldn't we?"

I shook my head. "We don't have time for that." I was already typing.

"You're wrong, Hank," Elvis said. "On television I saw a team do a makeover in less than three hours, including a manicure!"

Elvis went to answer the door and ushered in a very cosmopolitan, very stylish young man carrying a case.

"This is Jeremy," he announced. "Jeremy, are you going to do the makeover by yourself? Do you have queer eyes?"

Whatever he had, Jeremy couldn't take his eyes off of Elvis. "You are so good," he said. "You look just like him. I'd love to know who your surgeon was."

Elvis raised the curtain of his lip in an appreciative smile, and I explained what we needed.

"So, you don't need Larry here to look like somebody else in particular," he said, "because I could do him as a congressman I know from Arizona, or maybe this reporter I know in the *Times* Washington bureau."

"No, we just need for him not to look like himself," I said.

"Incognito," Jeremy said, and winked at Larry. "Gotcha. This will be fun."

So I worked on the statement while Jeremy and Larry retired to the bathroom. Elvis chose to follow them, expecting a better show than I was providing. At one point, I heard Jeremy on the phone, and at several points he went to answer the door, but I was absorbed in the tale I was spinning.

Jeremy made us late for the press conference because he couldn't decide whether to add a display handkerchief or not. Larry was by now a graying blond with styled hair, tortoiseshell glasses, a pale gray Hermés suit, and a collarless white shirt, buttoned up. To my astonishment, he'd also dressed Elvis in a black suit with a narrow lapel and a black shirt, open at the collar. How he'd come up with something that fit on such short notice I couldn't imagine. Elves?

"Stop worrying, Hank," Jeremy told me. "You never want to be on time to your own press conference. It just isn't done." He looked over Larry's shoulder at the image in the mirror. "No handkerchief," he said. "You're perfect the way you are. Well, we could improve on the shoes, of course, if we had more time.

"And you," he said, looking me over, "you could definitely use a new outfit."

I looked down at my rumpled chinos and knit pullover. "This *is* my new outfit."

Elvis was enthusiastic. "You look swell!" he said to Larry. "Give me six."

We'd drawn a respectable crowd, but I was relieved that it was no larger than it was. If we seemed dull enough, they'd all go away with nothing to report.

Elvis read the statement I'd prepared, and the reporters followed along. He made it all sound perfectly plausible, I thought. I would have preferred to stand in the back, but Larry thought it best that I sit with Elvis, in case he needed translation or restraint. Larry stood in the back with Alex O. and Jeremy and watched the reporters with an experienced eye.

"He'll take a few questions," I said when he'd finished, on Alex's advice. "But I'm sure you can appreciate that the delicate nature of his business negotiations make some topics off-limits." I felt my phone vibrate inside my pocket. I imagined that the angry buzz signaled a call from my sister.

The first question was innocuous enough. "Mr. Preston— Elvis—I understand that the mugger had a gun. Weren't you afraid of it?"

"The light was bad, ma'am," Elvis said, as I'd instructed him. "I didn't actually see the gun at first, when I made the scene." I breathed a sigh of relief. But the woman reporter was still looking at him expectantly, so he expanded. "Besides, in my country, I have some experience with law enforcement." I poked him under the table, and he shut up.

"Mr. Preston!" called a weasel-faced young man. "Surely you don't expect us to believe that your real name is 'Elvis Preston.'"

"I don't expect you to believe anything," Elvis said. He gave the man a disarming smile. "In your country, the press is supposed to question everything, isn't that right?"

This sally was greeted with good-natured laughter, and I hoped we'd put the matter to rest.

But one of the weasel's colleagues pressed the point. "But apart from your height, you look and sound like Elvis Presley," he said. "Is Elvis that big where you come from?"

"Not as big as I am," Elvis admitted, which brought him another laugh. "But in the world of rock and roll, he is the King. Everyone knows this."

A friendlier question followed. "Is this your first trip to Washington, Mr. Preston?"

"Yes," he said, "but I have always wanted to visit."

"Are you surprised by the street crime here?" someone asked.

"I am always surprised by crime," Elvis said, "even though—."

I poked him and he stopped short.

"Even though what?" the weasel's friend demanded.

"Even though crime is a natural product of an immature mind," he said smoothly. "Isn't that right?"

Nobody seemed inclined to disagree, especially since they didn't know what he was talking about.

"Are you doing any sightseeing while you're in town, Mr. Preston?" This from a tall, attractive brunette whose coy expression suggested that she wouldn't mind showing him around.

"Oh, yes," he said. "We were just returning from the Lincoln Memorial last night when—when the trouble occurred." He paused. "I was reading the Gettysburg Address. It is a swell speech."

"No more questions," I announced then. "Thank you, ladies and gentlemen."

I raised my hand to stem the tide, and Elvis slapped it.

CHAPTER EIGHT

"What we need," I said, "is a consultant."

We were sitting in the living room area of our new suite. Phone conversations with my mother and sister had left me feeling shaken, inadequate.

"But Hank," my mother had said, bafflement in her voice, "I thought you were looking forward to working on your dissertation over Spring Break. Isn't that what you should be doing? Can you afford a trip to Washington, D.C.?"

"What are you *doing*, Hank?" my sister had wanted to know. "Consultant to a couple of foreign businessmen? This makes no sense. We don't even have a cousin Mary. Tell me you haven't been forced to work for terrorists who are holding Anita hostage. That Elvis guy is downright creepy."

"I wouldn't cross the street to save Anita from terrorists," I'd muttered as I turned the phone off.

"Good for you, Hank!" Elvis had said. "She can't break your heart anymore. You will find another baby soon, I know. There were many dollies at the press conference."

Now, he said, "But Hank, you are our consultant, isn't that right?"

I shook my head. "I'm not a Washington insider. That's what we need. Pretty soon, some enterprising individual in Homeland Security or the F.B.I. is going to wonder how and when you entered the country. And when they can't find an 'Elvis Preston' or a

'Lawrence Smith' on any of the airlines' passenger lists, they'll get curious. It might not happen today or tomorrow, but it'll happen. And you know what happened the last time people got suspicious."

Elvis nodded. "Larry died."

I was confused. "Wait, he *died*? I thought he just got shot."

A look passed between them. "Very unpleasant, I'll admit," Larry said. He couldn't get used to the glasses, which were parked on top of his head. "I wouldn't mind avoiding that, if I could."

"But we did a good press conference, didn't we?" Elvis said.

Elvis liked praise as well as the next robot, and I didn't mind giving it to him. But the truth was, he was too charming not to excite interest. I'd hoped we could bore our audience. No such luck. As soon as he gave them that lopsided smile and drawled his first "ma'am," I watched the room divide into Elvis fans and skeptics. Both groups would be working overtime to find out more about him.

"Don't worry, Hank," Larry said. "I recognize that our time is short. But if we could manage another twenty-four hours even, I'd be grateful. I'm learning a great deal about your people and your culture. Perhaps I'm beginning to understand the mistakes I made last time."

The phone rang. It was Alex.

"Sorry to bother you, Hank, but there's a gentleman here who insists that he's an old friend of Mr. Smith's. He's very persistent, and claims that he's been holding some mail for Mr. Smith, which appears to be true. He also claims that if he could speak to Mr. Smith for just a moment, he could establish his identity, and Mr. Smith would want to see him. What should I do?"

I turned to look at Larry, sitting next to me on the couch. I was slouched and my feet were on the glass-topped cherry coffee table; his posture was impeccable and his legs were neatly crossed. "Put him on," I said, and passed the phone to Larry.

I didn't hear what the caller said, but I saw a smile of pleasurable recognition spread across Larry's face.

"Robbie!" he said. "How good to hear your voice. Oh, I—." He paused, and then seemed to put a mental finger on an entry in his lexicon. "Can't complain, I guess. How are you?" He listened, then said, "And you're just downstairs? Oh, yes, do come up. Let me talk to Mr. Otaryan."

The arrangements made, Larry hung up and turned to me in

what, for him, passed as excitement.

Elvis was on his feet. "*Our* Robbie? Was it really our Robbie?"

"The Cub Scout, right?" I said. "The one you hung out with when you came before."

"Yes," he said, and seemed genuinely happy for the first time since I'd met him.

"What did he say to you?"

Larry smiled. "He said, 'Klaptok zisto, you old son of a gun.'"

"Oh, he remembered!" Elvis's voice was thick and his eyes glinted. Clearly, he'd been designed with tear ducts as well as emotions. He turned to me. "That means, 'I come in peace' in our language. We taught Robbie how to say it."

"He will have changed," I said gently. "He's aged fifty-six years."

Larry sighed. "I know," he said. "I've changed, too—and I don't mean that my appearance has changed. Well, we'll see."

The man he ushered into the room a few minutes later was something of a surprise. It wasn't his age; he looked perhaps ten years younger than his age—mid-fifties rather than mid-sixties, I would have said, but still, his youthfulness alone wouldn't have surprised me. No, it was his type. Never having met the guy, I had no business with preconceptions of any kind, but nevertheless I'd expected the fresh-faced Cub Scout to have turned into a retired executive in a suit, or maybe leisure slacks and a golf shirt. Robbie Donovan was an aging hippie. He had white hair pulled back from a bald crown into a ponytail and a rather scruffy white beard. He wore capacious sky-blue patterned cotton trousers that tied at the waist and a tee shirt whose message I couldn't read under his gray hooded sweatshirt. On his feet he wore brown socks and leather sandals ugly enough to be original-model Birkenstocks. He was carrying an unbleached canvas bag that touted a local health food store. His grin stretched across wide cheeks. He had an arm slung across Larry's shoulder. As he entered, I caught a whiff of patchouli.

"Just look at you, man," he was saying. "You don't look a day older. Where you been keeping yourself? Outside time?"

"Something like that," Larry said.

Robbie slapped him on the back and said, "That's okay, man. No need to explain. Be over my head, I'm sure."

Elvis and I had stood up, and he noticed us now.

"Hey! That can't be—. No, no way! Is that the Yarpster?"

"Yes," Elvis said, fluttering his hands against his chest the way he did when he got excited. "Yes, it's me."

"No way!" He looked Elvis up and down with sincere wonder and admiration. "Well, it has to be, of course. How many seven-foot robots could you fit on that ship?" He threw his arms around Elvis for a long hug, then stood back and examined him again. "But look at you, dude! You're too much! What'd you do with the old Yarp?"

"I redesigned him, Robbie," he said. "Do you like my new look?"

Robbie shook his head in wonderment. "Far out," he said.

"And this is our friend, Hank," Larry said.

I was a little worried that Robbie Donovan might regard me as an interloper, someone who had taken his place, but he took my hand in both of his and shook it warmly. "Pleasure, man. So what do you think of these two characters? They're a trip, aren't they?"

He threw an arm around Elvis again, but could only reach to the middle of his back.

"How's that pitching arm?" he asked. Then he turned serious. "But listen. You guys got no idea how glad I am to see you. Last time I saw you—." He seemed to choke up. "Well, Mr. S., I didn't know whether you'd make it or not. If only I'd taught you how to read smoke signals, dudes, I could've warned you."

"Since we are such old friends, Robbie," Larry said, "I think you should call me 'Larry,' like everyone else."

Robbie laughed. "Sure thing, dude. Whatever you want. You're the boss."

"No skin off your wazoo, right, Robbie?" Elvis said.

This made Robbie laugh harder.

"I'll call you whatever you want, dudes." He laid a hand on Elvis's arm. "Just send me a news flash, bro, if you decide to change your name again to Mick Jaggar or Justin Timberlake or Beyoncé."

I was really starting to like this guy. What our team needed was a little levity. This business of saving the Earth—I'd been letting it get to me. Now that Robbie was here, the atmosphere in the room was effervescent. He didn't appear a likely candidate for the aid and advice we needed, but humor was no small contribution.

"Did you get your merit badge for aviation, Robbie?" Elvis asked.

Robbie made a dismissive gesture. "Nah, after all the parents went apeshit, I decided they weren't ready to digest a photograph of me standing in front of a flying saucer. But I appreciated what you did for me, and I still got the picture." He beamed at them, shaking his head. "Un-fucking-believable that you're here and I'm here, right here in Washington, D.C. I never thought I'd see you two again. Must be chuktok, huh?"

"I have to ask you something," I said to him, as he wiped his eyes. "How did you know who they were?" I indicated the Elvis look-alike and the incognito Larry.

"Oh, shit, I can see what you mean," Robbie said, regarding them. "It was something about the way Mr. Smith—Larry here— was standing. Can't explain it. His thinness, the set of his shoulders. One of the news reports showed him in the back of the room, you know. And I felt this weird sensation, like somebody tugging on my ponytail. I said, 'Who is that guy?' And somebody said, 'Elvis.' And I said, 'No, the other dude.' And then the news crawl gave his name—Lawrence Smith. And I thought, 'Far fucking out!'"

"But what are you doing in Washington, D.C., Robbie?" Elvis asked.

"I got a gig in a music store near Dupont Circle, sometimes run sound for local bands," he said. "Old story—I followed a chick here and just never split. Don't ask me why. Probably chuktok."

"Are your parents still living, Robbie?" Larry asked. He asked politely, as anybody might who hadn't been shot by one of the parties in question.

"My mother is," Robbie said.

"I liked your mother," Elvis said. "Betty was cool."

"She always liked you guys, too," Robbie said. "Well, it didn't hurt that you helped her bake cookies that one time, Yarp, or that you fixed her washing machine." He laughed again. "Wish I had a picture of you in that apron, dude."

"How is your mother, Robbie?" Larry asked.

"She has her good days and bad days," Robbie said. "She's got an assisted living apartment in Bethesda—in fact, we'll go see her. She uses a walker and plays Bingo most days, you know. She's forgetful, but she's still got most of her marbles. Probably more than me, come to think of it. I've smoked a lot of weed over the years— a lot of weed."

"Marijuana," I said. The clarification was automatic.

"A controlled substance in this country, isn't that right, Hank?" Elvis said. "Isn't smoking marijuana illegal, Robbie?" As usual, Elvis wasn't accusatory, just curious.

Robbie winked at him. "Only if you get caught, man. Only if you get caught."

I imagined Robbie a potential bad influence on Elvis, but I still couldn't help liking him. Not that I hadn't smoked grass myself, but Elvis had too few inhibitions as it was.

"So what have you been doing with your life since we saw you, Robbie?" Larry asked. He gestured for Robbie to sit down. Robbie sat, slipped his sandals off and crossed his legs.

"Oh, man, what have I been doing?" he said. "A little of this, a little of that. Those diamonds you gave me could have set me up for life, you know, if I'd been more interested in making something of myself and less interested in farting around. Dropped out of college, to my mother's dismay. Would've run off to Canada, if my number had come up in the damn draft, but it never did. Got certified in TM—."

"Transcendental meditation," I translated.

"—Traveled to India and Nepal, went to Senegal in the Peace Corps, played in some bands, managed a head shop and a music store. Oh, and for a while there I did sound for bands on tour. 'Sound consultant'—that's what it says on my tax returns."

"Hanks says we need a consultant," Elvis put in.

"Yeah?" Robbie said. "You taking the act on the road?"

"Tell him, Hank," Elvis said.

So I did. I had no illusions that a former head shop manager with an aptitude for acoustics was the answer to our prayers, but he listened attentively.

"So you need, like, a campaign manager?" he said at last.

"Kind of," I said. "Someone who's politically savvy, knows Washington, and has experience in public relations or advertising, something like that."

"I know just the person," he said.

"You do?" I was skeptical. I was afraid he'd bring me the head shop customer who'd silk-screened his tee shirt.

"Yeah, I do. Name's Ginger DiAngelo, a real fireball. She's run several political campaigns, worked with lobbyists, lots of shit like that. Don't know if she's busy, but I can give her a call. But hey, you're not going to give her that crap about representing a foreign manufacturer, are you? That was really lame."

"Can we trust her?"

Robbie had already pulled a cell phone out of his pocket and was dialing it.

"Yo, Ginger," he said, "it's Robbie. What're you up to these days?"

He listened for a while, and then said, "Well, hey, I hate to spoil your fun, but I've got kind of an emergency situation here that demands your attention."

I was mouthing, "Don't tell her over the phone," but he nodded at me and gave me a high sign.

"I'm at the Wardman Park Marriott." He laughed. "Yeah, that one. Uh-huh. Okay, babe, I'll give your name to the front desk. Bring your I.D."

He flipped the phone closed and grinned at us. "She's on her way. You'd better call the front desk, Hank."

As I reached for the phone, he said, "Oh, hey, I forgot. I brought you guys some of your mail. Mom's been collecting it all these years. She always said you'd come back for it." He reached down for his canvas bag. "I, uh, took the liberty of pitching all of Mr. S— Larry's—junk mail when I moved her out of her house five years ago. So most of the mail is Yarp's. Don't worry, big guy, I saved your *Reader's Digests*. Oh, and your secret decoder ring."

He emptied the bag on the coffee table.

Larry was puzzled. "This is all for us?" He turned to Elvis, who wouldn't meet his gaze.

"Hey, by the way, you still got a few of those diamonds, don't you, Larry?" Robbie said. "Reason I ask, Ginger's fees are pretty steep. I mean, she might give us an hour or two as a favor to me, or, you know, for the good of the cause and all that, but if we want more than that, we'll have to pay her."

"That's not a problem," Larry said.

"Oh, look!" Elvis was holding up a letter. "My application for a Diners Club card was approved in 1952!"

"Far out!" said Robbie.

CHAPTER NINE

Ginger DiAngelo was a petite dynamo. She entered talking on her cell phone, her free arm flung wide in animated expression. She stood maybe five feet in her platform pumps. She wore a black tailored short-skirted suit with a white open-collared silk blouse and carried a black leather briefcase slung over one shoulder. When she'd disposed of her caller, she shook hands briskly all around. She wasn't startled by Elvis—you could tell that she knew who he was—but she didn't tell what she knew, either.

By this time, we were having a late room-service lunch on a table near the kitchenette. She sat down at the table across from me. She had thick, wavy dark hair that just brushed her ear lobes and dark eyes that fixed me now, as she leaned forward with her chin resting on her fists, unnerving.

I told her everything. She didn't blink when I told her that Larry and Elvis had traveled some two hundred and fifty million miles to warn Earthlings not to deploy nuclear weapons in space. In fact, her lack of response made me wonder if this was the most surprising thing she'd heard all day, or if it had already been trumped by some hot item I couldn't guess at (President Inks Deal with Viagra Marketers? Texas to Secede from the Union?). When somebody else contributed a comment or clarification, her laser eyes shifted to them, but her expression never changed. When I finished, she sat back in her chair and gazed in the aliens' direction, but she didn't seem to be looking at them. She sat silent. Then she picked up her cell phone with one hand, and helped herself to a cold French fry with the other.

"I'll need to bring Howard and Anna in on this," she said, flipping open the phone. "And Jillian, of course. And I'll need to rearrange my schedule."

Panic bubbled in my throat. Who were these people? I hadn't even made up my mind yet about her, and now she was calling in back-up.

"Howard and Anna work for Ginger," Robbie said. "And Jillian's her personal assistant."

Ginger looked too young to have a personal assistant, but then I'd always been bad at guessing women's ages. I supposed, now that I studied her face, that she could have been in her forties—maybe even fifties, if she dyed her hair.

"Don't you have any questions for us?" I asked her.

She held the phone to her ear. "Hold on," she said into it. To me, she said, "You need to get the message out about nuclear weapons in space. You need to communicate with people across the world in a short amount of time, while protecting Larry and Elvis here. You need to convince people that the survival of the Earth depends on how they respond to this warning. Have I got it so far?"

"Well, yeah," I said.

She nodded, and began talking into the phone.

When she hung up, Elvis asked, "Will I still be able to go salsa dancing with Pedro and George tonight?"

"We'll see," she said, not unkindly.

I was feeling claustrophobic, so I changed into my sweatshirt and jeans, put on one of the pairs of sunglasses Jeremy had left with us, and covered my head with my hood. "I'm going for a walk," I announced.

I walked up Calvert toward the Naval Observatory and turned up Cleveland. By now it was four o'clock, and the street traffic was picking up. People passed me running, walking, and ambling; in cars or strollers, on bikes and motorbikes, skates and skateboards and Segways. Clusters of bulging plastic grocery bags bloomed from the ends of their fingers, or they carried briefcases or canvas bags slung over their shoulders or dangling from their elbows. Some were alone, some in groups, and some in couples. There were red-cheeked children in coats too warm for the weather; sallow-faced office workers wearing everything from conservative suits to business casual; sleek, sweat-drenched runners and bikers in skin-tight shorts and shirts; teenagers wearing jeans and sweatshirts, like me, and the occasional denim jacket; older women in dresses and stockings or designer warm-up suits or pantsuits and older men in Redskin jackets or union jackets. Their skin tones ran the gamut from coal black through the full range of umbers and siennas and olive, tan, and rose to translucent ecru. Many wore headphones. But most of them held a cell phone to one ear, elbow crooked. I wondered what an alien visitor would make of it, if he or she were unacquainted with our species and culture.

Unless we paid attention to our extraterrestrial visitors and their warning, all of these people, their hopes and frustrations, the people they loved and the ones they hated and feared, their tools and their toys, would vanish.

I wandered around for a while until my feet carried me into a bar, Murphy's, tucked away on 24th Street between Calvert and Connecticut. I found a vacant stool, ordered a beer, and looked up and into my own eyes.

I didn't look all that good on television, if you want to know the truth. It was partly the television's fault—my skin was too orange and my blond hair and beard glowed as if they'd been irradiated. But my eyes shifted and blinked too much, my posture was lousy, and I fiddled with a pen as if channeling my anxiety into it. I wouldn't have trusted me.

Elvis, on the other hand, was a natural. Sitting comfortably, he smiled his practiced, lopsided smile into the camera and took full advantage of his bedroom eyes when he dropped them to his statement to read. The camera loved him.

"Where'd he get that accent, that's what I want to know," said a man two stools down whose own accent pointed north toward Boston. "How does a guy from a foreign country wind up speaking like that?"

"Easy," said his companion. "He learned English from a Southerner, that's all."

"He learned English from watching Elvis Presley movies," said a third man. "Same place he got his haircut."

"That's another thing," said Number One, squinting at the set. "How'd he get to look so much like Elvis Presley? You tell me that. You think they got plastic surgeons over there in wherever the fuck he's from can do that?"

"Sure," said Number Three. "You give 'em a picture of Elvis Presley, tell 'em, 'I want to look like that.' Time they take the bandages off, you look just like him—or Brad Pitt or whoever the fuck you want to look like."

"I sure as hell wouldn't pick Elvis Presley," said Number One.

"At least he picked Elvis when he was young," said Two. "Not that fat fucker used to wear white jumpsuits and sing in Vegas."

"Some of these countries, they got better plastic surgeons than we do." Three pursued his favorite theory. "We train 'em, then they go back over there to Egypt or wherever. I heard it's all free over there, too. You walk in, say, 'I want a nose job,' fill out a form, and that's it."

"Don't get me started on the health care system," said One, who wanted nothing better.

By the time they'd chewed on the health care system and spit it out, the television had moved on to something else—the latest contestants on *American Idol* or *Dancing with the Stars*, I couldn't really tell which. But Number One wanted to return to a discussion of Elvis.

"I don't know," he said. "That Elvis guy, he just don't sound to me like he comes from a foreign country. I can usually tell."

"Yeah, but he don't sound one-hundred-percent Southern to me, either," said Number Two.

"I'll tell you one thing," Three said. "He shows up while I'm getting mugged, I ain't asking to see his Green Card."

"Listen, I get mugged—." Number One tapped the pocket of his Pipefitters Local jacket. "I can take care of myself."

"He can, too," Number Two affirmed. "I've seen him shoot at the range."

"You can't depend on nobody, so you got to depend on yourself, that's my motto," Number One said. "And I'll tell you something else." He pointed an index finger at the television and tapped the air for emphasis. "That other guy, the American? One sat next to the Elvis guy? That guy looked nervous as hell. I'm asking myself why."

I laid money on the bar and left.

Back at Central Command, the dining table was a beehive of activity in the midst of our former sanctuary. It was littered with three laptops, four cell phones, four little black boxes that might have been BlackBerries, two legal pads, three Styrofoam cups of coffee, and two cans of Diet Coke, plus random packets of artificial sweetener in three colors. On the floor in the near vicinity were several wads of paper, a rolling file, and a scattering of shoes in both genders.

I was introduced to the three newcomers: Howard, a tallish, thin young man in wire-rims who seemed almost as intense as his boss; Anna, a busty, cheerful-looking coffee-skinned young woman whose tidy corn rows hugged her head; and Jillian, whose frizzy auburn hair was constrained by a clip on the back of her head and whose irregular features made her face appear to have been designed by a committee.

Elvis was sitting on the couch playing a video game with Robbie. Larry was nowhere in sight. "Hank!" he called. "I get to go salsa dancing!"

"You're letting him go salsa dancing?" I said to Ginger.

"Sit down, Hank," she said. "Let us fill you in."

I sat. Howard was tapping away at his keyboard and Anna was on the phone.

"Okay," she said. "Operation E.T."

"E.T.?"

"For the first week, our focus will be on promoting Elvis and Larry as friendly, ordinary businessmen who are unintentional celebrities."

"The first week?" I said. "I'm supposed to be back in the classroom Monday morning."

She gave me a reproachful look. "Hank," she said, "do you want to save the Earth or teach a handful of freshmen how to write passable prose?"

"I'm not sure I can do either," I said. "But go ahead."

"What we're going to be doing, Hank," she said, "is building trust, so that when our friendly spacemen deliver the message they've come to deliver, people will trust them."

"Okay," I said.

"Now, research shows that the majority of people most trust someone like themselves," she said.

"Fifty-one percent in the U.S. on the Edelman Trust Barometer," Howard said. "Leads every category in North America, Latin America, and Europe. Comes in second only to physicians in Asia— don't ask me why. And people trust business more than the government or the media. Also, some celebrities they trust."

"How does Elvis fare?"

Ginger frowned. She was taking this seriously. "Well, at least he picked the young Elvis. We'd have a hard time selling him as a Vegas headliner."

"People don't trust Barry Manilow?" I said.

"Not on issues of planetary annihilation," Howard said.

"So, you want to turn him into a celebrity businessman who seems just like everybody else," I said.

"Not just him," she said. "Larry, too."

"It would help if one of them could cook," Howard mused. "Rachael Ray is very highly ranked among trustworthy celebs. She even beats Oprah."

"I can make cookies," Elvis called from the couch.

"We're concentrating first on beefing up their business cred," she said. "I sent Larry off to the ship to contact his people and see if we can establish trade relations. People may not trust their trading partners, but they don't expect governments to act against their trade interests, either."

"You mean, by annihilating their market?"

"Exactly. So if we could find something to export—."

"You know," Howard said. "Something we make that they want."

They couldn't be serious. But they were.

"Elvis C.D.'s?" I said.

"Better if it were made out of corn," Howard said. "Best, of course, if Earth could trade corn oil for crude oil."

"Do we know that C.D.'s aren't made out of corn?" Ginger said.

"I'll get right on it," Howard said.

"You think we'd stop manufacturing nuclear warheads if we could sell corn to the Andromeda Galaxy?" I said.

"That's the way it works, Hank," Ginger said. "We do it all the time—offer economic incentives—bribes, really—for disarmament."

"It boggles the mind," I said.

"Yes, well, the point is that we want Elvis to go salsa dancing. We want him to be seen out and about."

"Eating hot dogs and kissing babies," I said.

"You've got it. The more ordinary, the better."

"And Larry will go salsa dancing, too?" I said. This I wanted to see.

"Maybe. We thought of sending him to see *Blades of Glory*, but it doesn't maximize his exposure."

"*Blades of Glory*? Tell me you're kidding."

"We might send him to the Kennedy Center. Too bad we missed the jazz legends," she said. "Tomorrow we have them booked on a bus tour of Washington. Thursday we'll take them to the Smithsonian."

"I want to send them to Disney World," Howard said, "but Ginger isn't sold on the idea."

Elvis appeared. He was carrying some kind of gaming system console. "I want to go to the spy museum," he said.

"Bad idea," she said. "Too many negative associations. But don't worry. You'll love the Smithsonian. And afterwards, if the weather's nice, we'll have them fly kites on the Mall."

"Will we go shopping again?" Elvis asked hopefully.

"Tomorrow after the tour, unless you're too tired."

It wasn't clear to me that Elvis could be tired; I wasn't even sure whether he slept at night. I suspected that he spent the wee hours surfing the Web and watching old sci-fi flicks. He'd told me this morning that the aliens in *Close Encounters* looked a lot like a Quantifarian boogleball team. On another occasion, he'd smiled slyly and said, "Aren't you glad I came back as Elvis and not Barbarella, Hank?" I didn't want to go there.

Now he fluttered his fingers against his chest, and said to me, "I want to buy a guitar, Hank. Robbie's going to teach me to play."

He turned back to Ginger. "Ginger? Can we go to a drive-in movie? You know with the microphones"—he made a clipping motion with his hands—"hanging on the automobile window? I would like to see that fly-man movie." He had a thing for clip-on equipment that I didn't really understand—maybe it had some kind of retro appeal even for super-sophisticated aliens.

"*Spider-Man*," I corrected.

"Yesss!" Anna snapped her phone shut and pumped the air with her fist. "I got it!"

"Got what?" I said. It was obviously my job to play straight man around here.

"I got the rights to the John Williams score for *E.T.*" Howard gave her a high-five. "The basis for Elvis's new theme music."

"Theme music?" I said.

She leapt from her chair and did a little dance.

"Awesome!" Elvis said. "Far fucking out!"

CHAPTER TEN

I never said I knew how to dance. Drink, yes; dance, no. Anita always said I danced like a hibernating bear.

So how did I come to be sitting at a table, front and center, at the hottest dance club in D.C.? Yet another job for which I was spectacularly underqualified.

I was nursing a Dos Equis, wedged between two other people who showed no signs of joining in the merriment. To my left was Larry, who'd staged an impressive resistance to both *Blades of Glory* and the Kennedy Center; he sat intent as an anthropologist. On my right sat the woman I was coming to think of as "Jillian Of Course," who appeared to be the team gofer, dogsbody, and, at the moment, chaperone to the stars.

The star in question was on the dance floor, dancing with a tall, graceful Latina. And he was good. He could swivel his hips, snap his knees, and pop his shoulders just like the King, and he had the same air of abandoning himself to the music while remaining conscious of the audience he was entertaining. His eyes glittered with fun below the wild fringe of hair shaken loose from its Brylcreem. His teeth brushed his lower lip as he sent his smile around the dance floor.

Larry leaned my way. "There's a piece of fruit wedged in my beer bottle, Hank," he said.

"That's a lime," I said.

"You can leave it there, or take it out and run it around the edge of the bottle like this," Jillian said, and demonstrated.

He tried it, then held the lime wedge between a fastidious thumb and forefinger and drank. "Very tasty," he said. "But do all evening entertainments on this planet now involve drinking alcohol?"

"Pretty much," I admitted. "Unless it's a spaghetti dinner at the First Baptist Church."

He nodded. "Do people ever drink martinis anymore? I believe that was the fashionable drink when I was here before, although I never got to try one. The Siesta Coffee Shop and Frank's Atomic Diner did not serve alcohol."

Jillian told him that there were circles in which martinis were still fashionable, and circles in which they'd made a comeback, but that wine had largely replaced cocktails as a social lubricant.

I'd had hopes tonight of staying in my hotel room and catching up on my e-mail and phone mail, both of which were piling up. I'd even cherished hopes of a non-alcoholic night, so I sympathized with Larry.

"You don't have to drink alcohol, you know," I said to him. "We'll order you a Coke." I flagged down the waiter, who returned with a Coke. It was decorated with a maraschino cherry skewered by a pink plastic sword, which Larry eyed with interest.

I turned to Jillian and said, "So, do you ever get to say no to the Big Cheese?"

"Ginger?" she said. "No."

"What about your personal life?" I said.

"Excuse me?"

"Oh."

"What about *your* personal life?" she said.

"Missing in action since my girlfriend moved in with my dissertation director."

"I knew there was a reason why I was avoiding graduate school."

"Nothing but heartache," I said. "Take it from me. Of course, my students adore me."

"Really?"

"No."

She nodded.

Larry nudged me. "Tell her about your dissertation," he said.

"Larry, even I am not interested in my dissertation," I said.

He looked at Jillian. Her tangle of auburn hair was at half-mast; apparently, the clip that held it more or less pinned to the back of her head did not work overtime. "It's about semiotics," he said. "He can tell you fascinating things about ketchup and hot sauce bottles."

"Really?" she said.

"No," I said.

Elvis returned to the table to introduce his partner, who was wearing a short, red, spaghetti-strapped diaphanous number that I saw Jillian eyeing with envy. Jillian was still wearing a charcoal-gray pin-striped pantsuit.

"Come and dance, Larry," Elvis urged. To me he said, "Larry is a swell dancer. He's just shy." To the beautiful Lydia, he said, "Larry is enjoying a Coke right now—the pause that refreshes. Maybe when he's finished he'll get up and bust some moves."

"What would you study in grad school if you went?" I asked Jillian.

"I don't know," she said. "Public administration, maybe. Maybe law school."

"Wow!" I said. "That takes a lot of dedication."

"Why I'm not there," she said. "I don't know if I can do it—if I have the stamina."

"Are you kidding? If you keep up with Ginger DiAngelo, you have the stamina for anything."

She smiled at that. When she smiled I noticed something about her face. I said before that it was a face that looked like it had been designed by a committee. I now realized that every member of the committee had made his or her part perfect according to some personal model of perfection. They just hadn't consulted, or considered the whole effect. That made her not beautiful or even pretty, but unique and intriguing and, yes, appealing. She had large, wide-set hazel eyes that almost made you miss the delicate molding of her petite nose. She had a narrow, rather pointed chin under a mouth that seemed too broad for it. Her smile stretched a thin but well-defined upper lip across nice teeth and a full lower lip. The longer you looked, the more appealing it all was.

In any case, I should clarify that I'm not knocking uniqueness. I am perfectly well aware that I could be a grad student from Central Casting. If Hollywood ever seizes on grad school as the hotbed of lust and ambition that it really is, I'll be a shoo-in for the extra who speaks lines like, "But Professor Fliegl, we had an appointment at two-thirty. Don't you remember?" or "Still working in the library. And you?" or "I just can't decide whether to go on the job market this year as an A.B.D., or wait until next year when the diss is finished.”

“I’m learning a lot from her,” she said. “She’s the best at what she does.”

“Yeah,” I said. “I can see why she would be.”

Elvis was back on the dance floor, learning a line dance from Pedro and George, our hosts for the evening.

“Of course, some clients are easier to promote than others,” she said, watching Elvis.

“He’s a natural,” I admitted. “Just an ordinary android from outer space, with charisma.”

“Our bosses want him to appear tougher, more threatening,” Larry said. He was sucking on his cherry. “They regard him as something of a—what do you call it? A mess-up?”

“Screw-up,” I said, surprised.

“I chose him for this mission because I thought it would suit his talents,” he said. “Ginger says that we must build trust, and it’s obvious that he’s better at doing that than I am. We don’t have much time, after all. Our bosses are not in agreement about this mission, and I fear that we could be recalled any day.”

“So you went back to the ship this afternoon?” I said.

“There were pigeons sitting on it,” he said. “And lots of—.” He waved an expressive hand. “It was covered. I believe they can detect the hum. They seem to like it. But if anyone sees them, standing around on the air like that—.”

“They’ll think they’re hallucinating,” I said.

“So the ship’s really invisible?” Jillian asked. “How does that work?”

“Not very well, apparently,” Larry said.

Elvis boogied back to our table.

“Hank, come and dance with me,” he said. “Lydia’s taking a powder in the toilet.”

“Not a good idea, big guy,” I said.

“Why not?”

“Well, look at all the dancers out on the floor. What do you notice?”

He turned around and gazed at the dancers. He shrugged one shoulder, which appeared to be an alien equivalent to our two-shouldered variety. “They are all different shapes and colors. They are wearing different outfits.” Trust Elvis for the sartorial review. “Some of them are dancing along with the music, but maybe some of them are listening to a different tune in their heads."

"Who are they dancing with?"

"Other people." He seemed baffled.

"Do you see any men dancing with men?"

"No."

"No. That's because on Earth—." I caught myself. "In our culture, rather, men don't dance with men, they dance with women."

"Oh. So can I dance with Jillian?"

"Sure," I said. I'd been preparing an explanation, and was brought up short when he didn't ask for one. Probably he thought all of our customs were weird, and it was no use asking for an explanation that wouldn't make sense, anyway.

He dragged a protesting Jillian onto the dance floor. As she was led away, she mouthed something to me that looked like, "Terrible. I'm terrible!"

"So, Larry, did you contact your superiors?" I asked. "You guys find any Earth products to import?"

"Refrigerator magnets," he said. "We think they would be a big hit in the Peshtafoon Galaxy."

"Do they have a lot of refrigerators there?"

"No, but it's heavily populated by beings like Elvis."

I tried to imagine a galaxy of beings like Elvis, and couldn't.

"You know—androids with metallic skin. We would sell the magnets as body art. We are also considering bungee cords. Both of these items can be made out of corn."

"How about kitty litter?" I asked. "They make that out of corn these days. You guys got any need for an absorbent—something that would soak up fuel when your spaceships leaked?"

"No, we have microorganisms that do that," he said. "But perhaps the Hokkis could use it. They are extraordinary architects and engineers, the Hokkis, and they build most of their structures out of sand."

I pictured a race of hyperintelligent ants, but caught myself. There I go, I thought, assuming that Earth ants aren't hyperintelligent. If we were marooned together on a desert island, they'd certainly be better prepared to survive than I would. Semiotics will only get you so far.

"I know that Ginger was hoping for a McDonald's franchise, but I'm afraid we don't think that would work. It would involve transporting perishable food over too great a distance. But snack items—we might have a market for those. Twinkies and Ding Dongs and Ho Hos, cheese doodles and Little Debbies—those might sell well, especially among the more primitive beings of the Lesser Rhon Galaxy."

"Makes one giddy just to contemplate Ho Hos in space."

"And movies, of course. We want to import those. Especially Westerns and Bollywood."

"I can see the appeal," I said. "They are both genres with a strong moral dimension."

He nodded. "Of course, where I come from, nobody would root for the cowboys or the Indians. We would root for the horses."

"I'd love to read the reviews."

"It will take extensive negotiation, though," he said. "Much as we dread nuclear weapons in space, there are those who believe that advertising in space would be worse."

"I can see why they would," I said. "Look at Elvis."

"Yes," he said. "He has a great enthusiasm for American products. They are not things that he needs, or would actually use, but he is attracted to them by advertising."

I excused myself to go the bathroom, and when I came back, Larry was on the dance floor, demonstrating a dance. Elvis was right; he was good—or at least, I presumed he was. I took it on faith that the caterpillar undulations he was doing and the finger-fluttering that accompanied it were bona fide.

I should never have let Elvis talk me into trying it.

"But it's a line dance, Hank," he said, as he lifted me out of my chair by my elbow. "Boys can dance with boys in a line dance, as long as there are some girls, too."

Within ten minutes, I was bent over, clutching a chair and gasping for breath. My back, which was an ordinary hominid back, and not an especially strong one at that, was not designed to imitate a caterpillar, and it had gathered itself into a cowering, quivering mass of pain a hand's breadth below my ribcage. My fun was over before it had started.

When we entered our hotel room an hour later, I was leaning heavily on Elvis, so I had no choice but to go with him when he turned right around and left, motioning for Larry to follow.

In the hall, Elvis said, "We've been insected."

"Infected?" I said.

"Bugged," Larry said. "He means we've been bugged."

Elvis nodded. "With listening devices. Shall I disable them?"

"I have to pass on this decision," I said. "I'm in too much pain to care. Just set me up next to a bug and I'll drown out everything else with my moans and sobs."

Larry was rubbing his forehead and looking tired. "Go ahead," he said.

"It would be good to know where they came from," I said. "Be nice if we turned out to have business competitors we don't even know about, but that's probably just wishful thinking. I don't suppose, in this day and age, we'll find g-men skulking in the stairwell."

"I could find the receiver," Elvis said, "if you think the recording device would help."

"I doubt it," I said. "I'm betting it won't be tagged as property of the F.B.I."

"Then I'll disable them," Elvis said, "as soon as we put you in bed."

CHAPTER ELEVEN

My pitiable condition finally earned me the day off. I lay on my bed with an ice pack on my back. Alex O. had personally delivered the ice pack, and threatened to send a massage therapist.

Elvis had wanted to know if I had a headache. "If you do, we can get you some Speedy Alka Seltzer. When Congressmen debate a bill, headaches are a common ill, so they take Speedy Alka Seltzer."

I assured him that my head was the least of my problems.

Howard and Anna took the boys to the police station to make their statements about the foiled robbery, and I asked them to assure the cops that I'd be there as soon as I could stand up. I was not sorry to miss the bus tour of D.C., though I was a little sorry to miss Elvis's running commentary on the bus tour of D.C.

It was awkward to type, lying on my stomach and propped up on my elbows like that, but I wanted to catch up on my e-mail.

"Dear Rudy," I wrote. "Sorry to bother you over the break, but I just wanted to let you know that I'm questionable for Monday. I'm in D.C. with friends and I've thrown my back out. If you'll check the schedule, you'll see that my two sections of Elementary Comp meet MWF at 8 and 2. I'm sure that one of the other A.I.s will be happy to take them, and the kids won't be able to tell the difference. Hope you're having a relaxing break. Hank Jones."

"Dear Dick," I wrote. "I know you're expecting a chapter from me on Monday, but I just wanted to let you know that I've thrown my back out and so am running behind schedule. I did score a collection of rare 1950s TV dinner boxes on e-Bay, including the Swanson original (98¢!), so I'm eager to get back to work. Unfortunately, I'm stuck in D. C. until my back improves. Regards to Anita, Hank."

"Dear Bonnie," I wrote. "I imagine that by now Eco has let you know that I'm not around to feed him. I took an unexpected trip to D.C. on short notice, and I kind of forgot about him. He could stand to shed a few pounds, but could you make sure he has some Friskies in his dish? Unfortunately, I've thrown my back out and don't know when I'll be home, but I'll bring you a cool souvenir, I promise. Your repentant neighbor, Hank."

"Dear Amanda," I wrote. "I'm glad that you're having a good time in Florida. As for your research paper topic, I can understand why you might have developed an interest in shark attacks off the Florida coast, but please remember that you must take a position in this paper. Do you have a position on shark attacks or the best way to prevent them? Is there a pro-shark faction (e.g., animal rights activists) and an anti-shark faction? If not, you will need to come up with another topic. Feel free to e-mail me again if you like, as I am currently in D.C., where I have thrown out my back, and do not expect to return to Bloomington by class on Monday. Regards, Hank Jones. P.S. This does not mean that class has been canceled for Monday."

"Dear Professor Whipstan," I wrote. "I am indeed interested in contributing to the collection you're editing on American popular culture in the 1950s. What I have in mind is a semiotic analysis of TV dinner packaging from that era. I am writing to ask whether an extension on your original deadline would be possible, as I have thrown out my back while on a visit to D.C. Thanks for your consideration, Hank Jones."

I thought I heard a knock at the door, but I wasn't certain. Since we weren't supposed to have casual visitors, and the authorized ones all had access to keys and ought to know what kind of shape I was in, I went on typing.

"Dear Professor Dewbury," I wrote. "I see that you are organizing an MLA panel on American popular culture during the Cold War era. I would be interested in proposing a paper on the semiotics of cereal boxes during the 1950s. Please let me know if this is the kind of thing you have in mind. Regards, Hank Jones."

A man appeared in the doorway. He seemed surprised to see me.

He was about my age, in shirtsleeves and gray slacks. A gray patterned tie was pulled loose around his neck and he was carrying a briefcase. He had close-cropped light-brown hair and a neatly trimmed moustache. He stood still and looked at me.

"You the massage guy?" I said.

"Yes," he said. "That's me."

"I told Alex that I wasn't sure I wanted anybody touching me, you know? It hurts like hell," I said. "But he said that you were really good, and that I could tell you to lighten up. He promised I'd thank him afterward."

"Oh, yes?" he said.

"So I hope you can work on me right here, 'cause I don't think I can stand up."

"Oh, sure," he said. "That will be fine." He still didn't enter the room.

"Does the hotel make you guys dress up like that?" I said. "It seems kind of formal."

"Yes, well—." He cleared his throat. "It inspires confidence, I guess." He took a few steps into the room and set down his briefcase.

"You think so?" I said. "Me, I'd feel more confident if you were wearing a lab coat, or—wait, maybe not a lab coat. That would be too hokey. Maybe a tee shirt that said 'Gold's Gym' or something."

"I'd better wash my hands," he said, and gestured toward the bathroom. "Do you mind?"

"Go ahead," I said. To tell the truth, I was a little disconcerted. The way he'd said it, you'd have thought he just remembered something his mother told him. You wouldn't have thought he did this kind of thing for a living.

He picked up his briefcase and disappeared into the bathroom.

"Where'd you study?" I said, raising my voice over the sound of running water.

"Excuse me?"

"Where'd you study?" I repeated. At least he was taking the hand-washing seriously. He might cripple me, but he wouldn't infect me.

"Georgetown."

"You can study massage at Georgetown?"

Silence, except for rushing water. Then, "It's part of the sports medicine program."

"Oh. And when did you graduate from there? You seem kind of, well, young."

He emerged, wiping his hands on a towel. "I was at the top of my class," he said. "I did my best work in massage."

I nodded. "And when did you graduate?"

"2005."

There wasn't much to say to that, except, "No, thanks," and I didn't want to hurt his feelings. He removed the ice pack and set it to one side. He appeared to study my back. He rubbed his hands together, like a concert pianist preparing to tackle Tchaikovsky.

"I'm Hank, by the way," I said, and offered a hand. "I assume you knew that, but I figure it's better to make sure. You don't want to operate on the wrong guy."

"Dave," he said. We shook hands.

"Don't worry," I said. "My hands are clean."

He hesitated then, and looked toward the bathroom as if wondering whether I was testing him.

I tucked my thumbs inside the waistband of my pajama pants. "How 'bout I just pull these down a little? I don't think I can get them off, anyway."

I'm sure I sounded nervous, but he actually blushed. At first, I thought I must be hallucinating, but no, I saw a distinct red blossom at the base of his short sideburns and spread down his neck.

"You have done this before, right?" I said. "Outside of massage class, I mean."

"Oh, sure," he said. "Lots of times. My clients love me." Then he turned even redder, I swear.

I felt warm, tentative fingertips on my back, and turned my face away.

"Don't you need some kind of massage oil or something?" I said.

He paused, as if feeling for movement at the cellular level. "This is a new kind of massage," he said. "It's called 'dry massage.' Research shows it's more effective."

When he spread his palms on my back, they were slick with sweat. His tie was tickling the nape of my neck. "Sorry," he mumbled. The tickling sensation went away.

"Where does it hurt?" he asked. "Here?"

He was pressing my shoulder blades. "Lower," I said. Then, "Lower." And again, "Lower." He finally hit the spot. "There."

"Here?" He pressed his thumbs in.

I yelped.

"That must be it," he said. "You're supposed to breathe into it. Are you breathing?"

"No, I'm gasping in pain," I said.

"Well, breathe," he said.

I tried that, and it did help. He was circling the injured area with his thumbs, and the muscles were starting to yield.

"What were you doing when you screwed up your back, anyway?" he asked.

"The caterpillar crawl, I think, but upright, like in *Alice in Wonderland.*"

When he didn't comment, I said, "Dancing."

"Yeah? Where'd you go?"

"Place called Cabana's in Georgetown. You know it?"

"No, but I've heard of it. I'd like to go some time. My girlfriend's crazy about dancing."

I could feel my muscles rippling in combined pain and pleasure under his hands.

"There's a tight spot," he said. "I can feel it. Keep breathing. Are you breathing?"

"Have you given massages to any famous people in this hotel?"

"You're the most famous so far."

"I'm famous?"

"Well, sure. I mean, you were on the news and all."

"I'm just a consultant."

"Oh," he said. I felt his fingers pause. "What are you consulting about?"

"Mostly American culture," I said. "I'm not really qualified to consult about anything else."

"Yeah?" he said. "Is that what you do for a living? Consult with foreign businessmen on American culture?"

"I teach freshman comp for a living," I said, "and it's not much of a living at that. I'm a grad student."

"Oh," he said. "I'd better watch my grammar. Man, you're really tight in through here. You should get a massage more often."

I moaned as he pressed on a sore spot with his thumbs.

"How'd you end up with these guys, anyway, if you're a grad student?"

"Larry and Elvis? They're, like, friends of the family. My cousin Mary asked me to keep an eye on them, show them around." I was doing a pretty good job of keeping my story straight, under the circumstances. But if he pressed any harder, all bets were off.

"I saw part of the story on the news, but I didn't exactly understand why they didn't want to be seen or identified or anything like that," he said. "I mean, that Elvis guy isn't exactly inconspicuous. If they wanted to keep everything secret, why send a guy like that?"

"He's the world's leading expert on these aircraft stabilizer thingies they're trying to sell to the U.S. government and American manufacturers," I said. "Or so they tell me. Anyway, it's Larry who might be recognized. He's been in the business a long time."

I could feel him lean in to put weight behind his palms as he pushed on muscles along the edges of my ribcage. "I didn't know they made aircraft stabilizers over there in that place they're from."

"The Solomons," I said.

"Yeah, there," he said. "They have a lot of high-tech industry over there? Keep breathing."

"I wouldn't know," I said. "What I know about the Solomons you could fit in a Dixie cup. One thing I do know—they've got some killer dances."

"I'd like to see some of those," he said. "Hey, your neck's really tight, too. Want me to work on it?"

I said okay, and he started crunching the back of my neck, squeezing, holding, releasing. "How long these guys staying?"

"Why? You going to offer them a free massage?"

"I might. No, really, I'd like to see them dance. I'm sorry I missed it."

"So is this what you want to do with your life? Or are you planning a lucrative career in sports management?"

He paused. "What I really wanted to do, if you want to know, was play ball."

"What position?"

"Second base. Maybe shortstop. I used to be pretty good."

"So what happened?"

"Aw, I don't know. Didn't have the nerve, I guess. This was a nice, steady gig, and the pay's not too bad."

"Not what you'd make playing baseball, though, even in the minors."

"No," he admitted, "but I'm healthy. You play professional sports, you're going to trash your body, one way or another. Doesn't take much to end your career."

"I guess you've got to be in good shape to do massage," I said.

"You better believe it," he said, and demonstrated by applying his biceps to the muscles on the other side of my ribcage.

When he'd finished, he proposed that he put the ice pack back in the freezer and bring me some water to drink.

"You should drink a lot of water now," he said.

"Why?" I said.

"Well, you know—you've released a lot of, you know, endorphins."

"I thought endorphins were good things," I said. "I don't want to drown them, do I?"

"No, no, you need to, um, spread them around," he said. "That's what the water's for. Helps the endorphins to circulate through your body."

"Helps me piss 'em away, you mean," I said.

"Trust me," he said, picked up the ice pack and his briefcase and left the room.

He was gone a long time, so I was nearly asleep when he returned.

"Hank, let's get you turned over and see if you can sit up," he said, setting the little plastic bottle of water down on the night stand.

"I don't want to sit up," I said. "I want to sleep."

"You ought to sit up and drink some water," he said.

"Don't want to," I said. "You can't make me." I shut my eyes.

"Your funeral," he said, and that was the last thing I remember until my cell phone woke me up.

"Hangsta," said the voice on the phone.

"Oh, hey, Chris," I said groggily. "'S up?"

"What's up with you, man? One measly little appearance on national television and you're, like, totally AWOL. Just remember: fame don't last, dude. One of these days, when they toss you in the gutter and trample you on their way to the next superstar, you'll be thinking, 'Wonder what happened to my old pal Chris?'"

"How'd I look?"

"Scared shitless."

"Damn. I was hoping you'd say I reminded you of Matt Damon or something."

I tried a tentative turn on my side so that I could see the clock. It went pretty well. I felt a twinge, but it was hardly the teeth-rattling pain I'd felt earlier. That Dave—what a guy!

"Look at it this way, Hangmon. You don't have Brittany Spears's stage presence, but if you went head to head with her on *Jeopardy*, you'd eat her lunch."

"Especially if the Final Jeopardy category was critical theory and not primetime television."

"Damn straight. Good news is, when I asked Anita if she'd caught you on T.V., she went all pissy. You're getting to her, man. You're really getting to her. Bad news? I think your cat ran off with a lady of the evening. I saw him up on your fire escape with a Persian twice his size. He likes them big, doesn't he?"

"Listen," I said, "I probably won't make it to basketball on Sunday. I've thrown my back out, and I don't know how long I'm going to be stuck here."

"No problema, man," he said. "You know Jimmy Hernandez is dying to take your place."

"Another thing. You know that bar I go to sometimes—Jake's?"

"The one way out Tenth Street? Yeah, I know it."

"My car's in the parking lot, and my jacket's hanging on a hook inside the door. Do you think you could ask Bonnie to let you into my place, get my spare set of keys from the top desk drawer, and go retrieve them?"

"Yeah, okay, I'll ask Eddie to take me out there. He's looking for any excuse not to work on the diss."

We talked for a while longer. Finally, he said, "Well, enjoy your fifteen minutes of fame, man. But if you get tempted to move to the Solomons with your new buddies, ask yourself one question: if you were driving to the basket, would they set a pick on Nagley for you? You ask yourself that."

I ordered room service, and a cheerful Pakistani guy named Hussein brought it to me and helped me sit up to eat. The pain in my back had settled down to a dull ache, thanks to the massage. I spent the rest of the day watching mindless daytime television and surfing the Web, activities so stimulating that I was asleep again when I was roused by a hand on my shoulder.

"Wake up, Hank," Larry was saying.

"We've been bugged again, Hank," Elvis said, holding out a hand to display three tiny disks like watch batteries. They were dripping wet, as if they'd just emerged from a bath. "How did this happen?"

I squinted at them, groggy. "I don't know, man. I haven't been out of bed all day. I've been sleeping and watching television and messing around on the computer."

Something leapt a synapse in my brain and caused a chain

reaction.

"Oh, shit," I said. And I started to laugh. I laughed and laughed, until the tears curtained my cheek. I tried to tell them, but I couldn't stop laughing.

CHAPTER TWELVE

Another day of bed rest and I'd be ordering up *Blades of Glory* on pay-per-view. So I ratcheted myself to a standing position and let Jillian drive me to the police station to make my statement. Then we went to the Smithsonian with Larry and Elvis and Ginger, a bodyguard named Warren from a security firm Ginger had hired, and a bottle of Advil.

"Might as well give ol' Dave a clear field," I said, "let him plant his bugs in peace. Though I think he was kind of into the massage, once he got over the initial shock."

Ginger drove a Mercedes, but it was a tight squeeze with the two big men in the car, and my back took immediate umbrage. I shifted so that my back was pinned against Warren's steel-hard torso, and felt better.

"So, Ginger, are you my agent or is Hank my agent?" Elvis wanted to know. "I have received several offers to do product endorsements, and I think I'm supposed to refer them to my agent."

"I'll take a look at them," she said. "It wouldn't be a bad idea, if it projected the right image. Especially if you gave away the fees to child cancer victims or some cause like that."

"Defender Security wants me to wear a cape, like Superman," Elvis said, screwing his head around so that he could look at me. "Wouldn't that be awesome, Hank? The King sometimes wore a cape when he was performing in Las Vegas. This one would have the Defender Security logo on it, in sequence."

"Sequins," I corrected.

We didn't want to arouse suspicion by going straight to the exhibit we were most interested in, so we ambled past a lot of 18th- and 19th-century agricultural artifacts, First Ladies' ball gowns, Roman coins, and Chinese vases before making our way to the Air and Space Museum and its permanent exhibit, "Visitors from Outer Space." It was mostly photographic, but they did have scale models of two spaceships, a flying saucer and a cigar-shaped silver one that looked like a roadside diner. The control panels inside the models looked not unlike the one inside Larry and Elvis's ship, but without the paddleball. The exhibit also featured several "life-size" models of extraterrestrials as they were depicted in popular culture. These included, in addition to the generic bald ghost with big eyes, James Arness as a rampaging carrot in *The Thing*, Gort from *The Day the Earth Stood Still*, E.T., and a whole set from the *Star Wars* movies. They ran continuous audio of the 1938 radio broadcast of *War of the Worlds*.

"Earth people have some funny ideas about people from other planets, Hank," Elvis mused. "Why do they always think we are trying to invade?"

I glanced around and motioned for him to lower his voice. "Probably because they can't translate 'klaptok zisto.'"

"This one makes me sad," he said, moving closer to inspect The Thing. "The Air Force ignored the scientist and burned the alien alive in the end."

I admired his resistance to all the narrative cues intended to tell moviegoers whom to root for. Moviegoers in the fifties were not supposed to feel sad when the carrot bought it in the final reel.

"But I would still like to have my picture taken with him," Elvis said, handing me his cell phone, "so I can post it to *Facebook*." He slung one arm around the carrot's shoulders, if that's what they are, and grinned while I took his picture.

There were two banks of interactive question-and-answer games. I aced the ones on fifties sci-fi movies.

"Wow, you are really smart," Elvis said.

"It's called 'dissertation avoidance,' big guy." I did not ace the questions based on the official government reports on UFOs— Project Sign, Project Grudge, Project Bluebook and all the rest. I remembered that there'd been a rise in UFO sightings in the late forties and early fifties, and accepted the theory that these were based on cold war paranoia. But when I said so to Larry, he shook his head.

"Earth was a popular tourist destination for Meloxxans from the XXantu Galaxy in those days," he said. "Some of them were very careless."

Elvis nodded. "The Meloxxans were attracted to your square dancing, Hank. They are a very mathematical people, and the geometry of the dances appealed to them. They are also, of course, a very long-lived people, and so they have time to cruise the galaxies. They have opposed the destruction of Earth in intergalactic councils, even though they do not come here often anymore."

"They now go dancing in the Erlinalarian Galaxy," Larry said.

This gave me so much to ponder that I fell silent for a while.

Elvis was studying the replica of Gort. "Is that what they mean by 'heavy metal,' Hank?" he said with a playful smile. Then he lowered his voice. "That suit is so lame! I would be seriously embarrassed to show up on Earth dressed like that. But I liked that movie. The spacemen in that movie were a lot like Larry and me, but not so friendly. They tried to warn the Earth, too, but I suppose they were not taken seriously because they were in a movie."

The artifacts were sparse. For example, there was a broken tubular object, said to have been found in Colorado.

"What was it?" I asked Larry in a low voice. "Do you know?"

"A high-powered telescope," Larry said. "It's just a children's toy in our culture, but since we don't generally have a high estimation of Earthling sophistication, many tourists bring them for gifts. We have a closet full of them on the ship. Where I come from, they cost about the same as a flashlight here on Earth."

A little boy stared at Elvis and pointed. "Mommy, look at that really, really tall guy! Is he a spaceman?"

The mother smiled apologetically as she seized the pointing hand. "He's having a really hard time with the line between fact and fiction," she said to Elvis, who flashed her his lopsided grin.

"Aren't we all," I muttered.

Ginger had already snagged his elbow.

"We're going shopping?" he said.

She shook her head as she rushed him out. "Too much work to do."

We followed in her wake like baby ducklings.

Larry was silent in the car as Ginger talked to Howard and Anna on her cell phone and Elvis chattered on about the exhibit. Then

Elvis's attention snagged on something and he turned his head to look as we drove past.

"Ginger, can we drive through a car wash?" he said. "I have never done that."

I could tell that Ginger was on the verge of making her usual excuse about work, but she glanced at his eager face, and caught herself. "Sure," she said. "Why not? There's one two blocks up on the right."

Elvis had called shotgun, and since that was the only seat in the car that could accommodate his frame, nobody had objected. As we inched along the car wash track, he leaned close to the windshield.

"Wow," he said. "Far out! Look at the design the water makes on our window. Isn't that way cool, Larry?"

But Larry didn't respond.

"Larry is bummed because he doesn't think humans will be able to understand our message," Elvis told us. "He thinks you're more interested in what aliens look like than in what we have to say. He thinks humans are easily distracted. It is like Hank's semenotics, isn't it? Earth people are more interested in the packaging than in the product. Lighten up, dude," he said to Larry. "We can make sure they get it right." Elvis's speech was becoming a conglomeration of influences, from fifties expressions and Bobbie's sixties slang to Pedro's and George's more contemporary patter to the language he heard on television and read on the Web.

"How?" Larry said.

"We have Ginger," Elvis said. "Ginger will make sure they get it right."

"What, exactly, do you expect them to get wrong?" Jillian asked. I was glad she was the one to ask, because I didn't want to seem ignorant.

"Earth people are like people who live on an island, surrounded by water," Elvis said. "They believe that they are by themselves because they can't see anyone else around them. They lack imagination. It is like in New Mexico. They saw that we were different, and so they believed that we were communists. We don't even know what communists are. Or it is like the pod people in that movie. Do you know the one I mean, Hank?"

"*Invasion of the Body Snatchers*," I said.

"Why would we want to live inside the bodies of Earth people?" he said. "Why would anybody? That is just gross." He shuddered.

"We fear that Earth governments might want to involve us in their petty squabbles," Larry said.

Elvis nodded. "Immature minds, like Mr. Overstreet wrote about. They will want us to create world peace."

"It would make us seem like local law enforcement," Larry said.

"We don't care about world peace at all," Elvis said. "It's interplanetary and intergalactic peace we care about."

"We don't care what you do with your own planet," Larry said. "Much as we would hate to see it destroyed, it is your planet and therefore your responsibility."

"You could fight each other until your species became extinct and we wouldn't stop you," Elvis agreed. "It's only when you threaten other planets that we have to intervene."

"Well, don't worry, guys," Ginger said, rejoining the conversation. "We'll make sure they get it right. We start tomorrow, at a press conference in front of the Air and Space Museum. Now that I've seen it, I'm sure it's the right venue."

"I think the weather forecaster said it might snow tomorrow," said Jillian in a small voice.

"Doesn't matter," Ginger said. "If we have to, we can hover the damned spaceship over us to keep the snow off, right, boys?"

"But will I be able to speak to all of the nations at once?" Larry said.

"A Washington press conference is the closest thing," Ginger said. "And anyway, that's just for openers. Elvis, Howard will be at the hotel in an hour to help you launch your blog. I'll be working with Larry on his statement. Anna will be laying the groundwork for appearances in major television markets. Jillian will float. Oh, and get back to that screenwriter about a YouTube script. Hank, you'll—." She paused.

"I'm not seaworthy," I said. "I'll sink like an anchor." I wasn't fully upright yet, and my back was grateful that our tour had been cut short.

"You'll consult," she said.

"We should appear on the CBS television network, Ginger," Elvis said. "It's the most watched network. And CNN—that one is the most trusted name in news."

"We'll hit all of them," she assured him.

"But first we'll eat lunch, right, Ginger?" he said, as we blew past a McDonald's and he turned to watch it recede from view.

"Lunch?" she said.

In the chaos that followed, lunch did appear, courtesy of room service and Jillian. So did an entire rack of men's suits, a box of men's ties, two printers and a fax machine, a sound crew, a voice coach, and a half-dozen consultants. After Elvis had collected all the new bugs, we set them under a stack of metal plate covers and put the tray in the hall. I spent the afternoon on the couch, giving away my opinion whenever anyone asked for it, and shifting the ice pack on my back.

"Yo, Hank, what do you think? Elvis wants to open his first blog, 'Greetings, Earthlings,' but I think too many people would miss the humor. What do you think?"

"Tone it down, big guy," I said. "A lot of humorless people, including intelligence types, will be reading it."

"Hank, we've narrowed it down to the brown or the gray." Anna had a pencil stuck behind her ear and a hung suit in each hand. "What do you think?"

"Well, the brown's warmer, friendlier, but the gray is more trustworthy and serious, I think," I said. "I'd go with the gray."

"Hank." It was Ginger's turn. "Is it 'if I was the person in charge' or 'if I were the person in charge'?"

"If he was never in charge, it's 'were,'" I said. "Contrary to fact, so subjunctive mood."

"I can never figure that out," she said, and went back into the bedroom where she was holed up with Larry.

"Guys!" Anna called. "Jay Leno or David Letterman first?"

"If we want to be taken seriously, I say Letterman," I said.

"Second," said Jillian.

"Third," said Ginger from the bedroom, "unless it's going to be a guest host."

"Good point," said Jillian.

"If it's going to be a guest host, find out who it's likely to be," Ginger said. "Ditto with Leno."

At this point, Jillian was sitting on the couch with me, looking at some kind of media contacts list.

"What's she doing?" I asked, worried. "Calling up Letterman and asking if they'd like to host an extraterrestrial?"

"No, she's just making preliminary inquiries, leaving her phone number, that kind of thing," she said. "She'll never get through to anyone who matters with a story about an overgrown Elvis impersonator who saved two D.C. mugging victims. Not today, anyway. Tomorrow, they'll find her phone number fast enough."

"Hank, do you think it will hurt my image if I say that I hate easy listening and New Age music?" Elvis said.

"No, I think you're allowed to have preferences," I said.

"But not in Indiana during playoffs," he said.

"Right. I also think you should be prepared to be inundated with samples of easy listening and New Age from enthusiasts who want to convert you. In fact, I think that Alex and the hotel staff need to know what they're in for."

"I think Ginger said that we'd brief Alex tonight before he leaves," Jillian said.

"That'll give him a good night's sleep," I said.

Swayed as much by Larry's refusal to give up his parking place as by Jillian's weather report, Ginger had decided that the press conference should be indoors after all. She had called the director of the Air and Space Museum and explained what we needed. He did some calling around to check up on Ginger's reputation, and became convinced that she at least believed what she was saying, though he didn't really seem to believe that the spaceship was parked in Rock Creek Park. The Secretary of the Smithsonian didn't believe any of it. At some point that afternoon Larry, Ginger, and one of the security guards met up with the two men in Rock Creek to take them on a tour of the spaceship. They were suitably impressed and put the full resources of the museum at our disposal. The director didn't even waste time rebuking Ginger for contacting him at the last minute. I was beginning to appreciate that folks in Washington were used to crisis. The press conference would be in front of the Air and Space Museum's "Visitors from Outer Space" exhibit. We didn't object to giving the Smithsonian a little free publicity.

I took it upon myself to call Jeremy, the stylist. "We need you to come up some time before noon tomorrow and change Larry back into himself again."

"You guys are fun," Jeremy said. "Kinky, but fun."

At around five, Dave the masseur followed a consultant in from the hall. He was still wearing a suit and tie and carrying a briefcase. His smile looked a little uncertain.

"My man," I said, and shook his hand. "The man with the magic hands."

"You think so?" He looked pleased. "I came to see how you were doing, and if you wanted me to work on you some more."

"I don't think so," I said. "Things are kind of busy around here today."

Ginger appeared, her eyes on a legal pad. "Hank, is it 'Larry and Elvis's mission' or 'Larry's and Elvis's mission'?"

"The first one, if they have a joint mission that belongs to both of them," I said. It felt good to be needed for a change—that is, it felt good to be able to contribute what few skills I possessed.

"And 'Elvis' just gets an apostrophe, right?" She looked up, then started when she saw Dave.

"No, it's singular, so it gets apostrophe ess even though it ends in ess," I said. "Now, if he'd picked the name 'Jesus' or 'Moses' or 'Mister Rogers,' I wouldn't know what to tell you. The originals are exceptions to the rule, but I don't know about their namesakes. Last I heard, Elvis hadn't yet been promoted to their status." I waved a hand at Dave. "Ginger, this is my massage therapist, Dave. Dave, our publicist, Ginger."

They shook hands, and she left.

"What's going on around here, anyway?" Dave asked, looking around. "You guys have a publicist?"

"Don't ask me, I just work here," I said.

"I thought your friends were trying to avoid publicity, not generate it," Dave said. His eyes strayed to the list of media contacts Jillian had left on the coffee table.

"These days, Dave, you have to manage publicity," I said, "or so they tell me. Having a publicist is like having a personal trainer."

Elvis appeared. "Hank, would you like to read my first blog?"

He stopped short when he saw Dave, but from the way his eyes dropped to the briefcase, I got the impression he was seeing more than I was seeing.

I introduced them, and they shook hands.

"Listen, Dave," I said, "thanks for stopping by to check on me. I appreciate it. But we are pretty busy today, so maybe you could come back another time."

"Sure," he said. "If I could just use your bathroom before I go—"

"I think Jillian's in there," I said. "Sorry."

He accepted defeat and left. Elvis looked at me. "Why does he want to bug the bathroom, Hank? That craps me out."

"Creeps you out," I corrected. "It creeps me out, too. I think he just doesn't want to admit that his operation has been a total failure."

I read Elvis's first blog entry.

Hi, Everybody! it said.

My friends Ginger and Howard wanted me to start this blog so that you could learn something about me, so I said okay.

The first thing that people notice about me is that I'm tall and look like my favorite Earth person, Elvis Presley. Elvis Presley is my idol, and I was very sad when I returned to Earth and found out that he had died. We flew over Graceland once, but I want to go back and scatter sikshik flowers over his grave, which is what we do back home to show respect for someone who's died. We don't have live sikshik flowers, only dried ones because I forgot to water them, but those will work just as well if the feeling in my heart is true.

I would like to be a rock and roll singer like Elvis Presley, and my friend Robbie is going to teach me to play the guitar. We don't have guitars where I come from, only kyztars, which are kind of like your harps, and brgmos, which are kind of like your flutes. Where I come from, people love to sing and dance, just like Earth people, except that everybody does it. Nobody worries about how good they look doing it. My partner Larry is a very good dancer. He says that he is not so good at singing, but he sounds okay to me. Sometimes we sing along with The Ed Sullivan Show *to pass the time in outer space. Also, we can sing "Babaloo."*

Since we came back to Earth, I have learned about many other rock and roll singers, like Bill Haley and Sam Phillips and Chuck Berry and Bo Diddley and Little Richie and Big Joe Turner, and also about the blues. I like salsa music, too, and I have been salsa dancing once. I have discovered that I like most kinds of Earth music, except easy listening and New Age.

Well, Howard says I should keep this short, so I will wait until tomorrow to tell you about more of the things I like about Earth culture. Peace out, Elvis.

I looked up to see Elvis watching me anxiously.

"Do you think it's okay?" he asked.

"Terrific," I said. "Nice, reader-friendly voice, lots of concrete examples."

"Howard made me take out the part where I said that it would be a shame if Earth were destroyed after it had produced so much gravy music."

"Good move."

Alex showed up around six, and we sat him down—Ginger and Larry and I— and told him what we'd announce to the world the next day.

"Outer space," he said. "That's where you're from, you and Mr.

Preston. And you've come to warn us about the possibility of total annihilation. I see." He pinched the crease in his trousers.

"You're taking this pretty calmly," I said.

He shrugged. "It's Washington. If I reacted to every threat of total annihilation that came down the pike, I wouldn't last long here." He turned to Larry. "Thanks for telling me. I'll take appropriate measures to insure your security."

He stood and shook hands. I put a hand on his shoulder. "And Alex, one more thing. I can't tell you what to do, of course. You have to follow your own conscience. But we'd appreciate it if you didn't tell Dave or any of your other intelligence contacts before the press conference tomorrow. We'd just as soon avoid a strong military presence. Wouldn't be good publicity for the Marriott."

"I think we'll make this our little secret," he said, "as long as you can give me your word that you don't intend any kind of attack tomorrow."

"Certainly not." Larry was shocked.

We went to Citronelle in Georgetown for dinner, all of us plus Robbie and his girlfriend Eileen and a new Spartan Security bodyguard named Max. We spent an amount that approximated my annual salary, and I sat in a corner with a pillow behind my back. We toasted the success of our mission the next day, and when Eileen asked what that was, we told her and Max that we were holding a press conference. Everybody holds press conferences in D.C.—they are common as congressional pork—but neither Eileen nor Max objected to toasting one.

CHAPTER THIRTEEN

The weather on Friday was cold and wet—no snow but a steady rain.

The podium was placed in front of and to the right of the life-sized models of extraterrestrials so that well-positioned photographers could get all of the figures in the frame if Larry and Elvis stood together at the microphone. Hung suspended behind the podium and models were an American flag and another flag, and this visual effect had proven the most difficult to achieve on short notice. That day, Larry told everyone that it was the flag of the intergalactic mutual defense organization that had sent them, but Elvis told me later that the organization didn't have a flag, and that it was really the flag of the intergalactic police force, with a few extra stars and planets attached.

Reporters and photographers wandered in, soggy and ill-tempered. They had the resentful look of people who'd been taken off some juicy scandal to cover what would at best be a story about some financial deal between the U.S. and the Solomon Islands, wherever the fuck they were, to buy some aircraft part they wouldn't understand and could care less about. They regarded the black-and-white flag with disdain; what kind of two-bit country, their eyes said, would design a flag like that? Ginger had done her best to get the international press there, but I couldn't tell by looking whether or not she'd succeeded. I saw only one or two eager faces in the whole crowd—youngsters sent to cover an assignment nobody else wanted. I wished them well.

I had to hand it to Ginger: she knew what she was doing. When the Albert Einstein High School band struck up Robbie's arrangement of the theme to *E.T.*, I got a lump in my throat. Most of the reporters actually hung up their cell phones and craned their necks to see the podium.

The museum director stepped to the microphone, all smiles. When the theme music petered out, he spoke.

"Ladies and gentlemen, I've been asked to introduce to you two visitors who wish to speak to you on a topic of great importance," he said. "Indeed, I can think of no topic of greater importance."

Some of the veterans in the crowd rolled their eyes or exchanged jaded looks. They were expecting another lecture about climate change. Maybe the Solomons were about to disappear, which would save them the bother of figuring out where they were.

Larry and Elvis stepped from behind the flags and waited. I was glad that I'd talked Elvis out of wearing his new Witness Protection tee shirt. Larry looked distinguished, but Elvis looked as fashionable as he could have wished in a dark gray pinstripe and an open-collared light gray silk shirt. And even under the television lights, he looked cool.

The reporters shifted in their seats. Here were the same two clowns who'd already claimed their fifteen seconds of fame for rescuing a couple of tourists from a mugger on a slow news day. What did they want now? The Congressional Medal of Honor?

"Those of you who have seen our 'Visitors from Outer Space' exhibit will be familiar with the long history of government interest in the question of whether or not Earth has been visited by intelligent beings from other planets," the director continued. "Some of you have perhaps concluded, like many of the scientists and researchers who have studied the question, that such visits have in fact taken place. I am here today to confirm your supposition. We are being visited right now, this minute, as I speak. I now yield the podium to two of those visitors, whom you know as Mr. Lawrence Smith and Mr. Elvis Preston."

Some of the journalists were quicker than others, and their gasps identified them. Some of the veterans made other sounds expressing annoyance, exasperation, and incredulity. One or two leaned forward, eager to have a go at these publicity-seeking impostors. In the back row, a cynic on his cell phone had noticed the commotion around him, and was now asking his neighbors what he'd missed.

Elvis turned glowing eyes on him, and the cell phone disappeared from his hand. Elvis held it up for the crowd to see, and addressed the flabbergasted cynic sternly. "You should be quiet now and listen to what Larry has to say. We have come a long, long way to talk to you about the future of your planet."

I saw other cell phones being slipped into pockets, out of the line of fire. The young reporters were grinning ear to ear and writing madly in their notebooks.

Now it was Larry's turn. He shook hands with the director and smiled for the cameras. "Friends," he said, and tried to tamp down the unexpectedly enthusiastic applause. "Friends."

I caught Jillian's eye and raised my eyebrows in appreciation. A good rhetorical strategy, I thought.

She nodded. "Tough love," she whispered. "More carrot than stick."

"Nice move," I said.

"Friends," he said, "much as we enjoy visiting your planet, getting to know you, sampling your delicious cuisine, and, uh, participating in your culture—." Here there were a few snickers from those in the audience who had heard about their visit to the dance club. "Much as we enjoy all of those things, as I say, we are sorry to be sent here to deliver such a serious message. We are two hundred and fifty million of your Earth miles from our home galaxy, we're tired, and we miss our friends and families, just as you miss yours when you travel long distances. We come, not on a mission of world peace"—here he looked at his audience meaningfully, as if attempting to make eye contact with each of them—"but of intergalactic peace—universal peace."

They interrupted him with applause. "Universal peace" always drew a big round of applause, in my experience, until people were asked to give up the things they had to give up in order to achieve it.

"I represent a league of planets—an intergalactic United Nations, if you will—that is absolutely determined to eliminate aggression for the greater security of all planets. We cannot police the internecine squabbles that erupt on individual planets, nor do we wish to. But we will not tolerate violence and aggression directed at one planet by another. Let me be clear about what I mean here. We would regard the introduction of any nuclear weapons into outer space as an act of aggression, and we would act quickly to eliminate the aggressor.

By 'aggressor,' I mean the planet. We would not have the luxury of taking the time to ascertain the country or individuals responsible. Our police force, on which Elvis serves, has been given absolute power to enforce this rule of nonaggression, and it has done so very effectively for many Earth millennia. I am prepared, if necessary, to demonstrate that power in such a way that none of you will doubt not only the seriousness of our mission but our ability to carry out what we have promised. I hope I won't have to.

"Let me say again that we have grown fond of this planet and its people. Elvis here has grown particularly fond of your music and food." A ripple of laughter released some of the crowd's tension as Elvis smiled sheepishly. "We come as friends to warn you against pursuing the course you have set. We will not be back. If you don't heed our warning, the ones who will come after us will come not as friends but as destroyers. We sincerely hope that you don't allow that to happen."

There was a moment of awkwardness in which nobody clapped, and then somebody yelled, "Let the big guy speak." Other voices joined in.

Elvis approached the mike a little bashfully for a guy with two hundred and thirty-four friends on Facebook.

He looked down at the microphone. "Wow," he said, and swiped a hand across his brow. "This is probably the greatest honor I've ever had in my life."

Three people laughed and clapped, while the others stared at them.

I said to Jillian, "Is he quoting the person I think he's quoting?"

She nodded and shushed me.

"I wish I'd brought my guitar," Elvis said. "But seriously, folks, everything Larry said is true, so I hope you were all paying attention."

"Mr. Preston!" A middle-aged man with a receding hairline and a sour look was on his feet. "Is it true you can destroy a planet?"

"Well, not all by myself," Elvis said. "I might need a little help."

A man with his arms crossed didn't bother to stand. "You destroyed any lately?"

"Not lately, no," Elvis said.

I felt the sweat pop out along my scalp and under my beard.

"No? How many have you destroyed in total?"

"Two. Maybe three."

"'Maybe three?'" The voice dripped sarcasm. "You don't

remember?"

"It's kind of complicated. What's your name?" Elvis said in a conversational tone, not angry or defensive.

"Walcott, John Walcott, U.P.I." Walcott smirked at his cronies.

"Hi," Elvis said. "I'm Elvis."

The general laughter took some of the wind out of Walcott's sails.

"Well, Mr. Walcott, it's a long story, but one of those planets was dying anyway. See, the inhabitants ruined the atmosphere, and so it didn't have enough protection from the star it was orbiting, and the whole planet heated up so the life forms couldn't survive anymore. But the ones that were left attacked a neighboring planet, and that's when we got called in for the wash-up operation."

This explanation was greeted with silence. As if on cue, one of the more recently attached white dots came unglued from the black flag behind him and drifted to the floor.

Then one of the fresh-faced young women asked, "So is the Elvis look just a ploy or are you really a fan? How do you know about him, anyway?"

He gave her his lopsided grin. "We've been monitoring your television and radio transmissions from outer space." He glanced at Larry. "Well," he amended, "we were monitoring them until our scanner broke." We had decided not to mention the previous New Mexico visit, even though we weren't trying to hide Larry's identity anymore. "I'm a big fan. Read my blog tomorrow. Or ask Larry. He's pretty tired of hearing me sing 'Hound Dog.'

"But listen, dudes, you should be asking Larry questions about our mission. He's the one with all the brains. I'm just the prawn."

"Brawn," Jillian and I chorused softly.

"Mr. Smith," called a man in tortoiseshell glasses. "Dan Jordan of the *Times*. Are you asking us to sign an agreement, or join this interplanetary defense organization?"

Larry returned to the mike. "Frankly, Mr. Jordan, we don't really have much faith in signed agreements. Since we monitor your planet on an ongoing basis, we will know whether or not you've heeded our warning. As to whether or not you want to join the organization, that is entirely up to you."

"You got some literature on it?" said one wag.

"Meg Falconer of the *Wall Street Journal*, Mr. Smith," said a woman in a rather old-fashioned suit, standing up. "Will you be leaving right away now that you've delivered your message, or will you be staying to hear a reply?"

"We'll be staying for a little while," Larry said. "We don't know how long. We want to disseminate our message more widely. In addition, we want to give you the opportunity to think about what we've said and ask any questions you may have."

"Mr. Smith!" A man stood up in the back. "Harry Rosenthal, *The Nation*. What are your views on the wars in Iraq and Afghanistan?"

"I'm sorry, Mr. Rosenthal, but as I explained, it's not my purpose or my wish to insert myself into any wars taking place on Earth. For one thing, I'm not well-informed."

"That never stopped anybody else in this town," said the wag.

"I can only say that my people have learned to live without wars by acknowledging that all people want the same things—clean water, food, shelter, and safety for their children and their families. We are committed to meeting those basic needs. It's a way of life I can recommend to you."

He nodded to the director, who stepped in and ended the press conference.

The fresh-faced woman looked disappointed that she hadn't gotten the chance to ask her follow-up question about Elvis's transformation: how had he done it?

The boys were whisked away out of sight, but then somebody caught sight of me. There was a brief, frozen moment, before the hordes descended, when every eye in the room was on me, and I felt my stomach hit the floor. Then Jillian took my hand and said in my ear, "No comment." She began tugging me toward the exit.

"Hank! What can you tell us about these aliens? Can they really carry out their threat?"

"Mr. Jones! Where do these guys come from?"

"Hank, is there any connection between these two aliens and Osama Bin Laden?"

"Yo, Hank! If these guys come from outer space, where's their spaceship? It ain't parked on top of the Pentagon."

"Hank, there's a rumor going around that Elvis Preston is the reincarnation of Elvis Presley. Can you comment?"

"Mr. Jones, have you seen any demonstrations of the spacemen's special powers?"

They nearly trampled the Einstein High School band members in their eagerness to get to me, and the kids were scrambling for safety. I winced when a tuba hit the floor, but figured that the best thing that I could do was draw the mob away. In any case, Jillian had a grip on my hand that was tight as a Republican's pocket, and she had now broken into a run. As I looked back, I saw our bodyguard-of-the-day, in his black jacket and Spartan Security shirt, trying to run interference for us. He looked like he'd had a lot of experience with this maneuver on the gridiron. Before I met Elvis, I would've considered him huge.

Jillian pulled me under a rope and around a barrier that said "Exhibit Closed." We found the closest wall and leaned against it, trying to pant as quietly as we could. We heard footsteps rumbling past. In the dimly lit exhibit hall, I could see the shapes of four biplanes.

"If I could fly," I gasped, "I'd commandeer one of those and fly back to Indiana."

"Don't be silly," she gasped. "You're having a great time." She pushed off from the wall and approached one of the planes.

"I am?" I said. I pushed off from the wall and stifled a yelp when my back protested.

She was smiling and running a hand lovingly along the plane's flank. "It's a Mustang."

"It looks like a plane to me," I said.

"It's a P-57 Mustang. My grandmother flew these."

"Your grandmother was a pilot?"

She nodded. "A WASP, during the war. She also flew the C-47s on cargo transport missions. I guess she flew a lot of different planes, but she loved the Mustang. A lot of pilots did."

I tried to imagine either of my grandmothers piloting a plane, or my mother, either, for that matter. "I don't think my grandmothers had much to do with the war effort."

"Of course they did," Jillian said. "Everybody did. That was back in a time when everybody could support a war that was fought, like Larry said, to stop an aggressor. We weren't fighting for big business or to boost the president's ratings or because some right-wing Christian yahoo with the president's ear wanted to kill non-Christians. Even after Pearl Harbor, we weren't really fighting for revenge. Well, maybe some people were, but in those days the leaders of the free world didn't declare war for revenge. If we could get Americans mobilized for peace the way they were mobilized for war in the forties, we could save the planet."

"You think people were smarter back then?" I said, tracing a flame design on the Mustang's fuselage. "The majority of Americans still think there were Iraqis in the planes on 9/11, and that's why they supported the invasion of Iraq."

"I don't know," she said. "We can't seem to elect a quorum of leaders with the country's best interests at heart rather than their own."

"We can't elect a quorum of leaders with the I.Q. of a tadpole."

"We sure can't elect a quorum with both public-mindedness and intellect," she said. "Makes you wonder if we're capable of heeding Larry's warning, doesn't it?"

I rubbed a hand across my face. "The odd thing is, I want them to succeed, Larry and Elvis, because it means so much to them, but I don't give them much chance of success. I don't have that much faith in humanity."

We rejoined the others in a conference room, where the Einstein band members were being plied with cookies and punch and given the first crack at the spacemen. They were a pretty representative sample of their parents: some were asking Larry questions about outer space and the things he'd seen on his travels there, and some were asking Elvis what he really looked like and how he'd made himself look like Elvis Presley and whether he was married. I was gratified to note that the former were in the majority. Again, I had to hand it to Ginger, if she was the one who'd arranged this encounter. Larry and Elvis were both good with kids, and the kids would each take home with them snapshots of themselves with their pals, the aliens. In fact, I was a little surprised how well Larry interacted with young people. Given Robbie's experience, I guess I should have known better. It wasn't as if he dropped his reserve or his dignity. Maybe, I decided, he was good with kids because he treated them like intelligent beings. And let's face it, some of these high school students knew more about astrophysics than I did—way more. It was too bad, really, that some of the ones who were capable of asking Larry intelligent questions about space-time were probably still writing essays that began, "Their are many problem's in todays American society." Did that mean I wanted to dedicate my life to teaching them to write intelligently in their mother tongue? Not necessarily.

One girl asked Elvis if he was wearing a wig. He blinked coyly, responded with, "Only my hairdresser knows for sure."

Our departure marked the beginning of a new regimen, as far as security was concerned. We now traveled in Spartan Security vans, and our entourage had expanded to accommodate two additional bodyguards. Our security guard for the press conference had acquired a wire behind his ear. They tried to separate Larry and Elvis into two vans, but Elvis wouldn't have it.

"I'm Larry's main bodyguard," he said. "I stick to him like goo. We're like hot dogs and ketchup."

He didn't object to the other security guards. He accepted their usefulness.

"Dudes, I don't want to vaporize anybody if I don't have to," he said.

"Fair enough. Let's go back to the hotel and see what Anna's lined up for you," Ginger said.

"Can we stop at Taco Bell?" Elvis said.

CHAPTER FOURTEEN

For my money, the high point of the afternoon occurred when two I.N.S. agents showed up with handcuffs, a photographer, and a Colorado congressman who'd made his reputation as an advocate for tougher immigration laws. The older of the two agents looked sheepish. We'd been tipped off by our early warning system, and Alex followed them into the room. He looked more amused than concerned, which made me wonder what he knew that I didn't.

The older agent politely asked Larry and Elvis if he could see their passports.

"What does it look like?" Elvis asked.

This created a diversion, because of course nobody in the room was carrying one, so a fairly lengthy description was in order, and the two agents delivered it as a tag team.

When they'd satisfied Elvis's curiosity, he said, "No. I don't have one of those. But I have Diner's Club." He produced his card with a flourish, and then showed his disappointment that they weren't more impressed.

The older agent asked if they had any papers to confirm that they'd entered the country legally. Then he asked if they'd ever filled out any forms requesting to enter the country.

"No," Larry said. "As you know, we came on a diplomatic mission from a place where the forms are not available."

"But we can fill them out now," Elvis said, "if you help us."

"It's too late now, buster," said the congressman, baring his teeth for the photographer, "as you damn well know. You're going to be seeing the U.S.A. from behind bars, until we ship you back to where you came from."

Larry smiled at that, but Elvis said, "My name isn't Buster. It's Elvis."

"Yeah, right," the congressman snarled. "You got any proof of that?"

Elvis held up his Visa card.

The younger agent had his hand on his cuffs. The older agent was palming his forehead, but I saw a smile twitching at one corner of his mouth.

Dave the masseur chose that moment to arrive, and Alex let him in.

"Is this a bad time, Hank?" he said.

"No, Dave, it's a good time," I said. "These two gentlemen are I.N.S. agents, and they're about to arrest Larry and Elvis here as illegal aliens."

"Oh," he said, and walked out. He hadn't even set his briefcase down.

"Let me ask you something," the younger agent said, addressing Larry. "What was your port of entry?"

The older agent rolled his eyes.

"Into your airspace, do you mean?" Larry asked. "Or where did we first land?"

"Where'd you land?"

"In Bloomington, Indiana, isn't that right, Hank?" Larry said. "Somewhere in the vicinity of Charley's Bar."

The younger agent had his hands on his hips. "You just flew across the border, and got as far as Indiana. Running lights? Air traffic control contact?"

"No, we had a security shield up," Larry said. "It makes us invisible, both to human eyes and to your radar." He didn't say anything about pigeons, I noticed.

"And if that doesn't sound like a terrorist, I don't know what does," said the congressman.

"I wasn't aware that terrorists liked to congregate at Charley's Bar," Larry said.

I exchanged a look with Jillian. Larry as comedian? This was something new.

"You can tell that to the judge, bozo," the congressman said. "Go ahead, agent. Cuff him."

Now the boys from Spartan Security got into the act. A Hispanic guy built like a cement mixer stepped in front of Larry.

"I wouldn't do anything foolish," he said. He had some kind of Southern accent.

"You wouldn't, huh?" the congressman said. "Maybe we should check your green card, amigo."

The Hispanic guard turned to the congressman. "My name isn't 'amigo,' it's Francisco Alejandro Díaz de Cortez—Cisco to my friends, which doesn't include you. I grew up in a neighborhood in San Antonio where calling somebody out of his name could be a capital offense. My people fought with the Texans against the Mexicans at the Alamo and the Battle of San Jacinto. Now, I'm a peacekeeper. And so I'm just warning y'all, if he takes those cuffs off his belt, we're going to have us a breach of the peace here, and we Texans know what to do about that."

Ginger said, to nobody in particular, "We do not have time for this."

Alex answered a knock at the door and a new player entered. He was an older man in his sixties, with thin gray hair and a general air of weariness. He made eye contact with the older of the two I.N.S. agents.

"Agent? May I speak to you a moment?" he said.

I don't think the agent knew him, but my guess is that he recognized the type, and, with an air of relief, went to consult with the older man. The younger agent stayed where he was, cuffs still on his belt, and joined the congressman in glowering at Francisco Alejandro Díaz de Cortez.

The older agent returned and said to the younger agent, "Okay, we're done here." He turned to Larry and Elvis, "Sorry to have bothered you folks." He shook their hands.

"That's okay, man," Elvis said. "No skin off my tush. You're just doing your job." They exchanged one of those cop-to-cop smiles.

The younger agent was directing his resentment at the older man, but not conspicuously enough to get into trouble over it.

The congressman, however, was beside himself. "You're not going to arrest them? They're illegal aliens."

"No, sir, they're not," the older agent said. "They're guests of the United States government, which makes them legal aliens." He waved a hand at the rest of us. "You folks have a nice day."

The congressman followed them out in high dudgeon, but the photographer lingered long enough to confirm the spelling of Francisco Alejandro Díaz de Cortez.

Dave reappeared, briefcase in hand. "Hank," he said, "how about that massage?"

Two hours later, my back was relaxed but the rest of me was bored stiff. I called down to the hair salon. "Jeremy, I need a disguise. I'm desperate to get out of here."

"There's only so much I can do," he said, "unless you get rid of the beard. Or we can dye it black."

I thought. "Can I keep the moustache?"

"Better not," he said.

What the hell, I thought. I could always grow it all back.

"Who do you want to look like?" he asked.

"Nobody in particular," I said. "Look, I don't want a makeover, I just want to be able to walk around without being recognized— you know, like Madonna or Angelina Jolie."

"That's easy," he said. "Remove all your make-up, and don't wash your hair for a few days. Wear sweat pants. Leave your bodyguard and your kids at home."

He arrived half an hour later with his shaving gear and a collection of wigs and sunglasses. Elvis was busy working on his blog with Howard, Anna was returning phone calls from all the people who were suddenly returning her phone calls, Ginger and Larry were sitting at the table working on opening statements for different venues, Jillian was off running errands, a filmmaker named Anil was microwaving a cup of coffee and reading some papers he held in one hand, and the three bodyguards were watching NASCAR racing. Jeremy and I retired to the bathroom.

It was weird to be reintroduced to an upper lip and chin I hadn't seen for at least five years. I touched them with my fingers, and even though I was watching myself in the mirror, I was startled when the fingers made contact with bare skin.

Jeremy was also watching me in the mirror. He now produced a wig of wavy, longish, light-brown hair, dyed to look a little sun-bleached.

"This one's my favorite for you," he said, and slipped it over my dark blond hair, which was intended to be short but rarely achieved its intended length because I lacked either the money or the time to get it cut.

He fussed with the wig until it looked more natural on me.

"Voilà!" he said. "You could be Leonardo DiCaprio."

I replaced my wire-rim glasses, and studied myself in the mirror. Let me just clarify, there was no way I'd be mistaken for Leonardo DiCaprio. For one thing, in spite of the regular basketball games and fair-weather biking to campus and home, I had the lumpy, solid look of a guy who spends his days reading books and grading papers, with the beginnings of a beer belly, or more accurately, a beer-and-pizza belly. I looked like Leonardo DiCaprio after a three-month strike by his personal trainer maybe at a stretch and from a distance of fifty feet with a crowd of people obscuring your view. I looked like an aging Beach Boy. Leo had nothing to fear from me.

"Gee, thanks. I think."

He handed me a pair of dark glasses. "How blind are you?" he said.

It felt good to get outside and walk around again. The rain had stopped, but the air was thick with moisture. This was the kind of thing you noticed when more of your skin cells were making contact with the atmosphere. You also notice it when you aren't wearing your glasses and are having to depend more on your other senses for information about the world around you.

After I'd walked about half an hour, I sat down on a bench in a small park and watched the kids on the playground—or rather, I watched the moving shapes that I took to be kids. There was a time when you could do this without feeling like a sex offender, but those days were long past, so I looked at my watch as I sat down, resolved to stay no longer than fifteen minutes. I also wanted to convey the impression that I was waiting for someone. As I looked around, I noticed a dog park farther along, and thought I could probably get away with dogwatching, if I needed to change venues.

The bench was cold and damp, and the rainwater seeped through my jeans. I collected two alert glances from passing moms, and decided that the sunglasses were no help to my clean-cut image, so I took them off and stuffed them in the pocket of my sweatshirt. Squinting probably didn't do anything for my image, either. I tucked my hands into the small of my back and leaned back against them, for which my back seemed to be grateful. Then it occurred to me that I looked like a pervert who was trying to restrain himself, so I silently apologized to my back and removed my hands and crossed my arms. I was pondering my lot in life, trying to work up some enthusiasm for logging some time at the Library of Congress, or maybe going back to the Smithsonian to look at the Betty Crocker kitchen I'd been rushed past the day before, when I became aware that someone was sitting on the other end of the bench. I smelled her before I saw her—a faint whiff of some light, fruity scent found its way to my newly unobstructed nostrils. I adjusted the angle of my head to expand my peripheral vision.

She was tall and thin, wearing jeans, a denim jacket, and trainers. She had long hair, platinum blond. She wore glasses. She was reading a book. I coughed to cover another head adjustment. Oh, shit. She was reading Douglas Adams's *A Hitchhiker's Guide to the Galaxy*. Surely I'd been busted.

But she continued to read, seeming to take no notice of me. She was actually turning the pages. So my fifteen minutes turned into twenty as I sat waiting to see what she would do. I watched a little boy slide down the slide a dozen times, emitting the same squeal of delight every time, and a little girl being pushed on a swing by an older sister. It was odd to see the world so out of focus, as if I were under water. I heard occasional small explosions from my right indicating stifled laughter. This, too, was a good sign. If she'd been reading *War and Peace*, it would have made me suspicious, but Douglas Adams certainly warranted a few chuckles.

The next time my eyes slid in her direction she was eating an apple. She was close enough so that I could see she had nice, healthy teeth. A pair of toddlers started fighting over a Big Wheel in front of our bench, and she looked up. She smiled at them, shook her head, went back to her reading. Soon she was chuckling again.

I couldn't stand it. "What part are you reading now?" I asked.

She looked up as if startled, looked around, found me. "What?" she said.

I pointed at the book. "What part?"

"Oh," she smiled. "Ford's *Hitchhiker's Guide* entry for Earth: 'Mostly harmless.'"

"Yeah," I said. "His revision of the previous entry, the summary of all he's learned in fifteen years of living there incognito."

She laughed. "Adams cracks me up," she said. "But at the same time, it's thought-provoking, you know? And kind of, you know, like, visionary. I mean, he wrote this back in the seventies, and here it turns out that right now, today, we're being visited by space aliens." She shook her head. "Amazing."

"Well, some people say we've been having visitors for years," I pointed out.

"Well, yeah, I guess so," she said. "But I never really believed that stuff, did you?" She closed the book around her index finger, and scooted one scoot closer to me. "The way Mrs. Humphreys explained it—that was my seventh-grade social studies teacher, Mrs. Humphreys—all those flying saucer sightings? They were really Soviet aircraft, testing a lot of advanced weaponry."

"But you believe these new aliens—Lawrence Smith and Elvis Preston—are from outer space?"

"We-e-ell." She glanced down at the book in her hand. "Not exactly. I mean, I don't know what to think." She chewed her apple thoughtfully. "I heard someone on the radio say that this super-Elvis is the reincarnation of the real Elvis," she said, "and I don't believe that for a minute. He could be just a guy with a good plastic surgeon who took too many growth hormones."

"But you don't think these guys are Soviet agents?"

"They could still be Russians," she said. "Or maybe Osama bin Laden sent them."

"If Osama bin Laden sent them," I said, "and got them into the country without anyone knowing about it, why not just have them blow up the White House or the Pentagon? Why have them hold a press conference to say they don't care about the wars in Iraq and Afghanistan?"

"Maybe he's just messing with our heads," she said. "He likes to do that. Or he wants us to let our guard down, and buy into world peace, and then, blam! He'll blow something up."

I felt a little of Larry's impatience rising in me. What was our chance of survival if Earthlings never got the message right? "He said they don't care about world peace," I objected. "I mean, isn't that what he said?"

"Well, yeah, he said that," she admitted. "But didn't he also say something about non-aggression? I kind of thought he meant Iraq and Afghanistan when he said that, didn't you?"

"No," I said between clenched teeth. "Since he specifically said he wouldn't take a stand on those conflicts, I took him at his word."

"Well, you don't have to get all bent out of shape about it," she said. "I'm just telling you what I thought. I'm entitled to my opinion and you're entitled to your opinion. It's a free country, right? So unless you're going to tell me that you talked to these guys on the phone and you know exactly what they were thinking, your opinion is just your opinion."

"Sorry," I said, "you're right. I don't know why I get so worked up. It's just—well, it's possible that if we don't believe them, the Earth will be destroyed. That kind of upsets me."

She shrugged and looked away. "Well, it upsets me, too, but it's going to happen anyway, one way or another. We're destroying it ourselves, and we know we are, and what are we doing to stop it? Giving tax breaks for hybrid cars, handing out tips on weatherstripping your windows, blathering on about 'clean coal,' an oxymoron if there ever was one, and falling all over ourselves to drill for oil in the few places left on the planet that we haven't totally screwed up. We won't fucking sign the Kyoto Accord—no, that would be way too extreme. I'm sorry, but it's all going down the toilet, anyway, and who knows? Maybe a blast from some kind of super laser would be quicker and less painful than the way we're doing it."

"I see what you mean," I said.

She set down her apple core, wiped her hand on her jeans, and offered her hand to me.

"I'm Charlotte," she said. "Peace?"

"I'm all for it," I said. "Hank."

We shook.

"No kidding?" she said. "Hank. That's the name of the guy who's hanging out with the spacemen. You related?"

"He's my twin brother," I said. "He's Hank One, I'm Hank Two."

She grinned. "You don't look like him," she said.

"Fraternal twins."

There were two mothers now sitting on a bench opposite ours, one with a baby in a stroller. Both had toddlers of indeterminate gender in tow. As we watched, one toddler offered the other a cookie. The second kid crossed his eyes to focus on it, then snatched it, and with only a little prompting from its mother, mumbled through a mouthful of cookie something that could have been "thank you."

Charlotte nodded in their direction. "It's not as if humans can't learn to share."

"Yeah," I said. "Maybe we should send our world leaders back to kindergarten."

"Some of them skipped kindergarten altogether," she said. "I'm convinced."

"Or maybe we should just encourage more public crying," I said. "Maybe if world leaders just let everybody know when their feelings were hurt, the bullies would be shamed into behaving better."

"I'm pretty sure that one's been tried," she said. "Turned out there wasn't enough shame to go around."

We fell silent.

Then she said, "I haven't seen you around here before."

"No, I just moved into the neighborhood," I said. "You live around here?"

"Not too far," she said. "What do you do?"

"Oh," I said, and made a vague gesture. "I'm a consultant. You?"

"I'm a writer," she said. "I walk around the city, looking for inspiration and material."

"Find anything good lately?" I asked.

She cocked her head. "Maybe. Hard to say. I like to leave my options open. I might put you in a story, for example."

"Me?" I was astonished. "Boy, would that be a mistake! I'm totally boring."

"Really?" She eyed me in mock surprise. "I'll bet you're not. The people who think they're boring are never as boring as they think they are, and the ones who think they're fascinating are usually much more boring than the ones who think they're boring."

"I'm boring, and I know it," I said.

"Come on," she said. "What do you consult about?" She said this with the air of an investigative reporter on a mission.

"Oh—." I hunched my shoulders and moved restlessly on the bench. "You know—management kinds of stuff."

"Such as?"

"Well, like, anything to do with time management," I said. "Like, I consult with food packagers about how to make the biggest impact in the shortest amount of time in terms of package design. Did you know it only takes consumers an average of forty-seven seconds to choose a brand of a product they haven't bought before or don't regularly buy?"

"That doesn't quite sound like time management to me," she said.

"It is, though," I said, "because the package design is also impacted by the time it takes to produce the package and the time it takes a consumer to open the package, what we in the industry call 'openability.'"

"Openability," she echoed. "No shit."

"So what kinds of things do you write about?" I said. "Do you write stories or essays or what?"

She was rummaging in her bag now, out of sight on the bench on the other side of her. "Whatever I feel like," she said into her bag. "Sometimes stories, sometimes essays." She brought out something small and shiny. She tossed it to me.

It was a granola bar in a purple metallic wrapper.

"Okay, so let's say I made this wrapper, and I consulted you," she said. "What would you tell me?"

I scrutinized the wrapper. "Well, right off the bat I'd tell you to change the typeface and maybe increase the size of the font on the word 'delicious.' 'Delicious' comes second after 'power-packed,' but it should come first because it's the most important criterion to consumers, even athletes and health nuts—what we call the 'deal-breaker.'"

"And you think I wouldn't get as far as 'delicious' in forty-seven seconds?"

"You might, but why take chances?"

"Okay, tell me more."

"I can't tell you more without opening the package."

"So, open it."

I looked it over, then tried to insert my index finger under one of the flaps. She scooted closer to watch me.

"This is called the 'chimp test,'" I said. "If a chimp can open the package within ten seconds, it's a good package—strictly from the time management and marketing points of view, you understand."

"Yeah?" she said. "How many chimps you got working for you?"

"I'm not the boss," I said. "If you're asking about my co-workers, only two are chimps."

I'd tried both flaps, both sides. Nothing doing. I tried my teeth. You'd have thought the damn wrapper was made out of Kevlar. I expressed my frustration by making high-pitched chimp sounds, baring my teeth, and flinging the package away. The two mothers across from us ducked, and looked at me wide-eyed.

Charlotte's eyes followed the arc of the package, then returned to my face.

"You're so full of shit," she said.

I raised my eyebrows. "It's the truth," I insisted. "That's just what Schmo would have done—except that his aim would have been better. Which is why he makes big bucks at his job."

She went to retrieve the package. The mothers were herding their toddlers in quick retreat.

She stood in front of me, holding up the package. "Regardez," she said. She inserted a fingernail into a flap and had the thing open in well under ten seconds.

"That's why we hire chimps and not women," I said. "You see, women designers often forget that half of the world's consumers don't have fingernails like theirs. You add in the kids and the women who bite their fingernails, we're talking about more than half. I'm not complaining. It's more work for me when companies design bad packaging, and then wonder why their sales tank."

"Must be a revelation to them when the chimp rejects their package," she said.

"You have no idea," I said.

She glanced at her watch. "Well, I gotta be going. Listen, you want me to show you around the neighborhood some time?"

"Well," I said. I hesitated. "I'd really like that, but I don't know when I'm going to be working."

"Tomorrow's Saturday," she said. She stowed Douglas Adams in a canvas tote bag that she hung from her shoulder. "If you work on Saturdays, you've flunked your own time management consultation."

"Can I call you?" I said.

She found an ATM receipt in her bag and scrawled a number. She handed it to me. "I'll show you all the best places to shop for chimp gifts."

"Great," I said.

I watched her walk away, still undecided. Did she know who I was or didn't she? Was I developing an exaggerated sense of my own importance?

Probably.

CHAPTER FIFTEEN

When I got back to the room, I found Robbie hanging out with two bodyguards. He was uncharacteristically dressed up, wearing a restrained plaid sports coat over his Eric Clapton tee shirt, a pair of khakis and sneakers. He was waiting for Larry and Elvis, whom he was taking to his mother's retirement complex for dinner. Ginger and company had decamped, and Larry was in the bedroom helping Elvis decide what to wear.

"Hey, wow!" Robbie said when he saw me. "You're, like, totally transformed!"

I reached up and pulled off the wig, then stroked my bare chin self-consciously. I'd removed the dark glasses in the elevator so that I could read the buttons.

"What do you think?" I said.

"I don't know, man," he said, shaking his head. "Give me some time to get used to it."

This was not a response that inspired confidence.

I heard Elvis's voice, coming from the bedroom. "You don't think it makes me look too—."

"Too what?" Larry sounded baffled.

"Too—big?"

Robbie raised his voice. "Bigness is your thing, dude. Embrace your bigness."

Elvis appeared in the doorway. He was wearing a blue-green cable-knit sweater, cargo pants, and—I kid you not—blue suede shoes. "But, Robbie, don't you think this sweater makes me look fat?"

Robbie and I and the two bodyguards looked at each other. The two bodyguards had the appearance and builds of Samoans, and looked like brothers.

"Yo, man," one of them said, "that sweater is fly."

"Is that good?" Elvis said hopefully.

"It's the best," said the other. "It's dope."

"Who told you you looked fat, anyway?" Robbie asked. When Elvis didn't answer, he rolled his eyes. "Aw, man, I told you to lay off that television. The boob tube'll turn your mind to mush."

"You a big man," said the first bodyguard, "like us. Nothing wrong with that. Where we come from, all men are big. I don't hear no complaints from the ladies."

He and his brother laughed.

Elvis turned to me. "Hank?"

"Totally fly," I said.

"Then I'm almost ready," he said to Robbie, and retreated to the bedroom.

The Samoans went back to a video game they were playing that seemed to have something to do with extraterrestrial combat. I sat down on the other end of the couch from Robbie.

"How you doin', man?" he asked.

"Fine," I said. "You?"

He gave me an intense look. "No, I mean, how you *doin'*?"

I shrugged, a little confused.

"Let me tell you something," he said. "Hanging out with those two—it'll change your life, man. Did mine."

"Yeah?" I said.

"Damn straight," he said. "If Larry hadn't come along when he did, I'm convinced I would've ended up a corporate drone with a couple of divorces and a house in the 'burbs. Well, I got one divorce, but that's not my point. My point is, I would never have opened my eyes and looked around, man. And I don't just mean at the world, I mean at the whole friggin' thing, the whole enchilada. Know what I mean?"

"I'm not sure."

"The universe, man! Everything that's out there. I mean everything. God, too, 'cause he's out there—or she's out there. I mean everybody and everything that doesn't look like you and doesn't act like you and doesn't think like you—hell, probably doesn't even breathe like you. Infinity. Eternity. All of it."

"Uh-huh."

"You know how big the universe is? You ever thought about that? These guys traveled two hundred and fifty million miles—well, two hundred and fifty million from here to the edge of their galaxy, and who knows how big that fucker is. So, anyway, they traveled two hundred and fifty million miles, and it was like—oh, I don't know—driving from here to Tierra del Fuego, maybe, not even to China. And we're only talking about this dimension, this universe, not even taking into account all the other possibilities. You think about that?"

"I'm beginning to," I said.

He'd been leaning toward me, and now he sat back. "That's what I'm talking about. That's exactly what I'm talking about. You start thinking, you never stop. No end in sight. Sometimes I used to feel like my head was going to explode." He raised his hands to enact the explosion. "The Little Bang, know what I mean?" Then he leaned in again. "We live on this microscopic speck of dust in a remote corner of a dust cloud made up of a kazillion specks of dust circling around these amazingly intense energy fields, and ours is pretty small as energy fields go. We're so fucking primitive that it was practically yesterday, cosmologically speaking, we noticed that the damn universe doesn't revolve around us. Miserable and discontented as we are—I'm talking about humans, now—we think we're superior to every other life form on this planet. And yet these two guys traveled two hundred and fifty million miles to warn us to stop what we're doing or face annihilation. Twice. And one of them got shot for it last time. And came back. Now what is that?"

He searched my face. I was interested but unenlightened.

He sat back again. "That's love, man. What else could it be? What the hell else could it be?"

I didn't have an answer for that one, either.

He raised an index finger for emphasis. "And it ain't personal. That's the thing. They didn't know before they got here that they were going to meet up with a Robbie and Betty Donovan and a Hank Jones that they might be kind of sorry to annihilate, stupid as we are. It's like if you actually considered ants and their feelings before you stepped on them or mowed down their anthill. It's pure love of all creation—undeserved and unearned and, for that matter, unreturned. Once you start to think about that, man, your insides will change as much as your outside." He tapped my knee and winked at me. "More."

He stood up as Elvis and Larry re-entered the room. "Ready to boogie?" To the brothers, he said, "Which of you gents has the pleasure of being our escort for the evening?" One of them raised his hand, stood, and shrugged into his Spartan Security windbreaker. "You remember where you parked the Range Rover? Good. Sure you don't want to come along, Hank? It's Italian night. No? Can't tempt you? Okay, then. See you later."

After they left, I lay down on the couch. My back was feeling the strain of my little sojourn in the park and the conversation with Robbie had left me light-headed as well.

Joe, the remaining bodyguard, invited me to play whatever he was playing, but I declined.

"You don't have to babysit me, you know," I said. "The targets just walked out the door."

"Orders, man," he said. "Round-the-clock security. Anyway, what would happen if a hopped-up Rambo type showed up at the door right now, and found out that there was no spacemen here to blow away? You think he'd just say, 'Oh, okay, then. Sorry I bothered you'?"

"I see your point," I said.

"I don't mind telling you, though, I'd like to be here if that guy does show up when Elvis is here. They say he can incinerate a guy just by looking at him. You believe that?"

"I don't know," I said. "I don't especially want to see it."

"Well, I do," he said. "Long as it's a really bad dude, and not just room service or the air conditioner repair guy."

"You hungry?" I asked.

"I'm always hungry," he said.

"Well, maybe in another half hour, after I've rested my back for a while, we can go get something to eat."

The phone rang, and Joe answered it, then handed it to me. "Jillian," he said.

"Oh, god, I'm glad you're there," she said. "I think I left my Palm Pilot in the kitchenette. Could you look and see?"

"What does it look like?" I said.

Silence. "You're kidding, right?" she said.

"I don't get out much," I said. "My date book is not so crowded that I can't keep it all in my head. I know what an iPod is because my students all have them. But when they make appointments with me, they just write it on the backs of their hands."

"It looks kind of like a black cell phone, only thinner and wider."

"Hold on." I heaved myself off the couch and went to look. I found an object like the one she'd described on top of the microwave. I picked it up and went back to the phone. "Yeah, it's here."

"Great. Now, would you just look and see what time my hair appointment is tomorrow morning?"

"How do I do that?"

She talked me through it, and I told her when her appointment was.

"Great! Thanks a million, Hank," she said. "Hey, how come you're not at dinner? Didn't you want to meet Robbie's mom? Or is your back bothering you?"

"It's not too bad," I said. "I just thought they might appreciate a little privacy. After all, from her perspective, she hasn't seen him in more than fifty years."

"Are you kidding?" she said. "Have you ever been to dinner at a retirement complex? Privacy is the last thing they'll get. So what are you doing? And which bodyguard are you doing it with?"

"It's Samoan Joe. He's playing video games, and I'm just resting. In a little while, we'll go out to dinner."

"Hey, how'd it go with your new look? I'm sorry I wasn't there to see it."

"I don't know," I said. "I might've gotten picked up in the park. There was this woman there, and she came and sat on the same bench I was sitting on, and she was reading Douglas Adams."

"Uh-oh."

"She said she was a writer. And she brought up the spacemen. But she didn't act like she knew I was connected to them. I mean, she connected my name, but she didn't think I looked anything like the Hank that was hanging out with the aliens."

"Sounds bogus to me," she said.

"I told her I'd just moved into the neighborhood, and she offered to show me around tomorrow."

"Aren't you going to Mount Vernon tomorrow with the boys?"

"I don't know. Is that where they're going?"

"Yeah. But dress warm—you're going by boat, and it could be cold."

"Are you going?" I said.

"I'm thinking about it. I have kind of a date."

"Can't you bring him along?" I said.

"Maybe," she said. "We'll see."

I put on my wig and asked Joe to pick a restaurant, and we went to a great Latin American place where nobody seemed to recognize me. Then we walked around, and ended up at Murphy's again. It wasn't a neighborhood that ran to bars, and I didn't especially want to do my drinking at the Marriott with the conventioneers. There was a different crowd in the pub at this time of day, mostly young professionals from the neighborhood. Joe told me his life story, which was way more interesting than mine. He and his brother Paul were both studying to be personal trainers.

By eleven o'clock, all of the networks were running stories about a previous visit to Earth by spacemen Lawrence Smith and Elvis Preston. Somebody at Betty Donovan's retirement center had probably tipped them off. The newscasters hadn't yet located any witnesses, except for Betty and Robbie, who were too busy playing canasta to answer their questions, but I figured that it was only a matter of time before witnesses and false witnesses started coming out of the woodwork. The morning shows would each score at least one, I felt sure of that.

I lay in bed that night and imagined what it might feel like to be as excited about my prospective career as Joe was about his. The truth was that Joe was much more impressed by my impending Ph.D. than I was, and he was even more impressed that I had to write a book to get it.

"Wow, man, that's great," he'd said. "When they publish your book, I can say I know a famous author."

And I'd been too bored with myself, and with my rather threadbare dreams of life as Professor Jones, to correct his mistaken impression that dissertations led to acclaim and renown. Instead, I had changed the subject.

Now, I told myself, "It's Friday. On Monday morning, you're supposed to be back in the classroom. Okay, you've bought a few days of grace, but that's going to run out soon. What do you intend to do? You planning on walking away from all your coursework, not to mention the money you've invested, just because you bumped into a pair of spacemen in a bar when you were feeling down?"

I thought about everything Robbie had said about how meeting the spacemen had changed his whole perspective. I tried to imagine the infinitude of space, and pictured two superior extraterrestrial beings traveling through it to end up on barstools next to me in Bloomington, Indiana.

"Yeah," I said to myself. "That's exactly what I'm thinking about doing."

CHAPTER SIXTEEN

Something soft and wet against my cheek startled me awake. I felt a weight on my arm and a tickling as something brushed my shoulder. Warm puffs of air brought with them the odor of garlic. I opened my eyes.

My assailant yipped its approval and applied its tongue more vigorously.

In the ear that wasn't being tongued, I heard Elvis. "Oh, look! She likes you, Hank."

The phone rang. The dog barked at it excitedly. I reached around squirming dog and picked it up.

A woman's voice said something.

"Hold on, I can't hear," I said. "Elvis! Would you come get this dog out of my face?"

"She's just excited, Hank," he said, scooping up the dog and tucking her under his arm. "She's heard so much about you."

"I bet," I said. Into the phone, I said, "Would you repeat that?"

The woman's voice, sounding either exasperated or amused, I couldn't tell which, said, louder and more distinctly, "This is the White House calling. The President would like to speak to Mr. Smith."

"How do I know it's really you?" I said.

There was a brief silence, and then a sigh. "Mr. Jones, please. Already this morning we've hosted a No Child Left Behind breakfast for thirty-seven preschoolers, Barney just bit the undersecretary of

State, and the Russian ambassador is coming for lunch. Don't make my day any worse."

"Hang on," I said. As soon as my feet hit the floor, the dog wriggled free and tackled one ankle. I made slow progress with the dog attached, but then Larry appeared in the doorway. "The White House is on the line. The President wants to speak to you. Do you want to speak to him?"

"All right," Larry said, unimpressed. "I suppose that's progress."

I followed him out into the living room. "Just remember, he's not the same one as last time. This one is—."

Larry paused, hand on the phone, and raised his eyebrows at me.

"Well, he's not the same. Can I listen in?"

He nodded.

Elvis, behind me, bent to detach the dog from my leg. "She is really a very good dog, Hank," he said, with an emphasis I found rather discomfiting. "She's only excited, that's all."

I missed the beginning of the conversation, but when I picked up the phone again, the President was asking how the spacemen were enjoying the sights of Washington. Larry made a polite reply, and mentioned how much he appreciated re-reading Lincoln's speech at the Lincoln Memorial.

"Oh, yes, the Emancipation Proclamation," said the President. "That's one of my favorites."

Larry did not correct him, but went on to mention that they would be going to Mount Vernon that day.

"Yes, I heard that, I heard that," the President said. "Well, listen, I know you're busy, sightseeing and everything, but it seems to me that you and I should sit down for a little chat."

Larry sighed. "If you think it would help," Larry said, "I have no objection."

The President laughed at that, but it was a nervous laugh.

"I didn't come to Earth to speak with a single representative of a single government," Larry continued, "but if you have advice to give me on how to approach all of the other governments on your planet, I'd be very grateful to hear it."

I didn't think the President had any useful advice to give on approaching members of the local opposition, much less the whole planet, and they both knew it. But he invited Larry to Camp David anyway at some unspecified time in the future, and Larry agreed to go.

"Oh, before I forget," the President said, "I'm supposed to offer you some Secret Service agents to help out with your security."

To my relief, Larry politely declined. I've never been big on crowds, and our hotel room was definitely getting crowded.

Then the President asked to speak to Elvis, so I retrieved the dog and took her into the bathroom, where she could bounce her barks off the tile to her heart's content.

Elvis himself opened the door when the phone call was over. The dog threw herself at him in a joyful frenzy. "Hello, hello," he said to the animated mop. "I'm back. I just had to talk to the President." To me, he said, "Well, Hank, what do you think?"

"About the President's call?"

"About little Getlo," he said, doing that head-wave thing dog owners do when their chin is being tongue-washed.

"How would I know?" I said. "She doesn't stand still long enough for me to get a good look at her. Her name's Getlo? What kind of name is that?"

"You don't like it?"

"I didn't say that," I said. Now that I'd been liberated, I was washing my face the old-fashioned way.

"'Getlo' was the name of Elvis Presley's favorite dog," he said. "This dog died tragically young, and broke her master's heart. It is a very sad story. Elvis also had many horses and other dogs and a chimp named Scamper, but I don't like that name."

I was brushing my teeth and watching him in the mirror. From what I'd heard of the language he and Larry spoke, I could appreciate the appeal of 'Getlo,' with its hard consonants, labial el and long oh. It probably sounded beautiful in his ears.

"So." I spat toothpaste. "She's named for a doomed dog." When I bent to spit, my back objected. I realized then that the pain had been pretty constant since I first got out of bed, only I hadn't had the opportunity to notice.

He covered the dog's ears with his hand. One hand easily covered the two tufts that marked her ears. "Don't listen to him," he said. "You are named for a very special and loved dog."

I took two Advils and got dressed. Larry and Elvis were sitting at the table eating off a room service tray. Larry looked up when I appeared, and reached for the coffee pot.

"They didn't have any Kellogg's Pep, Hank," Elvis said apologetically. "I was hoping for a Buffalo Bill picture ring. But we have Wheaties, Breakfast of Champions."

The dog raced over to greet me.

"Where'd she come from, anyway?" I said. "Tell me you didn't sign a deal to do dog food commercials."

"She just followed us," Elvis said. "It was chuktok."

"It was what?"

"Chuktok."

"Is that something like fate?" I guessed.

"Yes," Larry said.

"No," Elvis said.

I paused in the act of spreading jam on toast, and looked at them. A brief dialogue in their native tongue ensued.

"It's kind of like what you call 'fate,'" Elvis said, "but it's more like divine wishing. You know, like the Almighty Spirit causes something to happen because it wishes that something to happen. But in the end, you must also wish it to happen. So Getlo here must also wish it, and we must, and you must."

"I don't see where I come into it," I said, eyeing the dog. She was kind of cute, in a ragamuffin way, as she chewed on one of the expensive sneakers that had been a gift from Anita, my ex. "Anyway, where was she, when all of this wishing came to fruition?"

"She was at Serenity Cove, Betty's retirement complex," Elvis said. "She was just walking around outside the building. Hank, have you ever played canasta? It is sweet."

I put my toast down, my appetite gone. I could see the headlines: "Alien Dognappers Strike Senior Center." There would be a photograph—two, actually. One of an elderly woman hugging little Getlo in happier times, and one of her in tears, probably leaning on her walker, with a caption that read, "I just want my baby back."

"Did you ask if she belonged to anybody in the complex?"

"Oh, she didn't belong to anybody, Hank," Elvis said. He leaned over and held out a piece of bacon. The dog sniffed, then took it delicately between her teeth and retreated a few steps to lie down and eat it. "She needs a new home. Look at her. She wanted to come with us."

I sighed. "But you didn't ask around." I looked at Larry, who shrugged.

"I told him we should," Larry said.

"Look," I said, "of course she wanted to go with you. Dogs like adventure, and friendly dogs will follow anybody."

"Especially if they are carrying meatballs," Larry said.

That explained the garlic breath. "Yes," I said, "especially then. But she probably belongs to someone in the complex. They let her out to do her business—." Elvis frowned. "To urinate and defecate. When they called her to come in, she was gone."

"She is not wearing an identification bracelet around her neck," Elvis pointed out. "She looked very sad."

Elvis was right about the collar. That was a hopeful sign. But this dog didn't look like she had a sad bone in her body.

"You have a point," I said. "But we still need to make sure that she doesn't belong to someone in the complex. She looks too well cared for to be a stray."

"Do I have to take her back?" Elvis said. I hadn't seen him this unhappy since he'd heard Elvis Presley was dead.

"I'll call the complex and see if anyone has reported a missing dog," I said.

It turned out that someone had reported a missing dog, so I was right about that. But Elvis appeared to be right about her needing a home. The dog's owner had recently been hospitalized, and then transferred to a nursing home, and would not be returning to Serenity Cove. A neighbor had been looking after the dog since that time, and was distraught when she'd disappeared, but the neighbor didn't want to keep the dog.

"Marge will be so pleased that she's found a good home," said the woman on the other end of the line.

"I don't think you should leap to any conclusions," I said. "It depends on whether she likes space travel."

"Oh, I'm sure she can handle it," the woman said. "She's a very easygoing dog. In fact, her name is 'Sweetie.'"

Elvis didn't have that annoying human habit of saying, "I told you so." When I told him the dog's story, he just nodded, and said, "I thought she needed a home. Hank, we must take her to visit Marge at the nursing home."

Then he said, "When are we leaving for Mount Wernon?"

"At eleven," I said.

"What time is it now?" he asked.

"Use your watch," Larry and I chorused. Elvis tended to forget about the watch, and when he remembered, he thought it was his cell phone.

"Oh," he said, and grinned sheepishly. He looked at his watch, and jumped to his feet. "Come on, Hank! We don't have much time."

"For what?" I said.

"Shopping," he said. "Put your shoes on."

"Shopping for what?" I said. I put down the corner crust and, standing, took one last sip of coffee.

"For dog things," he said. "She can't keep eating meatballs and bacon."

He bustled me out the door. Our current bodyguard, Simon, rushed to catch up with us at the elevator. As we crossed the hotel lobby, Dave accosted us.

"I was just coming to check in with you, Hank," Dave said. "Need my services today?"

"I'm sorry, but we're in a hurry," Elvis said. Then he grabbed Dave by the wrist—the one with the briefcase attached. "Come with me. I want you to meet somebody."

He dragged Dave over to a bank of couches where a middle-aged man was sitting, talking on his cell phone, laptop open on the coffee table in front of him. The man wore jeans that looked like they'd been starched and pressed, and a blue Izod shirt. He looked up in surprise.

"Hi, I'm Elvis," Elvis said, and held out a hand.

The surprised man shook it. "Curt," he said, caught off guard.

Elvis turned to Dave. "This is Curt. He's with the Central Intelligence Agency." To Curt he said, "This is Dave. He's with the F.B.I. Why don't you two stay here and talk while we go to the pet store? The dark-haired man over there, the one who is pretending to read a newspaper—he's with the Secret Service. He would probably enjoy talking to you, too." He scanned the lobby. Everybody else looked just as normal as these guys looked, except for a handful of reporters and photographers bearing down on us. "We'll take the press with us." He waved at the two men. "Later, gator."

I didn't bother to ask him how he knew not only who the spies were, but which agency they represented, but I made a note to ask later. If he could read minds, I was going to have to start censoring my thoughts.

The two clerks in the pet store were thrilled by our visit, even though the reporters and photographers took up all the available space. As we stood in front of the leash display, Elvis holding his hands up to indicate the approximate size of the dog, lights flashed and cameras whirred. They whirred again when he stopped to pet the resident cat, who didn't seem to register his size but only arched her back and stretched her toes in response to his stroke. When we arrived at the dog food aisle, the two clerks took their time pointing out the advantages and disadvantages of every type and brand of food. Elvis frowned in concentration and asked questions. The reporters, who at first had bombarded him with questions about pets where he came from, had fallen silent when he had turned a glinty eye on a nearby pen in motion and made it disappear. "Please, be quiet," he'd told them. "I have to talk to Jarod and Angie now."

Simon stood at his shoulder and glared at them, too, just for good measure, though he looked less menacing than he might have looked without a dayglo leash draped around his neck and a stuffed bear under his arm.

When we reached the toy aisle, Jarod asked what kind of a dog Getlo was. Elvis turned to me. I shrugged. "Yappy and energetic," I said. "Short."

"She's a Shih Tzu," Simon the bodyguard volunteered. "Maybe a mix, but she's definitely got Shih Tzu in her."

So we selected a few of the toys Shih Tzus favored.

At the checkout stand, Angie offered Elvis a refrigerator magnet, and when he stuck it to his forehead, the crowd went wild. Fortunately, I thought, the day was young, and the prospective photo-ops were many, so I was optimistic they'd find better pictures to print on the front page and run during the evening news. I wasn't sure that any of them had yet figured out why the refrigerator magnet had stuck, and I wasn't sure what difference if any it would make when they did figure it out. I found that I was most worried not about any political or military ramifications, but about Elvis's feelings.

As we re-crossed the hotel lobby, Elvis made a point of waving at Dave, Curt, and the blond guy from the Secret Service. Simon stepped into the path of a man who was advancing on Elvis. He was a droopy-jowled, gray-haired guy in a stained pair of chinos and a tired sportscoat.

"I have something for Mr. Preston," he said, holding up an envelope. It had the crisp, formal look of something legal.

"I'll take it," Simon said and made a grab for it.

"No can do," the man said, holding it out of Simon's reach. "I only get paid for delivery to Mr. Preston."

Elvis reached over Simon and took the envelope. He frowned at it as we walked to the elevator.

"Hank, what does 'es-queer' mean?" he asked.

"Esquire," I corrected. "It means an attorney. What is it?"

"What does 'vee ess period' mean?"

"Short for 'versus.' Usually refers to lawsuits."

"So if it says, 'Harney vee-ess Preston,' that means someone is suing me?"

"Yes," I said. "Who's suing you?"

"Someone who says I caused grave bodily harm to them." He looked up at me. "I don't remember causing grave bodily harm to anyone. Did I?"

"Harney," Simon said. "That was the mugger you caught."

"Do you mean the thief?" Elvis asked.

"His name was Harney?" I leaned back hard against the elevator, an expression of annoyance that my back did not appreciate. "Son of a bitch!"

"I didn't cause grave bodily harm to him," Elvis said in bewilderment. "I was very careful."

"I'm sure you were," I said. "Look, the guy's probably just trying to take advantage. He thinks because you're famous he'll get a lot of money out of you, one way or another."

"You were very careful, too, weren't you, Hank?" Elvis said. "He says you caused him grave bodily harm, too."

"Oh, shit," I said.

The trip to Mount Vernon was uneventful, or as uneventful as a trip can be when fifty members of the Washington press corps are trailing you, watching for your clumsiest move and goofiest expression. Larry made a creditable statement about Washington's greatness in rejecting absolute power when it had been offered to him. I happened to know that Ginger had helped to craft this statement, because I'd helped out again with the subjunctive mood ("If Washington were alive today . . . ."), but I also knew that it represented Larry's own sentiments. Elvis left a few new dents in the lintels, and I hoped we wouldn't be receiving another legal document tomorrow from the Mount Vernon Ladies' Association. Larry left a generous donation, Elvis bought the 2007 holiday ornament, and we seemed to depart on good terms.

Larry, Warren the bodyguard, and I took the service elevator up to our floor. Elvis and Simon went to the lobby because Elvis wanted to talk to Pedro and George. Elvis returned with the droopy-jowled process server we'd encountered in the lobby previously. Getlo threw herself at Elvis.

"You already gave us the papers," I protested.

"He says he has something for Larry," Elvis said. He picked up the dog and let her slobber all over his face.

Larry looked up from the desk, where he was checking phonemail messages. "For me?" he said.

"You Lawrence Smith?" the man said. When Larry said he was, the man handed him three envelopes. "You're a popular guy."

"What the hell?" I said.

The man left, and Larry and I sat down on the couch to read the documents. All three informed us that the plaintiff named therein was suing Lawrence Smith for an establishment of paternity. One of the plaintiffs was suing on behalf of her 56-year old son. The other two, a woman and a man, were suing on behalf of themselves.

"Can they do this?" I said.

Warren the bodyguard said, "No, man, they can't. Paternity laws apply to minors. I think you can only sue up until two years after a kid reaches adulthood. But I can ask my torts prof, if you want me to."

"So what do they want from me, these people?" Larry asked.

"Who knows?" Warren said. "Money, for sure. Maybe they're publicity junkies. One of them just might be off their rocker, and hoping you'll take them for a ride in a spaceship to wherever you came from."

"These are probably nuisance lawsuits," I said. "These people think that if they make you uncomfortable, you'll give them a diamond to go away."

Larry shrugged. "I don't mind giving diamonds to people who need them, but if this happens a lot, I won't have enough to go around."

"No, no, no, Larry," Simon, the other bodyguard, said. He held up a restraining hand. It happened to be holding a fluorescent pink squeak toy. "You don't give these losers nothing, man. They're just running a game on you. You don't want to reward bad behavior, or you'll see an epidemic."

"He's right," Warren said. "If you want to stop this kind of thing, you should counter-sue."

"You mean, in a court of law?" Larry frowned. "I don't have time for this nonsense."

"Doesn't have to take much time," Warren said. "Not your time, anyway. You hire the right lawyer and pay him enough to make the problem go away. If you didn't have the money, I wouldn't give you that advice. I'd tell you to ignore them all, make them drag your ass to court. By the time the court date rolls around, you'll be long gone anyway, right?"

"I certainly hope so," Larry said with a sigh.

"Warren's right," Simon said. "You get yourself a bad-ass attorney—a real mean son-of-a-bitch. He doesn't have to offer these people nothing. He just writes 'em all letters, threatening to throw the book at 'em if they don't back down." His eyes drifted to where Elvis was rolling on the floor with the dog, play-growling back at her. "Or, you don't want to spend any money on lawyers, you just send your boy Elvis here to pay those people a visit. You let him disappear their home entertainment centers or their Jacuzzis or their SUVs, you won't have any more trouble."

I shifted uneasily. "Then they'll sue for damages."

"What damages? You think they can prove in a court of law that Elvis here sent their flatscreen TV into orbit around Jupiter?"

"He has a point," Warren said, smiling. "I like it."

"What about Harney?"

"He'd be first on my list," Simon said.

"Mine, too," Warren said. "Pretty soon somebody's going to talk him into filing criminal assault charges, and then the cops are involved."

"You think a D.A. would let him?" I asked.

"I don't know, man," Warren said, shaking his head. "You never can tell. This is a political town. Everything depends on which way the wind is blowing. Let's say Homeland Security wants Elvis locked up, but they don't want to arrest him as a potential enemy combatant and send him to Guantanamo because they know he's got a couple hundred friends on Facebook, not to mention the gigs on Letterman and *Oprah*. So they, like, encourage the D.A. to file assault charges, and let the local cops take the heat."

"Earth sounds a lot like Rodabarb, Larry," Elvis said. To us, he said, "It is a planet in the ring galaxy you call 'Hoag's object.' The most common occupation of the people on that planet is a legal occupation—lawyers, judges, court clerks, other court officials, and delivery people like Gus, the man who delivered our lawsuit papers.

Those people are not happy unless they are involved in litigation. They have even attempted to take other planets to the intragalactic court, but after the first time or two, they were not permitted to file charges."

"Yes," Larry said, "it's gotten out of hand there. The life expectancy is quite low because they have no doctors. Everyone wants to work in the courts, and besides, practicing medicine would only attract lawsuits. Every Rodabarber is insured against lawsuits, of course, the way Earth people insure their cars. But no one could afford what you call medical malpractice insurance."

"Sounds like my idea of hell," I said.

"Oh!" Elvis said suddenly, sitting up. "What time is it?"

"Check your watch," Larry and I said.

He did. "Hank, you have to get ready."

"For what?"

He smiled slyly. "For your date."

"What date?"

"The one I made for you. Don't worry. I'm coming, too."

I started to protest, but he cut me off. "Hank, you have to get out and meet some chicks."

CHAPTER SEVENTEEN

The last thing I wanted was another night on the town, but Elvis told me just to wear sneakers and jeans. Simon produced a black Spartan Security tee shirt for me to wear. Elvis put on his Hoya sweats, a Bob Marley tee-shirt he'd picked up on the street in Adams Morgan, and his own mammoth high-tops. There was a changing of the guard while I was dressing, so when we headed out in the Spartan security SUV, the Samoan brothers, Joe and Paul, were sitting up front. Larry was in the back with us, wearing khakis and a pullover. Everybody seemed to know where we were going except me.

It was already dark by the time we reached Georgetown, and Joe parked on the street. Paul took a gym bag out of the back. We turned onto the Georgetown campus and headed for a large building that looked like a fieldhouse. I followed the others inside, where the distinctive bouquet of sweat, fermented gym socks, dust, disinfectant, and floor wax confirmed my guess. The gorgeous Lydia was leaning up against a cinderblock wall with a basketball under her arm. The last time I'd seen her, she'd been salsa dancing in a sexy dress; now, she and the other people around her were all wearing shorts, tee shirts, and gym shoes. There were two other women and four men. Lydia was almost as tall as the tallest of the men, but not as tall, of course, as Elvis. When she spotted us, she launched herself off the wall like a released spring.

Elvis turned to me and grinned. "Surprise!" he said. "We are going to play basketball, Hank, like you do at home."

To tell you the truth, something swelled in my throat. This activity had clearly been planned by Elvis as a pleasurable surprise for me—a gift. He had taken into account my tastes, but also my possible homesickness, not to mention my newly single status. He was beaming at me, ready to take delight in my happiness.

My back let out a yelp of protest. "Shut up," I said to it under my breath. I grinned at Elvis. "Cool!" I said, rubbing my hands together. "Let's do it."

We played basketball. It wasn't quite the way I played at home, because although my regular game was pretty intense, it was the intensity of non-athletes whose day-to-day exercise ran largely to turning pages, hefting small cylinders of chalk, and tapping keyboards. These people were good. It didn't take long to figure out that some of them might actually be retired college players. Then there was the Elvis factor. It was a whole different game with a seven-foot center under the basket. He was easy to pass to, and putting the ball in the basket was no effort for him. But like most of us, he wasn't content to play to his strengths. No, he was dying to dribble. And given his height and the quickness of his opponents, every time he put the ball on the floor, he lost it. Well, okay, not every time; his opponents, caught up in his enthusiasm, were cutting him a little slack. For his part, Elvis was clearly playing a more cautious game than he might have had he been surrounded by other indestructible seven-foot, metal-skinned players. He was quick to apologize if he thought he'd injured someone, though there was plenty of blame to go around.

Sitting out to catch my breath, I fell into conversation with a couple of tall onlookers dressed in Hoyas sweats.

"Big dude got game," one of them said, nodding at Elvis.

I filed this remark away, knowing that it would please Elvis when he heard it.

Elvis called a foul on himself, and the other onlooker said, "Where he learn to play?"

I couldn't tell whether or not they'd identified him as an alien visitor. If he sprouted an extra head, I had a feeling that it wouldn't disrupt their cool, unemotional contemplation of his movement.

"I think mostly he learned from watching television," I said.

One of the players threw an elbow in his direction and Elvis lost his balance. To avoid falling on someone else, he executed an undulating roll that ended in a hop that righted him.

"Which channel he watch?" said the second onlooker.

But when the game-ending injury happened, Elvis was nowhere near the injured player. This guy was the second tallest player on the court—a slender but muscular man with a head thick with blond curls like a big blond peony. His name was Sam. He moved in to take a charge, and went down hard. Somebody stepped on his ankle, and he yowled. Sitting on the floor, he shouted obscenities between clenched teeth as he reached for his ankle. All the color drained from his face.

Elvis looked around guiltily. Larry, who'd been sitting on the sidelines watching the game, got up and moved across the court. The onlookers and I followed.

Several players were crouched in a circle near Sam. Larry joined the circle of crouchers and reached out for the ankle.

"Don't touch it, man," Sam said. "It hurts like hell."

"I'll be very gentle," Larry said in a calm voice. "Okay?"

Sam looked at him, then nodded.

Larry first positioned his hands on either side of the injured ankle, but very close. He left them there for a few minutes as we all stared at his hands. Then, very slowly, he wrapped them around the ankle and held it. Time passed. Eventually, he looked up at Sam. "Better?" he asked. Sam nodded.

"Can we take him to the hospital now?" Lydia asked.

"Yes," Larry said. "The bone is broken, so he'll need treatment. Just make sure he doesn't put any weight on it."

So we all ended our evening at the hospital, minus a few players who had to go to work or go home to study. Seven of us sat in the waiting room at the Emergency Department, where a broken ankle was a low priority. They gave Sam an ice bag and pointed him to a roomful of plastic chairs.

"Man, I don't know what you did," he said to Larry, "but it was like you drained the pain right out of it."

Larry just smiled.

On the way over from the fieldhouse, a worried Elvis had asked whether the injury was his fault. I'd patted his shoulder. "No, big guy, you had nothing to do with it."

You could feel the recognition circle the waiting room like an electric current. It happened more slowly than it might have if we'd been hanging out in a place where people weren't so distracted by their own problems, but eventually, everybody in the room had noticed the seven-foot guy in Hoyas sweats who looked like Elvis Presley. Everybody except maybe a young couple at the far end of the room who seemed too wrapped up in their misery.

Two little girls approached, holding hands. They were all skin and bones with little pot bellies and wispy light-brown hair, fragile as baby birds. The older one waited to be acknowledged, but the younger one pointed at Elvis and asked, "Are you the spaceman?"

"Yes, that's me," he said, fluttering his fingertips against his chest.

The older one gave Larry an apologetic look, and said, "Our mom said we could come over and say hi."

Larry smiled and offered his hand. "My name is Larry, and my friend's name is Elvis. What's your name?"

We hadn't noticed the young couple's disappearance, but their return disrupted the exchange of pleasantries between Larry and the sisters. The woman's sobs seemed to demand a respectful silence. The two little girls turned to watch her, big-eyed. The man had his arm around her, and was speaking softly, but he, too, was crying. They headed straight for us.

She stopped a few feet away. She was a sturdy young woman deflated by grief. She swiped a hand across her cheek and said to Larry, "I know who you are. You're the spaceman that came a long time ago. They said on T.V. that they shot you and you were dead and now you're back. My baby——." She faltered, then made a visible effort to control her grief. "They told me that my baby was dead, but she can't be dead. She's only two. If you could see her—she's just the sweetest little girl, so bright and lively and she loves everybody. Can't you please bring her back to me? Can't you?"

She made her request and stopped. Everything stopped. Her sobs hung suspended in the air around us.

Larry's eyes were soft with pity. I expected him to explain to her, gently, that he couldn't bring back the dead. But a glance at Elvis gave me pause, and I looked back at Larry with renewed interest.

Larry was taking his time, with good reason. The success of his mission might depend on his answer. If he couldn't do anything, he had to find the right words to tell these grieving parents so. If he could, and if he became known as a miracle worker—well, I didn't have time to sort through all the possible ramifications, but I knew that they would be immense. Right here, right now, he had to weigh them against two broken hearts and the life of a little girl who had existed in the universe for less than the blink of an eye.

"I will help if I can," he said at last, very softly. "But you must understand that only the Almighty Spirit has the power of life and death. If the Spirit wishes me to succeed, I will."

I glanced around. In spite of the silence, most of the other people in the waiting room had not been close enough to hear the exchange—one of the advantages of traveling in large groups. When Larry rose and followed the woman and her husband through the automatic doors onto the ward, I asked Elvis, "Can he do it?"

Elvis shrugged one shoulder. "It depends," he said.

"Chuktok?" I said softly.

He nodded. "The Almighty Spirit must wish it, and the little girl must wish it, too. And there are other considerations."

To the others, I said in a low voice, "Okay, guys, listen up. If he pulls this off, you have to keep quiet about it, okay? He's got a mission here, and it doesn't involve healing the human race, one person at a time. Got that?"

Sam was called shortly afterward, and disappeared through the automatic doors. When Larry returned, alone, his expression was so serious that we all assumed he'd failed. We took leave of our new friends. Elvis and I were invited to play anytime, while we were in town.

Outside, I put a hand on Larry's shoulder. "I'm sorry you failed, man," I said. "At least you tried."

He looked up. "I didn't fail," he said.

"You didn't?" I said.

"No," he said. "The life force was very strong in that little girl. She revived."

We all exchanged looks of surprise, except for Elvis, who looked as somber as Larry.

"Then why the long face?" I said. "I mean, why aren't you happy?"

"It is a serious thing," he said, "a sacred thing, to be permitted to heal in that way. And besides, I am trying to figure out how I'm going to tell Ginger what I've been up to."

CHAPTER EIGHTEEN

I woke up to the sound of music. That is, I woke up to the sounds of a guitar, and another noise, which I eventually identified as the sound of someone belting out "You Ain't Nothin' But a Hound Dog." He sang badly. Very badly.

"Robbie is teaching me to play the guitar," Elvis said when I ventured out of my bedroom. He was sitting next to Robbie on the couch.

"He's a natural," Robbie said. Robbie was wearing a tie-dyed tee shirt and ripped jeans. These were jeans with real rips where the knees had worn through the fabric, not some teen fashion statement. He was sitting cross-legged on the floor, back against the couch, stroking Getlo's belly. Elvis was sitting on the couch with a guitar across his lap. Max the bodyguard was sitting in an armchair, looking through *The Elvis Songbook for Guitar.*

"Would you like to see me play 'Hound Dog,' Hank?" Elvis asked.

"Let's work on it some more first, big guy," Robbie said.

"You don't think I look like Elvis?" Elvis asked him.

"Dude, you're the spittin' image," Robbie said. "You got the moves. But what we got to work on now is sound. You don't sound quite right yet. Remember, man, Elvis didn't become Elvis overnight. You got to have patience."

Larry called me from the table, where he was sitting and working on the computer. When I sat down across from him, he looked up.

"Tomorrow is Monday," he said. "Today is the last day of your Spring Break. Do you want us to take you back to Indiana?"

The other end of the room got very quiet.

"Is your back still in pain?" Larry asked when I didn't answer.

"No," I said cautiously.

The night before, I'd asked him why he hadn't offered to heal my back. He'd said that normally, he didn't like to interfere with the healing systems in place in the native cultures he visited.

"Please," I'd said, pulling up my shirt and presenting my whimpering back to him. "Interfere."

So he'd gone to work on me. I couldn't see what he was doing, of course, and it's hard to describe how it felt. It was as if he made the whole area glow with warmth, and I felt my muscles, one by one, soften and let go, as if they'd turned to wax. Then I felt—I swear—warm fingers probing inside my back until they found the epicenter of pain, and it dissolved. The fingers withdrew slowly, as if they were swimming away, and I'd felt drowsy and relaxed and warm all over.

Now, when he asked me about my back, I was surprised to discover that I felt no pain at all, not even if I turned or bent or stretched. I said more firmly, "No, it's okay."

He still looked at me expectantly.

"My classes are covered for a few days. . ." I trailed off. I knew that I should go home. I had obligations, after all. Larry and Elvis didn't need me, not really. And surely Ginger could find another grammar expert in the Washington Metro area. If I stayed, I would just be another spaceman groupie in a swelling entourage. It wasn't even as if our time together were action-packed. I had often felt at loose ends in the past several days. And yet.

"I guess I'd like to stay a little while longer, if it's okay," I said.

"Yesss!" Elvis shouted and waved a fist in the air. He smiled at me. "You are one fun dude, Hank. You rock!"

Whatever image I had of myself, being a "fun dude" had no place in it. And I had three ex-girlfriends who would testify that in this, at least, my self-concept was dead on.

"Aren't you happy that Hank is staying, Robbie?" Elvis asked.

"Sure am," Robbie said. "But about that fist pump, dude. It goes up and down, not side to side."

At the breakfast table, I scanned both *U.S.A. Today* and *The Washington Post* for any mention of the spaceman's miracle healing. Nothing. Plenty of stories about death, though—in Afghanistan, in

Sri Lanka, in the Congo, in Iraq, in Darfur. And those were just the deaths caused by human conflicts. Mother Nature had contributed two earthquakes and a tsunami.

"I don't think the doctors and nurses believed that I did anything, Hank," Larry said. "They thought the little girl woke up from a very deep coma."

"Huh," I said. "Is that what the mother thought?"

"No," he said, and smiled. "But I don't think she'll give me away."

The phone rang and Elvis, who was closest to it, answered it.

"It's for you, Hank," he said, and added in a stage whisper heard in Baltimore, "And it's a chick!"

I took the phone. It was Charlotte, the girl from the park. I experienced a momentary confusion. Had I given her my number? "Oh, hi," I said. "Yeah, sure, I remember you. Sorry I haven't called. I've been kind of, well, busy."

She laughed. "Tell me about it. How was Mount Vernon?"

"Mount Vernon?"

"Right. Big house on the river, George Washington's desk, Martha's herb garden. Is this ringing a bell?"

I sighed. "How did you know it was me? Everybody says I look really different in the wig and no glasses."

"I'm just good with faces. I thought it was you in the pet shop photo, and when I saw the Mount Vernon footage, I knew it was you. Want to know what gave you away?"

"What?"

"You always had a hand on your back," she said. "You know, if your back hurts that badly, you should see a massage therapist."

"I have. He moonlights for the F.B.I."

"I'm serious," she said. "A real massage therapist. Know how you can tell? Ask them where they trained. If they say Quantico, keep looking."

"Well, my back's better now," I said. "They must do something right at Quantico."

I was uncomfortably aware of the three sets of ears, one of them the size of salad plates, tuned in to this conversation.

"So, do you want that tour or not?"

"You're not mad at me?"

"Why should I be mad at you? Did you really expect me to believe all that bullshit about being a time-management consultant for package designers?"

"Well, I was hoping."

"No, you weren't. What kind of a loser does that for a living?"

I resolved never to explain my dissertation topic to her.

"Okay," I said. "I'm up for a tour."

"I mean, you did just move into the neighborhood, right? Even if you don't plan to stay."

"Well, sure. I guess I'm going to be here for the next few days, at least."

"Good. So what are you doing now?"

"Now? You mean right this minute?"

"Yeah."

"I just got up."

"Want to meet me in the lobby in, say, thirty minutes?"

"Okay."

"Can you come out and play by yourself or do you have to bring your mates?"

"Uh, they're okay. I can come by myself. I should probably wear my disguise, though."

Max the bodyguard objected to my solo plans, and was joined in his objections by Marshall the bodyguard when Marshall returned from a video store run. I ignored them and kept on moving out the door. To my annoyance, Max followed me.

In the lobby, I found Charlotte. She gave me a kiss on the cheek that felt impersonal, but still intimate for someone you'd met only once and on a park bench at that. Still, I suspected that Washingtonians had all kinds of habits that Hoosiers would find strange, and it was certainly an ass-kissing town, so maybe it was a cheek-kissing town as well. The kiss startled me in another way, too. While she didn't make lip contact precisely in the area where my beard used to be, my face felt unguarded, and the sensation on my skin felt unfamiliar.

She looked me over with a critical eye. "The hair looks a little—"

"Like Leonardo DiCaprio?" I said.

"More like surfer-gone-to seed. Are you going to wear your sunglasses the whole time?"

"We'll see how it goes," I said.

Charlotte wore jeans, a quilted jacket, and boots that made her almost as tall as I was. When she leaned in for the kiss, I smelled again that light fruity scent, like overripe apples, that I'd smelled on the park bench.

"I have a tail," I said, and nodded across the lobby to Max, who was unwrapping a piece of chewing gum. He stuck it in his mouth. "Or at least, one that I know of."

"On the elevator you picked up a tail?" she said. "Is he a gumshoe?"

I shook my head. "Part of our security."

"Want to ditch him?" Her eyes glittered with mischief.

I sidled up close to her, scanned the room, and directed my question in a low voice to a potted plant nearby. "You got a plan?"

"Follow me," she said in the same conspiratorial stage whisper. "Do what I do."

I stumbled over a suitcase as we headed for the door because I couldn't see through the damn sunglasses. Max picked me up, asking me if I were hurt as if we were strangers. He fell back as we left the Wardman, cut over to Connecticut, strolled up to the main entrance to the National Zoo and passed through the gates.

Once inside, she picked up the pace until we were speedwalking— past the giant pandas, past the elephants, past the great apes.

"Aren't we going to visit any animals?" I asked, gasping.

"Do you want to ditch your tail or not?" she said.

"I do have this injury—," I began, putting a hand to my back, though in truth, my back felt fine. It was my legs and my lungs that were on fire.

She plunged into the Reptile Discovery Center. I followed, blinded by the sunglasses and the sudden dark. She grabbed my wrist and dragged me on.

As my eyes adjusted, I caught a glimpse of a snake or two, but apparently we hadn't reached our destination. We exited the building, and doubled back to sit on a bench in front of the Gorilla Grove.

"Is this your idea of a neighborhood tour?" I panted.

"It's a huge, dark building," she said. "It will take him forever to realize he's lost us. Come on, Hank, breathe."

"I'm trying," I gasped.

"Feel better now?" she asked.

To preserve oxygen, I shook my head.

I waited for my panting to subside. "I feel kind of mean," I admitted.

She nodded. "You're not cut out for life on the lam, I can see that."

She set a leisurely pace back to the main entrance, which hadn't moved any closer in the interim, and we left the zoo and turned toward the heart of Adams Morgan. We walked around for an hour or so and she showed me her favorites—her favorite ice cream place, her favorite bookstore, her favorite street hustler, her favorite Mexican take-out place, her favorite shoe repair shop. The glasses continued to obscure my vision until I mistook a street vendor for a trash can.

"How much of this tour are you able to see?" she asked.

The other problem was my hair, which, because the wind was picking up, kept blowing in my face. She caught me grimacing.

"It keeps getting in my mouth," I said. "Ick!"

"Welcome to my world," she said. "Girls put up with that all the time."

We ended up at a small Italian bistro. I took off my jacket, revealing a tee shirt that Alex O. had contributed to the cause: Kiss Me! I'm Armenian.

"Oh!" she said, and gestured at my shirt. "Your prime minister just died. I'm sorry."

"He did?" I said, and looked down at the shirt, baffled. I didn't remember what I was wearing.

"Yeah," she said. "He was just fifty-five. Heart attack, they assume. He had heart surgery in the late nineties."

"Huh," I said. "I was online right before I came over here and I didn't see anything about it. I probably would've changed tee shirts."

"Were you a fan?" she asked.

"Don't even know the man's name," I said. "But the guy who loaned me this shirt—he's probably a fan."

We talked easily over lunch. It didn't seem like a date. She wasn't flirting with me, or at least, I didn't think she was; my sister says my instincts are not reliable. We talked about the spacemen, but I didn't feel that she was leading me in that direction. She did ask if I'd show her where the ship was parked, but I said that I was sworn to secrecy.

"Besides," I said. "It's invisible. Nothing to see." I didn't mention the pigeons.

She eyed me skeptically. "It's not parked on the mall, is it? That would be pretty trippy, if it was there all the time and nobody could see it. Say, how come Larry still looks exactly the same as he looked in those photos from the early fifties? And how come Elvis doesn't?"

As I'd anticipated, the press had unearthed two photos of Larry from the New Mexico days, including the team photo of the Lobos at the Little League field.

"With Larry, it has to do with relativity and the whole space-time business," I said, "but don't ask me what. With Elvis, all I know is that he redesigned himself. Don't ask me how."

She was a little vague about her writing, until I pressed her. Then she described two articles she'd sold. One was about new trends in scrapbooking, and it had sold to a craft magazine. The other was about a Maryland artist who made giant papier maché animals as yard decorations. That one had gone to the AAA magazine.

"So you specialize in what? Popular arts? Kitsch?"

She smiled. "You could say that."

"Then you'll be gratified to know that the interplanetary alliance that Larry and Elvis represent wants to import refrigerator magnets from Earth."

Her eyes widened. "No, seriously? You're making that up."

"I'm not," I said. "I wish I were. I hate to think that some time, somewhere, on the planet Zepko, a robot will be walking around covered in yellow smiley face refrigerator magnets that say 'Have a Nice Day.'"

"Gee, maybe they'll want bobbleheads, too," she said.

After lunch, she walked me back to the hotel, kissed me on the cheek, and told me to call her.

CHAPTER NINETEEN

I entered through a side door, so no one had a chance to warn me.

There was a commotion in the lobby. I went over to see what was going on. By now, I'd replaced my dark glasses with my regular glasses, and as I'd come through the door, I'd absentmindedly pulled off the wig.

A small crowd of people was kneeling in the middle of the lobby. At the center stood a thin, stoop-shouldered, middle-aged man with a receding hairline and a beard like an overused Brillo pad. He was holding a large open Bible in one hand, pointing at the page with the other, and reading from the Book of Revelations. A knot of hotel employees stood off to the side, looking on, and I spotted Alex O. on the other side of the kneeling congregation. I sidled up to one of the bellboys.

"Are you guys holding church services now, or is this some kind of protest?" I said.

He glanced at me, then his expression changed to one of alarm. "Don't let them see you!" he hissed.

Too late. The finger lifted from the Bible and pointed straight at me. "There's one of Satan's henchmen now!" the thin man bellowed. The crowd gasped, and the kneelers leaned away from me. A few of the women, horror-struck, raised crossed index fingers in my direction. It would have made more sense to me somehow if they hadn't been wearing pastel polyester pantsuits and enough make-up to re-coat the Sistine Chapel.

I felt my eyebrows rise. I looked around to see who was behind me, then pointed at my chest and mouthed, "Me?"

"Do not try to deceive us, you wily demon," the thin man shouted, "with your tricks and disguises."

He'd spotted the wig in my hand.

He strode toward me, just as I caught a glimpse of blue uniform on Alex's side of the circle. The cavalry had arrived.

The thin man stood in front of me. Several of the male kneelers had gotten up from the floor and closed in behind him. I felt the bellboy sliding away from me.

"We are not deceived," the thin man raged. "We cannot be deceived. We are God's people, the warriors of the Almighty."

"As long as you don't carry weapons," I said, "that's fine with me. You can be warriors of the Great Shazam for all I care."

This seemed to stir him up more, not calm him down. "Blasphemy! Anathema!" he roared. "You are aiding and abetting the Antichrist!"

Past the thin man's fellow warriors, I saw the blue uniforms making their way toward us.

"We have no need of weapons," the thin man said. "All we need is God's holy word." And with that, he slammed me upside the head with his mammoth Bible.

Somebody yelled "Ow!" It was probably me. My mind flew out of my mouth and my eyes watched the whole scene tilt until something hard struck me on the other side of the head and I went under. Later, I would conclude from the bruises that sprouted in various locations that God's warriors got in a few licks before the cops pulled them off me. I would also have this theory confirmed by a news photograph showing a mob of men attacking someone on the ground who was wearing my sneakers—someone near whose limp hand was something brown and hairy like a long-haired guinea pig that had given up the ghost.

I came to just in time to see that brick of a Bible sailing through the air, pages flapping, until it landed on my outstretched hand. "Ow," I said again, but dreamily. Someone in a dark suit and wearing an ear bud was wrestling with the thin man. How I registered, much less remembered, the ear bud is one of the mysteries of the human brain.

There was still a lot of shouting and scuffling going on and in the distance I could hear sirens. I wondered hazily if flashing lights were a symptom of concussion but then realized that I was surrounded by news photographers. I closed my eyes against the light but Alex's voice in my ear said firmly, "Open your eyes, Hank. Wake up."

Another familiar voice spoke in my other ear, the one that had caught the full force of the Bible belt. I couldn't understand it, but after a minute I identified it as Charlotte's.

By the time the medics arrived, I was alert enough to contemplate the gurney with distaste. I'd already given the press enough photographic fodder for one night. I didn't want my mother to open the paper and see me strapped in and surrounded by white uniforms, like a mental patient. With help, I stood up. The onlookers, the ones who had not been arrested and carted away, clapped, as if I'd been decked by an inside fast ball. Alex, Charlotte, and the medics kept trying to head me toward the exit—presumably toward an ambulance. But I refused to go.

"Look, I'm fine," I said. "A little wobbly is all."

"Hank, you could have a concussion," Charlotte said, now speaking loudly in my good ear, or rather, the ear that had made contact with the floor rather than the Bible.

"I'm fine," I said again. "Look, let them give me their tests. I'll prove it."

I won't say that I aced the tests, but I didn't fail them, either, so they finally made me sign a release and let me go. I refused to let Charlotte help me upstairs. "Alex will take me," I said. "Thanks just the same. Really."

I could see well enough, even through my cracked glasses, to know that she was disappointed.

On the elevator, Alex continued to lobby for a visit to the hospital, or at the very least, a house call from the hotel physician.

I finally agreed to the latter, but added, "I'm not going to sue you, okay, Alex?"

"I know lawyers who say that's the first sign of concussion—the reluctance to sue," he said.

"I'm sorry you got called out on your night off," I said. "Especially with your prime minister dead and all."

"Thanks, Hank," he said. "It comes with the territory."

He told me that nobody had called up to the room to let them know what was going on in the lobby.

Max opened the door and glared at me.

"Hi, Dad, I'm home," I said.

I got no sympathy from Max. "Whatever happened to you," he said, "you had it coming."

"Fair enough," I muttered as I limped past him.

They had all been watching a movie. A new bodyguard, Germaine, brought me some ice for my head, while Elvis plied me with questions. What had I been hit with? And why? Who were these people? And why did they think that Larry was Satan?

This last seemed to be the biggest puzzle to Elvis. For one thing, nobody where he came from believed in a figure of evil incarnate, as Larry explained. But even once Elvis had accepted that some Earth people believed in such a figure, he couldn't understand why they would confuse Larry with an evil being. "But Larry is a very good person," he said. "Larry has come all this way to warn the Earth people, to save them from destruction."

I couldn't explain it, except to say, "They don't know Larry. They know that he's powerful, and because he's warned them about destruction, they think he's the destroyer. They don't get it that Earth people are the ones who will destroy Earth."

"This guy—the Reverend Barnaby Pippin, as he calls himself— he's a well known crackpot in the D. C. area," Alex put in. Seeing Elvis's frown, he added, "A crackpot—you know, a lunatic, a crazy person."

"But why did he strike Hank with this book of holy scriptures?" Elvis asked.

"Because it was handy," I said, "and it weighed a ton. Even with apocrypha and a concordance, you wouldn't think a Bible could be so damned heavy."

"It's good that you remember that much," Alex said. "Maybe you don't have a concussion."

The doctor, a heavyset woman with a cheerful disposition, showed up and gave me some of the same tests the medics had, and some different. She asked questions about my medical history, my medications, and how long I'd been unconscious.

"Congratulations," she said at last. "You have a very hard head." She handed me some extra-strength Tylenol and gave me some instructions about icing both sides of my head.

"Do we have to keep him awake?" Germaine asked.

"No, but if he develops nausea or dizziness, take him to the hospital." She snapped her bag shut, and departed with Alex.

In the meantime, a businesslike young woman in hotel livery had retrieved my glasses, promising to have them repaired by morning.

Ten minutes later, the phone rang, and I got an earful from Ginger about security. She clearly didn't know about the evening's festivities, and I wasn't going to be the one to tell her.

"Come on, Ginger," I said. "I'm just—."

"You're just the guy whose face has appeared in almost every photo published," she snapped. "You're known, Hank. And if you don't like that, I'm sorry, but it can't be undone. Someone could get to them through you.

"You just don't think, Hank. But you don't have to think. That's what you pay me for. And I pay the best security firm in Washington to think about your security, twenty-four seven. Because that's when the loonies are active, Hank. Twenty-four seven."

"I was wearing my disguise," I said sulkily. Well, most of the time.

"I don't care. You compromised security, Hank, and not just yours, theirs."

"Okay."

"Who were you with, anyway?"

"This girl I know." If I hadn't just been dressed down for endangering Larry and Elvis and potentially undermining their mission, I probably would have told her that it wasn't any of her business. But I now had an uncomfortable sense that it was her business, and she was about to tell me why. Besides, my head was throbbing.

"A girl. When did you meet her?"

"A few days ago."

"When exactly?"

"Christ, Ginger, I wasn't looking at my watch! I'm not planning to record the event for posterity."

"What day?"

"Let's see. Um, I think it was Friday."

"Friday. After the press conference."

"Well, yeah."

"And you met her where?"

"In the park."

"In the park."

"You don't have to repeat everything I say, you know. I know what I said."

"Yes, but you don't hear yourself," she said. "You meet a girl in a park on the very day you appear on television screens all across

America, and you don't suspect anything. Jesus, Hank, this is D.C., not fucking Mister Rogers' Neighborhood. You have to suspect everybody."

"I'd just had my beard shaved off, and I was wearing a wig and dark glasses. Give me some credit, Ginger."

"Okay, fair enough. I'll give you some credit. Who spoke first?"

"I did."

"And why was that?"

I felt like I was in the witness box. "Well, she was reading, and I asked her what she was reading."

"And what was she reading?"

"Well, let's see. I think it was Douglas Adams."

"Never heard of him. So, what's her last name, this girl?"

"Actually, she's not a girl, she's a woman. I misspoke."

"Don't try to distract me with gender politics. What's her last name?"

"I don't know. I don't think she's mentioned it."

Silence. Then she said, "She gave you her phone number, didn't she?"

"Well, yeah, but she just wrote 'Charlotte.'"

"So what does Charlotte do?"

"She's a writer."

"A writer."

"Not like a reporter. She's free-lance. She writes about things like scrapbooking and papier maché art, stuff like that."

"Okay, give me the phone number. I'll get Howard on it."

I gave her the number.

"I'll see you tomorrow, bright and early," she said. "In the meantime, don't you dare set foot outside your suite without a minder."

"Yes, ma'am."

I sat down on my bed and contemplated my fate. Maybe I should go home after all. Maybe Ginger was right and I was jeopardizing the mission. Maybe I couldn't be trusted. Shortly afterward, I heard whispering outside the door, and then the pad of little dog paws, and Getlo appeared with her leash in her mouth.

"You're barking up the wrong tree, kid," I told her. "My leash is shorter than yours."

In the middle of the night I got up to pee and then wandered out into the sitting room to find Elvis engrossed in that night's Creature

Feature, *It Came from Outer Space*. I went and stood behind him.

"I like this one, Hank," he said. "The spacemen are the good guys."

It occurred to me that he would have absorbed the concept of good guys and bad guys from hanging out with ten-year-olds in the early fifties.

"Yeah," I said ruefully. "And the Earth people are still out to get them."

"Except for the heroes," he said, then added, "Like you, Hank. You're a hero."

I shook my head and patted his shoulder. "No, big guy, I'm just a hitchhiker from another galaxy."

"What Earth needs," he said soberly, "is more heroes."

I couldn't argue with that.

CHAPTER TWENTY

Just after the efficient hotel staff person returned my glasses the next morning, good as new, Ginger swept in, trailed by Howard, Anna, and Jillian. Jillian made eye contact with me and drew her finger across her throat, but I wasn't sure whether she was signaling me to keep quiet or commit hara-kiri.

Ginger threw a pile of paper in the middle of the breakfast table, causing a piece of bagel to go skittering off the edge, where Getlo caught it. On top of the pile was a glossy headshot of Charlotte, my Charlotte, looking very professional.

"That your girl?" Ginger asked.

"Yes," I said, although I had leaned away from the photo when it landed. I wasn't exactly cringing, but my whole body was on cringe alert.

"Charlotte," she said, "writes as 'C. R. Manning.' At one time she wrote about scrapbooking and papier maché art, but she's moved on from that. She is, as you said, free-lance, but her biggest customers are the *Washington Post*, the *Wall Street Journal*, and the newsweeklies. Word on the street is, the President is afraid of her. The President's cabinet is afraid of her. In fact, the whole fucking Congress is afraid of her." She threw her hands in the air. "God, send me one man who doesn't think with his dick."

"I don't think with my dick, Ginger," Elvis said, and gave her his lopsided grin.

It blew her anger away in one gust. She started to laugh. She folded one arm across her stomach, dropped her head on her free hand, and laughed. Everyone else's laughter was tentative, except for Elvis's.

"Thank God for that," she said. "If I didn't know better, I'd say it's a miracle. Now, somebody bring me a chair. I have to talk to this dickhead here about which of our secrets he spilled."

I'd spent much of the night lying on my bed and replaying my conversation with Charlotte with this very question in mind. I thought the only thing of any significance that I'd told her concerned the prospective trade in refrigerator magnets. I really had been pretty circumspect, and I told Ginger that.

"Okay, let's hope so. We'll know soon enough. In the meantime, I want it clearly understood that nobody leaves this room without a bodyguard, not even the dog." To my astonishment, she leaned down, took Getlo's head in both her hands, and shook it playfully. "Especially not the dog." The dog woofed.

Elvis raised his hand.

"No, Elvis, you don't count as a bodyguard, not for our purposes," she said. "I'm sure you're a terrific cop, but you don't know the neighborhood, and these guys do." She gestured in the direction of the couch, where Simon was reading the paper and Pete was reading a management textbook. "As a cop, you know how important that is. Besides, if someone comes after you, we want these guys to deal with it, not you. Let them shoot the guy and take the heat. We've been over this."

Elvis put his hand down.

"Now, Oprah's advance people should be here any minute, so we need to clean this place up a little. Larry, how does the spaceship look? She wants a tour."

"It's fine," Larry said.

"There are some empty Dr. Pepper bottles on top of the disaggregator, and maybe some Twinkies wrappers on the floor by the hovercraft port," Elvis volunteered.

"We'll need to send somebody over to pick up. Jillian? Larry, can Jillian get into the ship?"

"I can get her in, if she can find it," Larry said.

"I'll go with her," I said.

"Oprah will be here by noon, you'll have lunch with her in a room downstairs, come back up here for an interview, then on to the ship. They leave at three-thirty, which is when the NBC crew arrives with

Tim Russert." She looked at Larry. "They leave at five. Are you absolutely sure that you can make it to *Larry King Live* by eight-thirty, L.A. time? That's eleven-thirty our time."

Larry nodded.

"Drive-by food for dinner?" Elvis asked. "Or Chinese take-out?"

I was wondering when I was going to get my nap.

I overheard Elvis say to Jillian, "IMHO, that outfit is really flippy, Jillian." He pronounced "IMHO" as if it were a word.

"Excuse me?"

"That outfit is really flippy," he repeated, with less certainty.

"Gee, thanks, big guy," she said, and then added under her breath as she turned away, "I think."

Jillian and I left for the ship with our officially designated bodyguard, Simon, who had won the coin toss. Later, when Oprah visited the ship, Pete would get to see it as well.

It was raining, so I held the umbrella. Jillian had her hands in her jacket pockets, shoulders hunched against the damp cold.

"Sorry you got yelled at," she said, as if she were my kid sister. Then, strengthening the impression, she began to berate me. "But honestly, Hank, how could you be so naïve? She was reading Douglas Adams, for crissakes. You thought that was just a coincidence?"

"Lots of people read Douglas Adams," I said.

She glanced at me. "On the same fucking park bench as a guy who hangs out with extraterrestrials?"

"Well, I'm sure some people read Adams on park benches," I said.

"You do remember that in the book the woman who goes off with what's his face—."

"Zaphod Beeblebrox."

"Right, him. You do remember that the woman who leaves the other guy and goes off with him is a broadcast journalist?"

"You think Charlotte is trying to hitch a ride to deep space? You think she's planning to break my heart or something? We only went out one time, for crying out loud. It wasn't even a date."

"I'm just saying."

"What?"

"Elvis told me about your girlfriend. You're vulnerable."

"Yeah, well. Give me some credit."

We found the place where, even in the rain, pigeons were

roosting in mid-air. Jillian had to call Larry on the cell, and he opened up the ship. The ramp descended, and then, from the top, a Slinky—the old-fashioned, all-metal kind—began its rhythmic progress down the ramp.

"Doodoo, doodoo, doodoo, doodoo," Jillian chanted as she watched it. "Is it alive?"

"Nah, it probably just got dislodged the last time the ramp closed. This place is pretty neat for a bachelor pad, but it is a bachelor pad," I said.

We went in. Jillian pulled a trash bag out of her pocket and we picked up. Simon and Jillian tried all the seats, but when Jillian extended a hand to the instrument panel, I warned her off.

"There are all these touch sensors," I said. "If you touch the one that tells it to fly, we're in big trouble."

As we got ready to leave, I held the Slinky in my hands. "Should we re-set the Slinky for Oprah?"

We grinned at each other. I found something to prop it up with, but the others had plenty of advice about placement, positioning, angle of tilt, and so on.

As the ramp disappeared, I said, "I have to admit, I don't really get the Oprah gig. I like Oprah, though I can't say I've seen her show very much. But isn't it targeted at a female audience? And isn't it mostly feel-good stories about love and romance and happy families and miracles? What's the connection with saving the planet? You'd think Barbara Walters would be able to discuss foreign policy more knowledgeably."

"We're still negotiating with ABC," Jillian said. "The point about Oprah is that she's got millions of fans. People respect her. If she gives this mission her stamp of approval, that will count for something, at least with Americans. And she makes her guests look good. She doesn't ask embarrassing personal questions, the way Walters does. She'll humanize the boys, and make them seem like they're trying to help us and not just threaten us."

"They are trying to help us," I said. "It would probably be easier just to wipe out the planet than to keep sending emissaries to tell us to behave. Cheaper too, I'll bet, unless the clean-up is expensive."

A little later, I said, "But I still think Ginger is over the top on this security business. I mean, Elvis is indestructible, as far as I can figure out, and he's got Larry's back. So what's the problem?"

Jillian and Simon exchanged looks of exasperation.

"The problem is their gonzo sidekick, who's going to wander off by himself and get himself kidnapped by some terrorist group who wants to hold him hostage until our spacemen destroy the United States," Jillian said.

"They'd never do that," I said.

Simon smiled. "That's good, Hank. That's very good. Say it just like that to the terrorist assholes, and see where it gets you."

"I still don't see why anybody would want to kill them," I grumbled.

"Why does anybody want to kill John Lennon?" Jillian said.

"Why does anybody want to kill Gianni Versace?" Simon said.

And since I didn't have any answers, I shut up. Which was a good thing, because, as we'd later discover, we'd already received the first death threat. And Jillian, as it turned out, was a frigging Cassandra.

CHAPTER TWENTY ONE

The mail rode up in the elevator with us. That's all there was room for, the four sacks of mail, a luggage cart full of boxes and oversized envelopes, the bellboy who was delivering it, and us. The Oprah team was already setting up lights in the living room, so we stashed it in my room and closed the door.

Oprah herself was warm and gracious. She appreciated Elvis's sense of humor, so they got along famously. She'd also brought a bag of gourmet organic dog treats for Getlo, a gesture which won his heart. She gave both Larry and Elvis Chicago Cubs hats. Elvis gave her a diamond that Ginger had gotten mounted in a necklace. Her eyes opened wide when she saw it.

On camera, she had a serious talk with Larry about the message he wanted to deliver to the world. She never interrupted him. She asked questions about the world and the society he'd come from, so I learned a few things, and asked whether he missed his family. She asked him why he'd been chosen for this mission, or whether he'd volunteered. He said that he'd been asked because his superiors had a high regard for his engineering expertise and diplomatic skills, but that he could have refused.

"Larry is a very good person," Elvis put in. "He would never refuse to go where he's needed."

"So what about you, big E?" Oprah asked. "Did you volunteer?"

Elvis gave her his curtained smile. "I was too young to know any better, Oprah."

So eventually she got around to asking for a performance of "Hound Dog," and he gave it his best shot, after warning her that he was still working on it. But she loved it, and to my dismay gave him the kind of encouragement that would guarantee more practice sessions.

Then she asked me what it was like to hang with these guys. I saw the camera swing in my direction. I hadn't expected this. "Uh, never a dull moment," I said, which, if not quite true, had the ring of truth. And compared to my normal life, it was certainly true.

When the camera swung back, I glanced at my watch. In my normal life, I should at this moment be walking a roomful of freshmen through a rhetorical analysis of a reading assignment that some hadn't read, some had read at 3 a.m., and some had "read" with technopunk blasting their ears while they updated their *Facebook* status. I'd be telling Sean for the umpteenth time to put his cell phone in his pocket rather than hiding it in his sleeve so that he could text his soccer teammates, and Tiffany would just be arriving, twenty minutes into class, slipping into the back clutching a plastic container of French fries to sustain her through the remaining thirty minutes of class. Jamal would be asleep, head on his book, and Stacey, who would have actually read the assignment, would have her hand in the air to make some loopy observation that would challenge my own verbal agility and diplomatic skills.

At the ship, the Slinky was a big hit. The giant roller skate we'd failed to remove from the circular corridor was not, however, although the cameraman who tripped over it while walking backward did manage to prevent the camera from hitting the floor. Oprah admired everything, from the control panel to the little lavatory. She asked if they had a promotional deal with Cashmere Bouquet.

"No," Elvis said. "Should we?"

Everybody got hugs when she left, even Ginger and her crew, Simon and Pete, and me.

Back at the hotel, the NBC crew was already setting up lights in a hotel conference room, and Alex O. was standing by with Tim Russert, from whom I wasn't expecting a parting hug. They were discussing the death of the Armenian prime minister. I added my own condolences again, a little surprised at Alex's show of emotion. But then, there's nothing like hanging out with journalists to make a guy feel ill-informed; apparently, Prime Minister Margaryan was a nationalist hero. No wonder Charlotte had known about the death; she'd probably read it off an A.P. wire.

After the interview, we headed back to the ship, picking up Chinese take-out on the way. Jillian came along as our minder. When Elvis had heard that he'd be visiting the Ed Sullivan Theater where Elvis Presley had made one of his historic television appearances, he'd insisted on dressing to honor the King. Somewhere, somehow, Jeremy had scored for him a yoked shirt with full sleeves and a pair of black pants, and of course he was wearing his blue suede shoes. Larry had lobbied for a more conventional, conservative outfit, but Elvis had been adamant, and Larry had backed down. But Larry got his way on one matter: the guitar stayed home.

The show went okay, I guess, though from Larry's perspective, it could have gone better. When I say "okay," I mean that the guys didn't make any faux pas, and not a single audience member had to be sent into Time Out in the sixth dimension. Paul Shaffer had the band play the *E.T.* theme when the aliens were announced, and though I couldn't see it from where I was sitting in the audience, the camera captured the tears of emotion in Elvis's eyes when he stood on the stage where Elvis had once sung "Love Me Tender" and "Hound Dog." Letterman asked a few intelligent questions about their mission, but too quickly the interview veered into comedy, with Letterman volunteering Ten Signs That You're Talking to an Alien. He had some fun with robot humor, which Elvis didn't seem to understand, and then chatted with Elvis about dogs.

To his credit, Elvis tried to return the conversation to the more serious topic of their mission. "David, you should not be talking to me about dogs," he said, frowning. "You should be talking to Larry about the potential annihilation of your planet."

"You're right," Letterman said. "But if we talked too much about that, our viewers would change the channel." After a pause for laughter, he continued, "But seriously, Big Guy, are all the droids where you come from like you?"

"Tall?" Elvis asked, puzzled.

"Reserved," Letterman said, evoking another laugh. "You play your cards pretty close to your chest."

Elvis looked down, confused. When the audience laughed again, he gave an uncertain smile. "Oh, you are pushing my leg."

"Jesus," I said to Jillian as the audience dissolved around us.

Jillian was shaking her head.

Larry was too polite to re-direct the conversation himself, but I could tell by his body language that he was growing impatient. He sat stiff and silent during a commercial break as Letterman talked to Elvis, leaning over to lay a hand on his shoulder.

When the show resumed and Letterman asked Elvis to sing a song, Elvis glanced at Larry. "I did not bring my guitar," he said. "And anyway, I am just learning to play. I am not ready for crimetime."

But Paul Shaffer handed him a guitar and the audience clapped encouragement, so he succumbed to temptation. His rendition of "Hound Dog" would be the hottest new video on YouTube the next morning.

We all felt low-spirited on the quick flight back to D.C.

"I am sorry, Larry," Elvis said. "He should have talked to you more about our mission."

Larry sighed. "It isn't your fault," he said. "We must contend with the immature mind of the average television viewer. Overstreet was right."

"The mature insights were lost on the immature mind," Elvis agreed. "That is what Mr. Overstreet would say."

Jillian patted Elvis's hand. "But it must have been thrilling to stand and sing where Elvis did."

"Yes," Elvis told her. In a voice choked with emotion, he said, "It was out of sight. I will remember that moment for the rest of my life. I am all shook up."

As we set down in Rock Creek, I said, "Well, let's look on the bright side. Nobody took our parking place."

CHAPTER TWENTY TWO

I was awakened by the dog, who was worrying a mail bag with her teeth, barking in frustration, determined to get at something inside. I sat up in bed and looked around. "What is all this crap?" I said aloud.

Elvis appeared in the doorway. "Oh, here she is," he said.

"Have you been ordering online again?" I asked, eyeing the piles of mailbags, boxes and padded envelopes.

"Oh! Do you think my iPod is here already?" He looked around.

"I don't know, but I think the dog treats are," I said.

"I didn't order any dog treats," he said, trying to detach Getlo from the bag so that he could look inside.

"Maybe someone sent her a present," I said.

In fact, most of the boxes contained presents, from homemade cookies to a digital camera sent by Canon, its Canon logo big enough to be picked up by news photographers at twenty paces, and a pair of Air Jordans. There were tee shirts, most of them in size XXL, advertising everything from bagels to towing services to exterminators. There were also: a harmonica; four caps from four local sports teams from Vermont to Georgia (I assumed that the ones from farther afield would take another day or two to get here); two squeak toys for dogs, five rawhide chews, and three boxes of dog biscuits; ten books from authors hoping the spacemen would be seen holding a copy; an odd-looking instrument for interplanetary communication, or so its inventor claimed; a packet of coupons for free pizza from a nearby pizza parlor; a Tupperware container of dried rose petals for Elvis to sprinkle over Elvis Presley's grave; a radio-controlled, battery-operated miniature flying saucer; a jar of maple syrup; a jar of peach preserves; five dozen chocolate chip cookies from different sources; two dozen brownies; and a mood ring (extra large). Elvis memorabilia formed a whole category of its own: Elvis ash trays; Elvis auto-mugs; a Friend for Life Elvis bear, whose connection to Elvis seemed to me tenuous, at best; an Elvis soap dispenser; a life-size stand-up cut-out of Elvis dressed as a gunfighter and firing a pistol; an Elvis dog costume (white half-jumpsuit with gold sparkles, cuffs, and collar, and a matching cape—I kid you not); and three bumper stickers, again from different sources: one said "Honk If You Believe Elvis Is Still Alive," one said "Honk If You Love Elvis," and one said "Honk If You ARE Elvis." And of course, there was music—not only the styles and genres Elvis had expressed enthusiasm for on his blog, but, as I'd predicted, easy listening and New Age music intended to win him over. There were also two amateur CDs from punk garage bands hoping for his endorsement.

Larry, who'd been shot the last time he'd landed on Earth, was clearly bemused by this outpouring of generosity.

"Hank," Elvis said, "why is everybody sending us presents?"

"Well, I think we can assume that a third of them really like you and were moved to make a kind gesture. A third of them clearly want you to promote something—their business, their band, their book, their invention. A third of them probably want some kind of fame by proxy. They like to think you've touched something they've touched, and they're gratified to imagine that their soap dispenser may be headed for another galaxy soon. I could have the proportions wrong, but that's my theory."

"But we don't need a soap dispenser," he said. "Can't we give it away to someone who needs one?"

"Sure," I said. "But we might have trouble identifying someone who needs an Elvis dog costume."

"You are right," he said through a mouthful of cookie. "I do not think dogs like to wear costumes."

"Hey!" I grabbed the wrist that was on the way to his mouth. "Don't eat this stuff. We have to make sure it's safe."

"Safe?" he echoed.

"It's probably fine, but we don't know that. It could be poisoned.

Look, I know it sounds crazy," I said, "but you guys tend to be polarizing figures. Some people love you, some people hate you." He started to speak but I cut him off. "I know that they don't know you. They're not responding to who you really are. It's not personal. You represent something to them."

"Hank, are you talking about the way pictures on the cereal boxes and T.V. dinners represent something?" he asked, not critical, just asking for information.

"Well, sort of, yeah," I said. "See, Americans have a really warped relationship to celebrity. In this country, people can become famous just for being famous."

"But how do they get famous to begin with?" He noticed the dog licking crumbs off the carpet at his feet, and picked her up, squirming. He tickled her belly and said, "Getlo, we have to listen to Hank now."

"It doesn't matter. The point is, you're famous. Some people will love you because you're famous. Some people will hate you because you're famous. Some people who want to become famous might conclude that the way to become famous is to hurt you, or even kill you. Then they would get their picture in the papers, and everybody would know their names."

He was frowning in concentration. "Because they have immature minds."

I sighed. "I suppose so."

He nodded, then raised his lip in Elvis Presley's trademark grin. "Then it is a good thing that they can't kill me." He set Getlo down and popped the rest of the cookie in his mouth. "I will taste all the cookies to make sure they're not poisoned. This one is fine."

But the mood at the breakfast table was somber.

"It's not working," Larry said. "We are going to fail again."

"Listen to this, Hank," Elvis said. He had a book propped against a pitcher of orange juice. "'A mature truth told to immature minds ceases, in those minds, to be that same mature truth. Immature minds take from it only what immature minds can assimilate. In the end, even though they may give it lip-service—.'"Here he curled his own lip and looked up from the book. "I know what that means. It means you talk about something, but don't do anything." His eyes went back to the page in front of him. "'Even though they may give it lip-service and may raise institutions in its name, they turn the mature truth into an applied immaturity.' That is what Mr.

Overstreet says."

"He sounds like a smart guy," I conceded.

"Perhaps your people will only respond to threats," Larry said.

"I have been re-reading our other book," Elvis said, extracting a second book from behind *The Mature Mind*. "I had forgotten about it, but I found it last night when I searched for Mr. Overstreet's book."

"Your other book?" I asked.

He turned it around to show me the cover: *How I Raised Myself from Failure to Success in Selling* by Frank Bettger.

"I think you have read this book, Hank," Elvis said.

"No, I never heard of it."

His eyebrows levitated. "Never? But Hank, it is all about selling, like your advertisements. It is a very popular book. It is endorsed by Mr. Dale Carnegie and Dr. Norman Vincent Peale. I believe they are very famous people."

He handed it to me and I turned to the copyright page: 1947.

"Mr. Bettger was a baseball player who became injured and started selling life insurance," Elvis told me as I flipped through the book. "I am not sure that I understand what life insurance is, but I know that we are not selling it."

I looked up. "In a way, that's exactly what you're selling, big guy."

He smiled, pleased. "Okay. I was going to say that we are selling dislegging."

"Disarming," I corrected, then corrected myself. "Disarmament."

"Yes, that," he said. "And I know that Ginger is very smart and skillful about designing a media campaign and crafting our image and insuring maximum exposure." He picked his way carefully across these last phrases, which he'd learned from hanging out with Ginger and her crew. "But I think Mr. Bettger gives lots of good advice about selling."

"Such as?" I handed the book back to him.

He opened it and put his finger on a page. "Here it says that the one idea that transformed Mr. Bettger's career was to act enthusiastic."

"Act enthusiastic?"

"Yes." He used his finger as a bookmark and looked up at me. "How do we do that?"

Warren the bodyguard had joined us at the table with a whole-wheat bagel sandwich of peanut butter and bean sprouts. From somewhere in the suite, we could hear the other bodyguard on duty, Cisco, speaking to someone on his cell phone in loud Spanish. Warren and I exchanged a look. His said, "This one's all yours, bro."

"You already act enthusiastic," I said.

"I don't think so," Elvis said. "If I did, we would be succeeding more. I think that maybe I act enthusiastic about Elvis Presley, and rock and roll music, but those are not the things we're trying to sell. And Larry never acts enthusiastic." He didn't say this accusingly; he was just making an observation. His eyes were on the toast he was smearing with jelly.

Larry didn't seem to take offense. He seemed to be listening with interest.

Elvis looked up. "We are on a very serious mission. We would like to save your planet from being destroyed. That is what we need to act enthusiastic about." He bit a corner off of the toast triangle, and chewed. After he had swallowed, he said, "It will not be easy for Larry, I think. He has a serious nature and he is sad because he has been away from his family so long. But perhaps we could take a course in public speaking, like the one Mr. Bettger took from Mr. Carnegie."

Larry's eyes dropped and I could see him mentally adding six weeks to a mission that was already seriously behind schedule.

"Here is another thing Mr. Bettger says," Elvis continued, wiping his fingers on a napkin and picking up the book again. "We must tell our story earnestly, and we must find out what people want, and help them to get it. I think that is where the refrigerator magnets come in, don't you? Ginger was very smart about that, but perhaps she has read Mr. Bettger's book. But I don't think that the refrigerator magnets are the whole grimtigrog."

Warren paused with his bagel sandwich poised for a bite. "The what?"

Larry smiled. "A grimtigrog is a very large animal that has evolved on the planet Kirsk. It is capable of breaking into pieces, even very small pieces, and then reassembling itself, sometimes in a different shape."

"No shit," Warren said. "A grimtigrog."

Elvis looked at Warren and me. "Don't you think that if we are trying to sell disarmingment, the something that people want needs to be connected to that in some way?"

"Makes sense to me," I said.

"So what do Earth people want?"

I sighed. "Bigger, more powerful weapons systems."

Warren said, "Let us think about it, and get back to you, Big E."

Elvis turned a few more pages. "Ginger and Jillian are doing a good job of keeping us organized, so we don't need to worry about that, I think. And they make appointments for us, and prepare us, and even give us notes. I am looking at the basic principles to use in making the sale." He looked up. "But Mr. Bettger says we must ask questions. I don't think we have asked enough questions. Larry, you must ask more questions, and not just tell people what they must do all the time."

"What kinds of questions?" Larry said.

"You must ask them why they are not buying what you are selling." Larry made a gesture of impatience, and Elvis continued. "You see? You always become impatient. You should not get so bent. You must remember that you are dealing with immature minds." To Warren and me, he said, "Larry has always been good with children. He is very patient with children. He must learn to be the same way with adults on Earth." To Larry, he said, "You should read this book, Larry. Mr. Bettger was a very successful salesman, and he sold to Earth people. They are your bull's-eye market."

Larry reached out a hand and Elvis passed him the open book. Larry ran his eyes down the page, then smiled.

"You haven't mentioned principles six and seven yet," he said. "Principle six is 'explode dynamite—do something startling, surprising.' Principle seven is 'arouse fear.'" He looked up. "At last—something at which I believe that I could succeed."

CHAPTER TWENTY THREE

"I guess you've been busy lately," she said. I caught the familiar citrus scent a split-second too late to be forewarned.

"Well, if it isn't C. R. Manning, ace reporter," I said. "I guess you've been busy yourself."

She grinned, but when she tried to fall into step beside me, Warren blocked her, and the suddenness of his move caused Getlo to yip in surprise. Yeah, that was me: practically a Ph.D. and now the designated dog-walker—with a bodyguard, no less.

"Sorry, ma'am," Warren said. "Security."

She stepped back and put her hands on her hips. "Hank, will you please tell your bodyguard that I'm a friend?"

"No comment," I said, and kept walking.

"Oh, come on, Hank," she said, irritation in her voice. "What's that supposed to mean?"

I kept walking. By now, Getlo had spotted the other dogs and was dragging me forward, so my gait wasn't projecting the image of cool indifference I'd been going for, especially since I was wearing the sunglasses again and couldn't see very well.

"It's Washington, for crissake!" she called after me. "You're not supposed to trust anybody!"

Good to know, I thought. Sooner would have been better.

I knew I was being an asshole. If I were honest with myself, I had nobody to blame but myself for getting into so much hot water with Ginger. But self-directed honesty is way overrated, in my opinion, and C. R. Manning made such a convenient scapegoat.

Warren and I entered the dog park enclosure and bent together to unclip Getlo's leash. This was part of our act as a gay couple on an outing with our dog. As I fumbled with the clip, Warren brushed my hand aside, and said in a low voice, "Don't get any ideas."

"Thanks for the protection," I said.

"Part of my job," he said, and straightened. "In fact, given that she's a major security risk, I was specifically warned to keep her away from you."

I felt my face grow pink.

I had never been to a dog park, but it struck me now as I looked around that there were probably few places on Earth where one could witness such uncomplicated, unbridled joy. Dogs were running, jumping, waddling, rolling, sniffing, pawing, panting, and lolling, chasing Frisbees, balls, people and other dogs. To the other humans in the park, Getlo was in disguise—a small perpetually moving monument to Jeremy's inventiveness—but to the other dogs, she was simply herself. One sniff at her butt and they knew all they needed to know about her. As I sat on a picnic bench watching Warren throw a koosh ball for her to chase, I thought what a terrible shame it would be if the dogs ended up getting sacrificed to human stupidity. I thought that on the whole the universe would be no worse off if it lost six billion human beings, but dogs? That would be a tragedy.

Warren lobbed the ball. Getlo's eyes followed it, and her feet followed her eyes. She didn't see the big retriever until she slammed into him. She lay sprawled on the ground. I launched myself off the park bench.

But the first person to bend over her and pick her up wasn't Warren. It was Dave the masseur.

"I'm really sorry," he said, "but I think she's fine."

Getlo wagged her tail in affirmation. The big dog had turned to regard her.

I stared at Dave in confusion. What was a G-man doing in the dog park? Had his failure at electronic surveillance demoted him to dog-tailing? He was crouched down, petting both Getlo and the Golden. He was in shirtsleeves, his tie pulled loose. Then I noticed the plastic grocery bag tucked into his belt—universal badge of dog ownership. Of course, the dog could have been an agent, too, but he didn't look like one. A retired agent, maybe.

"Clyde," he was saying now, "say you're sorry."

"No harm, no foul, man," Warren was saying. "Wasn't Clyde's fault."

"His hearing isn't so good," Dave said, fondling the big dog's ears. "In his younger days, he would have heard her coming." Clyde lowered his head slowly to touch noses with Getlo. He had the tentative movements and bony protrusions of an old, arthritic dog.

"What are you doing here, Dave?" I said. "You bring your dog on a stakeout?"

He looked sheepish. "I don't like to leave him at home by himself. He's always liked riding in the car, and we've always spent a lot of time together. So, I—." He made a vague gesture. "When the weather warms up, I won't be able to, of course. But he's got his dog bed and his water dish, and he's perfectly happy until I get back to walk him." He looked around. "He loves the dog park. I think he comes here to remember his youth."

I introduced him to Warren as my massage therapist. Warren said "oh," and studied him keenly. Dave and I sat down on a bench.

"How's your back?" Dave asked.

"Great. I finally asked Larry to work on it."

"Yeah? What'd he do?" Dave seemed genuinely interested.

"Don't know," I said. "I couldn't see. I don't think he even touched me—not really. It was like he penetrated my body with these fingers of energy or something."

"Huh," Dave said. "No shit."

We watched Warren playing with both dogs. He'd throw the ball for Getlo to chase, and she'd return it to the Golden. Then he'd pick it up as gently as a pheasant and take it to Warren.

"She looks great," Dave said. "I mean, she looks awful, but that's great. Nobody would know it's the same dog. Did Jeremy do that?"

"Yeah, with a bucket of fill dirt from the construction site up the street."

We sat in companionable silence. Then he said, "I've been thinking about what we talked about."

"Yeah?" I said. I wasn't sure what he meant. In my peripheral vision I could tell that he was still watching the dogs.

"I looked into those fantasy baseball camps—you know, the ones where ordinary adults get to live out their dreams and play with hall-of-famers? I'm thinking of going to one next winter," he said. Then he added, "If we're all still here, of course."

I looked at him. "Wow, that's great, Dave!"

He shrugged. "It's a long time away. A lot could happen."

"Well, sure," I said. "That's always true."

"That's what I've been thinking," he said. "I mean, I could wake up dead tomorrow, and then I'd be kicking myself that I never played while I had the chance."

I watched a pack of assorted dogs circling a youngish kid in a parka. He appeared to be mentally handicapped, and he was spinning around and shrieking so that at first I was worried about him. But just when I was about to go rescue him, he collapsed in the middle of the pack and came up giggling, throwing his arm around the nearest dog as the others crowded in to lick his face. I smiled.

"Can I ask you something?" Dave said.

"Sure."

"If I'm out of line, just tell me, and I'll back off."

I turned to him.

"If they do destroy Earth," he said, "do you know anything about the time frame? I mean, are they the guys who'll push the button? There's something about physics, I know—about time being different in outer space and all. I know that time passes a lot slower in space than it does here on Earth, but I don't know how much slower. So—I was just wondering."

I laughed and clapped him on the back. "Just send in the fucking deposit, Dave. Just do it."

CHAPTER TWENTY FOUR

Jillian met us at the door when we got back. Getlo threw herself at Jillian as if we'd been gone for days.

"Did we miss *Oprah*?" I asked, bending to unclip the leash.

She shushed me, looking worriedly over my shoulder into the hallway. "The less said about that, the better."

"Too much spaceship tour, too little message?"

She nodded as Warren came in and closed the door behind him. "Where's Larry?" she asked.

"I don't know," I said. "Isn't he here?"

I glanced at her, then registered the alarm rising in her eyes.

"No," she said. "We thought he was with you."

"You think Ginger would have let him out of here without a full contingent of bodyguards?"

"No, but he isn't here, so I assumed—." Her voice trailed off and she swallowed. "Hank, there have been death threats. Where is he?"

I noticed now that there were more people in the living room than there had been when I left. Several of them were wearing black Spartan Security tees, but some looked like Dave clones, in shirtsleeves and ties and showing wires behind their ears.

There was a knock on the door, and I turned around to open it. Dave stood there, with Clyde, the golden retriever.

"I didn't want to take the time to—," he said apologetically, nodding at the dog. "They told me to come right away."

"Getlo will be thrilled," I said. "Come on in." I turned to Jillian.

"Now tell me what's going on."

Ginger appeared, a cell phone to one ear. "Where's Larry?" she said, looking around in surprise as if he'd maybe decided to hide in the coat closet.

"Not with us," I said.

"I'll call you back," she said into the phone, and snapped it shut. "He's not with you," she said. "That means he's missing. Somebody has taken out a ten-thousand-dollar hit on him, and now he's missing. Bloody hell." She re-opened her cell phone, and pushed a button. "Come on, pick up, pick up," she said under her breath. She heaved a sigh. "Voicemail." Then she said, "Larry, it's Ginger. You need to call me immediately—I mean immediately—when you get this message."

"Ten thousand dollars?" I echoed, trailing them.

"On the Internet," Jillian said. "It could be a hoax, but we've been going through the mail, and we've found ten death threats so far." She gestured at two agents and two Spartan Security people seated around the table. Each had a mailbag on the floor next to them, and was opening mail with gloved hands. "Elvis has received six threats in his e-mail."

Elvis entered from the bedroom. "But Jillian, I have also received many very friendly e-mails." To me, he said, "I have received three proposals of marriage." He squatted down to greet Getlo. "Getlo, you have made a friend too."

Ginger said, "Elvis, Larry's missing. We thought he went with Hank and Warren to walk the dog, but apparently, he didn't." She looked at her watch. "That means he's been missing for an hour and a half, at least. We have to find him. Do you know where he is?"

The big guy straightened, his expression sober. "No, Ginger, I don't know. Maybe he went to the ship."

Ginger looked relieved. "Yes, yes, that's likely. That's probably where he is. Hank, could you take Warren and Jillian and check? You know where it is, right? Good. On second thought, better take Max, too."

One of the suits, a white-haired man, said, "We'll send an agent with them. McGreevy!" A tall, broad-shouldered redhead came forward. "Go with them."

I wasn't keen on leading the F.B.I. to the spaceship, but under the circumstances, I couldn't think of a good argument not to. Larry had been shot the last time he set foot on the planet, so I knew he was vulnerable. And in those days, he'd had only a small group of paranoid dads to contend with. Now, there was a psycho on every street corner—in the District, probably two. And I didn't think they'd be deterred by the District's handgun ban.

I didn't bother with the wig and sunglasses. Being able to see was a top priority, and I didn't care about being seen. Max drove to save time. We parked on Beach and I led them through the woods. In the car I'd asked about the credibility of the death threats. McGreevy had shrugged.

"Hard to say," he'd said. "Most of them probably aren't very credible. The Internet one's probably a fake. But we have to check them all out. Thing is, successful assassins don't usually advertise their intentions first. What we do take seriously is the level of anger the threats represent."

Under different circumstances, I could tell that the pigeons would have been a major source of entertainment. As it was, Warren just said, "Son of a bitch. Would you look at that?" I called Elvis, and the ramp appeared out of thin air.

The ship was just as we'd left it—empty. I called Elvis again for instructions. I needed to check all of the closets and storage spaces, just to make sure. I got clipped by a frip-frip racquet when I opened that door, but I didn't even try to cram all the sports equipment back inside.

Outside the ship again, the ramp disappearing behind us, I called Ginger again. "Have you looked for a note?" I asked.

"No note," she said. "We've looked everywhere."

I put a hand to the temple that had started to throb, only partly from contact with the racquet. "Okay, okay," I said. "I think somebody should go down and check out the Lincoln Memorial. I think we should scour the neighborhood."

"Okay, Hank, but be as discreet as possible," she said.

"We will," I said. The last thing we wanted was an APB on a missing spaceman.

"Anyplace else you can think of?" Ginger asked.

She sighed. "Nothing we haven't already tried."

I paused. "Are we convinced that Elvis doesn't know where he is?"

"No, I'm not," she said. "But I'm convinced that if he does know, he's not going to tell us."

Max drove the car back while the rest of us walked. We came up behind the zoo and checked the shops and restaurants along Calvert, Connecticut, and Woodley. I stuck my head in Murphy's.

"Of course, with the subway stop right here," I said, "he could be anywhere by now."

We divided up Adams Morgan, but an hour's search turned up nothing more suspicious than a few more suits with short haircuts scouring the same area. We went home in defeat.

Elvis was working on his blog. Howard was nowhere in sight, so maybe he had joined a search party.

"You don't seem too concerned about Larry," I said. "The last time you let him out of your sight on this planet, he got himself shot."

"Yes, and I am worried about that," Elvis admitted, his eyes on the screen. "But Larry will do what he wants to do." Then he turned to me, "You know, Hank, we have been living in the spaceship together for a very long time. And this is a very beautiful planet. He has been living inside this hotel room ever since we arrived. I cannot blame him for wanting to go outside for a while. I would like to take Getlo to the dog park." He said this last wistfully. He turned back to the screen with a sigh. "And anyway, back on Larry's planet, this is a special time for him. On your planet, you would call it an anniversary, I think."

"It is?"

"Yes. One of his children died at this time—that is, when we adjust for distance and motion. So he is always sad when it comes because he remembers this child."

"Larry lost a child?" I said. I felt my image of him shifting, rearranging itself in my head. "He couldn't—well, revive the child?"

"As he explained to you, Hank, everything depends on the Almighty Spirit. It was this child's time to return, so no, he couldn't revive the child."

"Jesus," I said. I sank down on the bed. "I'm sorry. I don't know how parents survive a thing like that."

"You must not say anything to Larry," he said, typing. "He might not want me to tell you. He is a very private person."

"How long ago did this happen?" I asked.

"That is hard to say," Elvis said. "Some people might think it was a very long time ago. But maybe if you had lost a child yourself, you would think it happened only yesterday. There are many different ways of experiencing time."

I sat with my elbows on my knees, my chin in my palms, contemplating life. Somewhere in the vast, unimaginable reaches of space, there were planets with names I couldn't pronounce inhabited by life forms I couldn't envision. And yet, among these beings there were parents and children who felt some of the same emotions we felt and experienced some of the same crises of pain and loss that we did.

In the background, I was barely aware of the staccato clicks of Elvis's furious typing. I'd never asked how he learned to type, even though it was clear he'd mastered it much more quickly than he'd mastered the guitar.

"Now will you read my blog?" he asked.

I got up from the bed and went to stand behind him, leaning over to read the screen.

Today I want to write about our mission, he'd written. *I am very, very enthusiastic about our mission, because I want us to succeed and prevent Earth from being destroyed. I will tell you a very interesting story. When we heard that Earth was trying to send atomic weapons into space—this was back on Larry's home planet, where I had lived only for a few gluks—Larry and I said, "Oh, we would love to go and save the Earth!" We had heard that Earth was a very beautiful planet with many interesting life forms, and so we thought that it would be a shame for Earth to disappear.*

We traveled for a very long time to get here, but we couldn't wait to arrive and deliver our message! The Earth people did not seem to want to save their planet, however, and they attacked us. We went away, but when our leaders asked if we wanted to try again, we said Yes! We did not think that Earth adults were very friendly, but their planet was beautiful, and we were very enthusiastic about saving it from annihilation.

When we came back, we found that Earth people had become very friendly while we were gone. They have sent many, many presents to Larry and me and my little dog Getlo. But they still do not seem very interested in universal peace.

So I am asking all of you out there who are reading this blog to write and tell me what Earth people want, and why you are not interested in peace.

Adios for now,

Elvis

p.s. Larry says that soon we will have to do something that will surprise you. But I wanted to try this first. So please put on your thinking cats, and tell me how we can make disarmingment more appealing to you.

I patted his shoulder.

"Is it all right?" he asked.

"Well, *I* like it," I said. "But you should probably ask Howard and Anna and Ginger. Diplomacy is their department. And Larry, of course, when he comes back."

I drifted to the window and gazed out. Where the hell could he be? The answer, of course, was "anywhere." From the distance my gaze dropped, and I had a thought. Maybe some places were more likely than others.

Now if I could only run the gamut of G-men and security guards, not to mention two dogs, and slip out unnoticed. With a wig under my jacket.

CHAPTER TWENTY FIVE

I stopped at a CVS and bought clip-on sun filters for my glasses. I had to be able to see, since I didn't have my bodyguard and my seeing-eye Shih Tzu.

It was the kind of day that not only brought dogs to the dog park, but mothers and kids to the National Zoo. I stopped only briefly to contemplate the map. I couldn't guess which animal would most attract Larry's attention, but I suspected that it was the ones outside of the cages and enclosures that would interest him most. So I picked a path at random.

I started out at a pretty steady clip, aware that the afternoon was getting on, and the zoo would close at five. But my attention kept snagging on the animals. I slowed my steps at the Giant Pandas, and finally came to a complete standstill in front of the flamingo enclosure. I'd seen my share of plastic flamingos, of course—who hasn't?—but these were the real deal—pink-tinted balls of fluff with long, extravagant ess-curved necks, pinhole eyes, spats on their beaks, and toothpick-stilted legs, only one of which seemed to be in general use, the other folded neatly under their bodies. I stood rooted to the spot.

"Jesus!" I said under my breath. "Would you look at that?"

When I finally willed my feet to move again, I circled the bird house and walked up the path past the giant pandas and the elephants. I was consulting my map, wondering whether I could devise a better, more systematic search plan, when a security guard passed me at a run. Turning, I saw another guard ahead, also running, a walkie-talkie to his ear. I took off after them, adrenaline flooding my body.

Then I heard a woman screaming. She was shrieking, hysterical. It was an ear-shattering cry of pure panic. The guards pushed past people, although by now the foot traffic was flowing in the same direction. I stayed on their heels though my lungs were burning. Finally, the guards plunged into a crowd, and I followed.

The drama was playing out inside the lion exhibit. What I saw was a small child—just a flash of blond hair and red jacket—flailing in the water of the moat. Two lions, male and female, stood in the lower yard close to the edge of the moat, watching with curiosity. The other figure in the water looked familiar. He reached the child as the blond head went under and lifted it in his arms. I saw in my peripheral vision a zookeeper with a gun of some kind, and as I turned my head to see, heard Larry speak a sharp, commanding "No!" The zookeeper hesitated. He didn't set the gun down, but he didn't fire, either.

Larry set the sobbing child on the edge of the pool, then hoisted himself up in one graceful movement until he sat next to the child, which clung to him now. The lioness stepped forward, stretching her neck and opening her mouth slightly the way Eco does whenever he's detected a particularly fascinating odor. The crowd emitted a collective gasp, and the hysterical woman began keening, "No, oh, no, oh, no." Larry regarded the lioness placidly, and seemed willing to wait until she'd made up her mind. Then, shielding the child with his body, he raised his arm slowly and let her sniff his hand. The zookeeper made a protest I couldn't hear, and clenched the gun, sighting down its barrel. Then the lioness gently butted Larry's hand, and he laid it on her forehead. She turned, shot the zookeeper a look, and walked to her mate, who also turned away and preceded her across the yard. They leapt gracefully up to the next level and retreated into the semi-privacy of their concrete cave.

Some of the onlookers broke into applause as Larry picked up the child and approached the zookeeper. Some of them, I realized as I looked around, were too busy snapping photographs or holding their cell phones up to capture the moment on video. I sighed. The story wouldn't make the six o'clock news, but I'd surely see it replayed at eleven. I wondered whether Ginger would be pleased or angry. She would certainly be pissed off about his disappearing act, and he was certain to get a tongue-lashing about that. But I didn't think it would bother him. Unlike Elvis, he seemed impervious to criticism. I wondered who had designed Elvis to be so emotionally vulnerable. Not Larry, surely.

Larry was limping, as if he'd injured himself when he'd jumped the fence. The onlookers, mostly young mothers and a few grandparents and tourists, chattered excitedly, apparently astonished that Larry hadn't been mauled by the lioness. I was astonished that nobody seemed to have recognized him—a testament to his bland, forgettable features, I supposed.

The mother was following a guard around the side of the enclosure, and the crowd trailed them. The mother was pushing a stroller which contained a smaller child, who appeared to have slept through the crisis, and another child, wearing a petulant expression on a face smeared with something red, was clutching the hem of her jacket. Larry emerged with the zookeeper, still carrying the child, which had its head buried in his shoulder. I couldn't tell if it was a boy or girl.

And now, surrounded by tourists, mothers, and grandparents, I could see other reasons why he hadn't been recognized. He was dressed in khaki slacks, a beige Izod shirt, complete with alligator, and a nondescript tan windbreaker. And of course, he was soaking wet. Everybody looks different with their hair plastered to their head, even spacemen.

The mother launched herself at them, but instead of embracing Larry in gratitude, as I'd expected, she wrenched the soggy child from him and, clamping one arm around the waist of the shrieking, sobbing, flailing toddler, she began to beat Larry with her free fist.

"You pushed him, you bastard! You tried to kill my Jakey!" she screeched. "Bastard! You bastard! You bastard!" She punctuated her words with blows.

A guard tried to restrain her, but Larry looked at her with mild bemusement. "Now, ma'am," the guard was saying.

The zookeeper was less propitiatory. "Listen, lady, you're lucky the kid's alive. You ought to thank this man for saving his life."

She turned her wrath on him, but continued to strike out at Larry, whose raised arm took most of the blows. "You'll pay for this, too!" she cried. "This place isn't safe for kids! I'll sue! I'll sue all of you bastards!"

A medic was trying to pry the child from her viselike grip,

presumably to check it for injuries. She swung on him, snapping the boy's head back. The kid's foot struck his sister in the forehead and she yelped. "You get away from him! Don't you touch him! I'll sue!"

Now one of the onlookers, a thin, feisty-looking woman in a Redskins cap, got involved. "Lady, you ain't got no right to cuss them out!" she said. "I saw what happened. You was too busy smacking your little girl around to pay attention to that little boy. He didn't have no business climbing up on that wall, and if you'da been watching him like you should've, he wouldn't never have fallen over."

There was a murmur of approval from the crowd, and another mom with a child in a stroller said, "Uh-huh, she's right. I saw it, too."

Beside herself with fury, the mother rushed at her first critic. "Don't you dare! Don't you dare, you bitch, tell me I'm a bad mother!" She slapped the woman across the face. A male tourist tried to restrain her as his wife pointed the video camera at them.

Redskins cap slapped her back, hard. "Don't you be calling me a bitch!" she said. "Wasn't my child who fell in the lion pit."

Pandemonium broke out. People who tried to separate the combatants got elbowed, trodden on, and smacked. At least two children, Jakey and his sister, were now wailing at the top of their lungs. As would-be interceders got flung aside, they landed on other people, some of them children, whose families joined the fray. Someone got clobbered with a camcorder, so that introduced blood into the mix. I saw a flash of dark blue as a Metropolitan Police Officer waded into the crowd. Larry, meanwhile, was quietly retreating in my peripheral vision, so I slipped past the ring of videographers.

I followed the trail of wet footprints, caught up with him by Lemur Island and fell into step. "Nice save, dude," I said.

He gave a wry smile. "At least I rescued the child."

"What I can't believe is the way the mother turned on you," I said.

"That was interesting," he said in his anthropologist's voice. "She acted out of fear. She was expressing the fear she'd felt when the little boy fell, but also, I think, fear of just that accusation that the other woman made—that she was a bad mother. I saw the little boy falling and reached out to catch him, but I wasn't quick enough. I suppose she could have thought that I pushed him."

I didn't ask why he'd gone off on his own. I didn't even tell him how many people had been out looking for him; he would have guessed that. I just said, "You're in Ginger's doghouse, you know." This he also knew.

He said, "At least I'll be in good company with Getlo."

I grinned at him. But the smile he gave me was minimal, and it didn't reach his eyes.

"What did you say to the lion back there?" I asked.

I was half-kidding, but only half, and he replied, matter-of-factly, "I told her that the boy was a baby human in training. Most living creatures understand about babies. I apologized for disturbing her peace, but she was very gracious." He finger-combed his hair. "How bad do I look?" he asked.

Surprised, I said, "Not bad." I'd never known him to be concerned about his appearance before.

"Good enough to stop by Murphy's Pub for a beer?" he said.

CHAPTER TWENTY SIX

The *Washington Post* headline read, "SPACEMAN SAVES CHILD FROM LION." The accompanying photo showed the lioness nuzzling Larry's hand while the unfortunate Jakey sobbed into his other shoulder. It had been shot with a telephoto lens, so Larry's calm facial expression was as clearly visible as his sodden hair and clothing. The byline was "C. R. Manning."

I hadn't spotted her in the crowd, but then, I hadn't been looking for her. The only person I'd been looking for had been Larry.

Until the morning paper appeared, Larry had been known to the local media and its audience only as a "good Samaritan." Astonishingly, not only had no one recognized him, but no one had connected his disappearance with the disappearance of Elvis after the foiled mugging attempt. But C. R. Manning had recognized him, probably because she'd been following me, and I'd led her to the scoop that would no doubt make her week.

There was also a photograph of the melee that had followed, as well as a close-up of Jakey and his mother, she with a towel held to one temple and an expression suggesting that she'd just been given the news about the spaceman. I fully expected us to hear from her lawyer as soon as she found out about Larry's diamonds. Or she might opt for the book contract, with the national book tour and appearances on *Good Morning, America* and *Oprah*. I wanted to bet on the latter, but I couldn't find anyone who would take me up on it.

"Too bad there are no Calaverians here, Hank," Elvis told me.

"They will bet on anything."

Ginger, to my surprise, was rather pleased with the publicity, even though she was still furious with Larry.

But Larry was as impervious to her approval as he was to her wrath. "It's not working, Ginger. I have received a very gracious offer from the president of the American Association for the Advancement of Science to arrange an international forum of scientists, but I fear it will be a waste of time without a demonstration of the gravity of our enterprise."

No one spoke. Then at last Ginger said with resignation, "What do you intend to do and when do you intend to do it?"

"I can't tell you that," he said. "I don't know."

Elvis raised his hand. "I have a suggestion."

For once, he was ignored.

She sighed. "Will you tell me when you do know?"

"Probably not," he said, not unkindly. "I'm sorry."

"Okay," she said slowly, as if adjusting to this new turn of events. "Okay. You have an appointment at a video production facility at ten to film some footage for the YouTube video. Do you want me to cancel it?"

"No," Larry said. "I have a statement to read that should air as soon as our demonstration—whatever it is—is complete. I'd like to film that."

She studied his face. "You're not going to hurt anyone, are you?"

"I don't intend to," he said. "But I can't insure everyone's safety, either. It will all depend upon how your people react. If they behave rationally, no one should be injured."

"That's a big 'if,'" I muttered.

Larry looked at me. "I'm not optimistic," he said.

I didn't feel needed. In fact, I thought my little Washington adventure was drawing to a close. So I slipped out while nobody was looking, put on my wig and clip-on shades and took the Metro to the Smithsonian to check out their advertising collection. I left Elvis rolling on the floor with Getlo, while Warren and a handful of F.B.I. agents sat at the table opening the mail. Larry was in his room, Ginger and Anna were on the phone, and Jillian was out running errands.

I won't pretend I didn't get a kick out of reading Eskimo Pie ads from the twenties, but still, I was distracted. It was that old conundrum: what do you want to be doing when the world ends? I didn't know. I knew that I didn't want to be standing in front of a class of drowsy freshmen, trying to explain apostrophe use. I didn't want to be sitting at the computer, composing a trenchant analysis of T.V. dinner boxes from the fifties. There was a time when I would have wanted to be in bed with Anita, but I found to my surprise that I was pretty much over that. I would prefer, I realized, to be in bed with Eco the cat, playing Trap-the-tail or Undercover Monster Foot.

My interest in American history flagged, and I wandered over to the Museum of Natural History. I was in the mood for contemplating evolution before it ended altogether. In fact, I grew so engrossed that I didn't notice the time slipping away until my stomach growled loudly enough to set off giggles in a cluster of schoolgirls next to me. I found my way to the Atrium Café.

Just as I was about to bite into my burger, my cell phone rang.

"Where are you?" Ginger.

"What's wrong?"

"Everything," she said. "I'm missing two E.T.s and a P.A.—and you, of course."

"Jesus!" I said. I knew that she wouldn't give me details over the cell phone, so I swallowed all of my automatic responses, such as, "How did that happen?" and "How is that possible?" and other helpful questions of that ilk. "I'm at the Museum of Natural History. Where are you?"

"At the hotel. Get back here as soon as possible." Then, as an afterthought, she added, "Please," and disconnected.

I took a cab. It didn't make sense. Both Larry and Elvis were missing? And the P.A.—that must be Jillian? I didn't actually know what Howard's and Anna's titles were, but I was pretty sure they didn't qualify as P.A.s. Surely, the three M.I.A.s were together somewhere. You didn't lose three people at the same time without some connection between those disappearances. Had Larry and Elvis persuaded Jillian to help them escape?

The cab slowed, then stopped.

I looked around in confusion. This wasn't my hotel. In fact, we were in the middle of the roundabout at Dupont Circle. The driver was cursing, turning his key, pounding the steering wheel. Then I heard something else: voices, and only voices. What I expected to hear was a cacophony of horns and curses. Instead, I heard only curses. We were stuck in gridlock. I scanned our surroundings through the cab window, making a three hundred and sixty-degree turn. No car was moving. More than that: no radio was blaring, no sirens were wailing, there were no electronic beeps or burps to litter the air. People on the sidewalk were dropping their arms to stare at their cell phones, then gaze around them in bewilderment.

I threw money at the driver, bolted from the cab, and ran. I had more than ten blocks to cover, uphill. And I was the only thing moving.

I was vaguely aware that I was creating panic in my wake. People must have thought I'd seen something to run from. Whatever was happening must be happening downtown, they thought. I heard the firestorm of hysteria ignite behind me, and then more running footsteps. I felt like the lead extra in a Godzilla movie. I kept running, head up, eyes on the distance. Adrenaline would get me there. I could die later, when it was more convenient.

At Calvert Street, I hesitated. Making the decision before the exhaustion could catch up to me, I continued jogging straight up Connecticut past the zoo and then turned toward Rock Creek Park.

I stopped at last, gasping, on a bluff overlooking the creek. I saw no pigeons sunning themselves on an invisible shelf, detected no low hum of engine noise. The spaceship was gone.

CHAPTER TWENTY SEVEN

I bent over, hands on my knees, eyes squeezed shut, doubled over as much by a sense of overwhelming loss as by exhaustion. I let my knees buckle and knelt on the soft loam. I could hear the twittering of birds, an animal cry from the zoo, and a faint drone that might have been human.

When I finally hauled my leaden body upright, my wig slipped. In frustration I yanked it off and sent it sailing over the bluff. Immediately, I regretted the desecration, but then reassured myself that it would make a warm, comfortable home—or an exotic mate— for some small furry creature.

"Okay, okay," I said to myself under my breath. "Larry wanted to scare us and he's succeeded. It doesn't mean they're gone for good. And it doesn't mean that the planet is doomed. As for Jillian, she's probably up there with them, enjoying the view."

Slowly, I walked back to the hotel, conserving my energy for the long climb up to our suite. My perceptions had a dreamy, underwater quality to them.

Yet gradually I realized that I wasn't the only one moving in slow motion. When I emerged onto Connecticut, no one was running anymore. I saw a few weepers, including women hugging their children to their breasts, but mostly I saw knots of people, standing together or sitting on stoops or on top of stalled cars, talking. I heard snatches of their conversations as I passed.

"Ain't never seen nothing like this," one man said.

"Seems like I saw it in a movie once," another said. "Can't recollect which one, though."

"You don't think it's permanent?" someone said anxiously.

"Naw," said the second man. "They tryin' to save Earth, not destroy it."

"*If* we can believe them," a cynic put in.

I found it both gratifying and worrying that nobody questioned the source of the current state of affairs.

"Well, I don't care," a woman said. "Don't know why the boss was in such a rush for these papers anyway. He can just cool his heels."

Someone drawled, "No skin off your buttocks, huh?" And everyone laughed.

"People I feel sorry for is the ones down in the Metro," said an elderly man. "Wouldn't want to be caught down there, no, sir!"

"Yeah, I bet it's stuffy," said a mother with a child on one hip. "But what about the folks in the hospitals? What about the babies?"

"And the planes in the air?" someone added.

As if on cue, we heard the rhythmic *thwap* of helicopter rotor blades and a police helicopter passed overhead. In the distance we could see a plane headed for Reagan. I hoped that the control tower was operational, but then I supposed that planes had been landed before control towers were invented.

"I wonder how they do that," a young man said. "How they pull the plug on some things, and not others."

"They smart, that's how," someone said.

"You'd better believe they're smart!" someone else said.

"Ain't me got to do the believing," retorted the first person. "It's the damn gov'ment better be paying attention."

""You think this is happening all over, or just in Washington?" a woman asked. "Or just in America? You s'pose over there in Iraq and Korea and Africa and places like that they standing around talking right now, just like us?"

A man snorted. "Sure, that's exactly what they're doing. And I'll bet they're wishing they didn't have nincompoops in charge of the planet's future, just like we are."

"'Cept in some of those places, they didn't vote the nincompoops in, like we did," a woman said softly.

"Well, long as the world's ending, I'm glad I didn't file my income tax yet." A Hispanic accent, male.

"Not me. I'm getting a refund this year, and I want everything the government owes me." A woman's voice.

"You shouldn't be joking about taxes at a time like this," a young woman said, her voice shaking with emotion. "You should be down on your knees—we all should—asking God to forgive us poor sinners, telling him we're sorry for all our sins."

"Honey, the Lord know me well enough by now to know what I'm sorry for and what I'm not," said an older woman.

"Where they at, right now, those spacemen, I wonder," said a woman.

"I wonder if they feel sorry for us," said another.

"I wish I knew where they were. If I knew, I'd go home and get my gun and shove it up in their faces. Then we see who's sorry." A young male voice, angry.

"Aww, dog, what you think?" Another young male voice. "You think them spacemen scared of your sorry ass and that little popgun you carry? Man, you point that thing at them, Elvis going to disintegrate it right out your hand."

So it went.

The glass doors to the hotel lobby were propped open and the lobby was thick with reporters and civilians. What I'd expected was an angry mob. To my amazement, though, the atmosphere that predominated was almost festive. There were pockets of rage and outrage, with spokespeople vying for the reporters' attention. But the reporters were too busy chatting amiably with each other, and the angriest rants were drowned out by snatches of communal song, including "We Are the World" and, for a humorous encore, "It's a Small World After All," and that perennial favorite, "We Shall Overcome," before morphing into a medley of Elvis Presley songs. Several balloons bounced from hand to hand above the heads of the crowd. I caught a whiff of marijuana. From the edge of the crowd, I spotted the bored reporter from the back row of the Smithsonian press conference, but he didn't look bored now.

I was wondering how I was going to penetrate the mass of people in order to cross the lobby to the stairs when I felt a hand on my elbow.

I turned and saw Robbie grinning at me. He was wearing some kind of pale green polyester medical uniform jacket over flowered drawstring trousers and Birkies. "Wait here," he said.

When he returned he was pushing a long, flat cart, a piece of catering equipment, if I could judge by the tablecloths it was draped in. He lifted a tablecloth and nodded his head at it. "Hop on," he said.

So I lay down on the cart, which was just a little short for me, and he covered me up to my eyes with the tablecloth. My sneakered feet hung off the edge like a cowcatcher on a backward engine. I heard a clang as he dropped something on the bottom shelf. He took hold of the cart near my head and began to shout, "Coming through! Medical emergency! Coming through, there!"

I couldn't see what was happening from where I lay, but the cart rolled forward and we threaded our way through the crowd. I closed my eyes. It felt good to get off my feet. And it was just possible that any second now, I'd have a heart attack, and we really would have a medical emergency. At last I felt the tablecloth lifted off my face, and I opened my eyes to see two cops standing over me, studying my face as if in a morgue identification.

"Yeah, that's him, all right," one said. "Let him through."

The other one opened the door they were guarding, and we began to ascend the stairs.

"Where'd you get the jacket?" I asked.

"Got a neighbor who's a dental hygienist. She left it hanging in the laundry room, so it's still a little damp, but I thought it might come in handy."

"How'd you get here so fast?"

"Borrowed roller blades from my other neighbor."

"Don't suppose you know where the boys are," I gasped. I could have used a longer rest after my sprint up Connecticut to Rock Creek.

He shook his head. "But don't worry. They'll be back."

The door to the suite stood open, and the hall and living room were crowded with short-haired suits wearing ear buds. Robbie nudged me, grinning. "Part of the uniform, when you're a G-man. Don't matter that the suckers don't work." Then he dropped his voice still lower. "Would have loved to catch sight of them, a whole platoon of G-men on bicycles, pedaling up Connecticut."

It was odd to see them standing around, talking to each other instead of into cell phones or hidden microphones or walkie-talkies.

"Hank, finally! Thank god."

Getlo's joyous greeting I'd come to expect, but Ginger's surprised me a little. I hadn't honestly felt like I was all that important to the team effort; I was more of a bench warmer.

I looked around. "I went to the spaceship first. It isn't there, as far as I can tell. Isn't Jillian back?" I said.

"Come sit down, Hank," Ginger said. "You, too, Robbie. I have bad news."

She perched on the coffee table, flanked by Anna and Howard, standing. We sat on the couch, Getlo between us, belly up.

"Jillian has been kidnapped," Ginger said.

I looked from Ginger to Anna to Howard, and finally to Robbie. He was frowning in concentration.

"Kidnapped by whom?" I said at last. "Why?"

"We don't know who," Ginger said. "As for why, they've made certain demands of Larry."

"Such as?"

"They want a particular Afghani prison opened, and all of the prisoners freed," she said. "They're apparently trying to rescue their leader."

"What does Larry have to do with that?"

Ginger shrugged. Anna said, "They obviously think he's all-powerful. They think he can do anything."

"The F.B.I. profiler thinks that there will be additional demands if the first one is met," Howard said.

"I thought she was with the guys," I said. A stupid thing to say, I knew, but I couldn't think of anything better.

"The guys disappeared from a men's room at the television studio," Anna said. "They locked Cisco in a janitor's closet."

"Cisco said they were really sorry," Howard said. "They were probably sorry about the wall, too."

"Wait, you let Elvis go to the men's room?" I said. I wasn't really sure what happened to all the food and drink he put away, but I didn't think it came out through the usual human channels.

Ginger raised a palm. "Don't start with me, Hank. Just don't even go there."

"And what happened to Jillian?" I asked.

"We sent her for take-out. She left the studio maybe half an hour before the boys disappeared."

"We kind of forgot about her after that," Anna said. "I mean, this time we lost both spacemen. And then a half hour after that, the power went off."

"So, wait, how do you know she's been kidnapped?"

"One of the F.B.I. agents found a note in his pocket about twenty minutes ago," Ginger said. "He'd been down in the lobby—well, I guess you've seen the crowd. We don't think the note could have been there very long. We're lucky he found it so quickly."

"There's a deadline," Howard said.

"A deadline?"

Ginger stood suddenly and crossed the room to the window. We watched her, then turned back to Howard.

In a low voice, he said, "If the leader's not free by midnight, there will be consequences."

"So the thing to do now is to find Jillian," Robbie said.

"The F.B.I. has dispatched a couple of their agents and a D.C. cop to canvas the area where she disappeared," Anna said. "But it will take them a while to get there, even if they manage to commandeer bikes or something. They said they couldn't afford to take too many people away from here, because even if Larry and Elvis aren't here, they're afraid of a riot. The cops are short-handed because they're dealing with the power outage. They have to guard the hospitals because those are the only places that have power. And maybe Larry and Elvis could help if they were here, but they're not. I'm scared, Hank."

"How long has the power been off?" I asked, looking at my watch. My watch had stopped at 1:07.

"It's been more than an hour, Hank," she said. "Who knows how long they intend to keep it off." She gestured toward the window. "The weather's mild. They won't have to worry about the elderly and the kids."

"The weather's fine here, Anna," Robbie said. "But what we have to remember is that what they've done probably affects the whole planet. Remember, they're not interested in local politics, so they probably wouldn't target New York City, or even the whole U.S. Australia's in the middle of a severe drought, and there's a tropical depression forming in the North Atlantic. I don't think they'll want to endanger anybody in cold or hot places, so it probably won't be much longer."

Ginger was back. "Hank, do you have any idea where they could be?"

I shook my head. "They could be in another dimension. You've tried their cells again, right?"

"Dude, if they're in another dimension, you think they took a cell tower with them?" Robbie said.

"Anyway, I've tried—like, every five minutes," Ginger said. "And—."

The lights came on. The air conditioner started to hum. Something beeped. And, after the briefest of pauses, the air was filled with the music of cell phone ringtones, including my own.

I didn't recognize the number.

"Hank, it's Charlotte," the voice said. "Don't—."

I hung up.

Everyone else in the room was talking on their cells. I wanted to turn mine off, but I didn't think I could do that in the middle of a crisis. When it started to ring again, I glanced at the display, and ignored it.

"I'm going to ask the agent in charge if he's going to dispatch more agents to search the area where Jillian disappeared," Ginger said, and turned on her heel. I hoped she could get someone to stop talking on the phone long enough to listen to her.

My phone rang. This time I glanced at the display, and answered.

"Where the hell are you?" I said in spite of myself. It was hardly the critical question of the moment.

"Hi, Hank," Elvis said. "What's up, dude? We are just laying doggo until the excitement blows under. The power failure was my idea—from the movie. Do you think it will work?"

I stuck a finger in my other ear. "Laying what?" I said.

Uncertainty leaked into his voice. "Laying doggo. Isn't that right? It means what you said before—laying slow. Doesn't it?"

I palmed my forehead. "Yeah, I guess, in some neighborhoods. Look, we have a crisis here. Jillian's been kidnapped." I couldn't afford to be overly scrupulous about cell phone security right now. And with Elvis, I had to be direct.

"Kidnapped?" I heard him say something to Larry in their own language, and then the soft rumble of Larry's voice in reply. Into the phone, he said, "No! But why? Who would do such a thing?"

"Someone who wants something from you and Larry," I said. "Someone who's threatened to kill her if they don't get what they want. But we can't talk about it over the phone. The line's not secure, understand?"

"Yes, I understand. We will come right back." I heard Larry's voice in the background again. "Do you know where this happened, Hank?"

"Around the place where you disappeared," I said.

"You must bring the car and meet us at the ship, Hank. That will save time."

I didn't argue, or ask what they had in mind. No point in wasting time. If they had any kind of a plan, they were two legs up on me.

CHAPTER TWENTY EIGHT

As Elvis emerged from the invisible ship, he was already talking.

"Larry wants to know if his YouTube video has been shown yet," he said. "We were in a hurry at the studio, and all the time we've been gone, he's been thinking of things he should have said."

"Not yet," I said. "But the priority now is to find Jillian before anything happens to her."

Waiting in the Spartan Security van were Joe and Paul, the Samoan brothers, and Robbie. I'd managed to take Ginger aside and speak to her quietly, and although she'd protested vehemently that two bodyguards were inadequate security for two spacemen who had just deprived the greater D.C. area, not to mention the planet, of more than an hour of computer, cell phone, and television use, she'd finally given in.

"You've got to let them run their game, Ginger," I'd said. "They're going to do it anyway. We can either get in their way or stand back and let them do their jobs."

In the van on the way to the studio, we filled in Larry and Elvis on the kidnapping.

"The F.B.I. thinks there will be more demands," I concluded.

"We cannot do as they wish, Hank," Larry said. "I'm sorry."

"We are not permitted to interfere in the internal politics or disputes of the planets we visit, Hank," Elvis said somberly.

I had expected them to say this, but the words still spiked my anxiety for Jillian.

"But don't worry," Elvis said. "We will find her. We are very, very good at our jobs."

We began at the studio, where a cop had been and gone. Nobody seemed to know anything. Nobody had seen Jillian leave the studio.

"Where was she going, Hank?" Elvis asked. He seemed to be taking the lead now, and I noticed that Larry was hanging back. They were both, as Elvis had affirmed, good at their jobs, but diplomacy wasn't needed right now. Police work was.

"City Lights on Dupont Circle," Robbie said.

I looked at him, impressed. Under his mellow exterior, I was beginning to realize, he had a good head in a crisis. Whatever drugs he'd done in his lifetime hadn't addled his brain.

"Which direction is that, Robbie?" Elvis asked. When Robbie pointed, Elvis asked a passing studio tech if the building had a back door.

The back door led to an alley. Elvis walked the alley, studying the ground. Larry stood against the building wall and watched him. When Elvis reached the sidewalk along 21st Street, he called Larry, and we followed.

Elvis said something to Larry in their language, and Larry looked down the sidewalk. A tree stood in a small plot carved out of the easement, and a squirrel was busy burying something in the dirt. Larry approached the squirrel alone, and squatted down. Elvis signaled us to stay back. We couldn't see what was happening from where we stood at the entrance to the alley. Then, to our amazement, the squirrel came hopping along the sidewalk in our direction, and we stepped back in unison to give it some space. The squirrel passed the alley, continued for a yard or two, and hopped over the curb. Larry, who was behind the squirrel, squatted down again. Once the squirrel had scampered off to the next tree, Larry waved us over.

"Not too close," Elvis cautioned, and we stopped. He moved forward alone.

What we saw was a white take-out bag, crushed by tire marks, its contents smashed and scattered. There was an intact packet of soy sauce a foot from the epicenter, but the squirrels and birds had clearly removed most of the edibles.

Elvis and Larry crouched over the spill and conversed in their language, turning their heads to look up and down the street. Larry pointed, and we all followed his finger, though most of us didn't know what we were looking for.

They both stood and Elvis approached us. "What we need are sniffer dogs," he said.

"What?" I said. He turned to Larry.

"Body hounds," Larry said. "He means we need body hounds." He was reaching for his translator when I got it.

"You mean bloodhounds?" I asked.

"They are called bloodhounds?" Elvis said. You wouldn't think an extraterrestrial Robocop would be squeamish, but his face registered mild disgust.

"Yeah, 'cause that's what we usually give them to smell," Paul put in.

"But actually," Joe said, "Elvis is right. There's a whole category of dogs called 'sniffer dogs,' and they're not all bloodhounds. Some of them sniff drugs and bombs and stuff like that."

Paul said, "But if Jillian got into the car with them, they won't be able to track her scent."

"Not necessarily true, dude," Robbie put in. "I read an article about it. A good bloodhound can track a scent coming through the ventilation system on a car."

"It's not just Jillian he wants the dogs to smell," I said, smiling as realization dawned. "It's the car. Or rather, one of the tires on the car." I was beginning to realize that I hadn't taken Elvis seriously up to this point. He was a trained intergalactic peace officer, after all, and presumably experienced or they wouldn't have sent him, not even to save an insignificant little planet like Earth.

"Can they do that?" Paul asked.

"Only one way to find out," I said, and dialed my cell phone.

Two uniforms were first on the scene, followed by a grumpy detective who supervised the cordoning off of the crime scene. We mollified him by confirming the boys' account that they hadn't touched anything. By now, Elvis had been recognized, and a few more uniforms showed up for crowd control. The press with their satellite-dish vans weren't far behind, but nobody answered their questions about what was going on.

The grumpy detective had scoffed at the idea of dogs, but he had been overruled by someone higher up. Ginger had also pulled strings to get two dogs and their trainers to the site. By the time the dogs showed up, it was almost six. We had six hours until midnight, and maybe an hour of daylight left.

Larry studied the dogs. One was a bloodhound and one was a

beagle. By now, I suspected that he was communicating with the dogs. But I couldn't tell because they weren't looking at him necessarily. I saw him point to one and speak to the trainer. By this time more suits had shown up, and another squad car or two. Ginger had also been escorted through the police barricade. She was carrying a plastic food bag with something navy blue inside: an article of Jillian's clothing. With her were reinforcements from Spartan Security, Cisco, Warren, and Max.

The trainer that Larry had indicated ducked under the crime-scene tape and walked the beagle to the curb to smell the contents of the takeout bag. The other trainer took the bag from Ginger and was offering a blue sweatshirt to the bloodhound's nose.

"We will follow in our own van," Elvis said. "If we are lucky, we will only have to go to Arlington, Virginia."

Joe said, "I'll walk with these guys." He gestured toward the other guards, who were surrounding the van. I noticed that a few short-haired ear-budded suits had also shown up, and they joined the security circle.

It would have been the friendly thing to do to offer to walk with them. But my legs were still complaining about the earlier sprint up Connecticut, and I consoled myself that our bodyguards probably wouldn't have let any of us walk, especially not now, when our space visitors had stirred up so much anger. Still, it was going to be hard to see my endurance outstripped by a beagle.

The dogs were preceded by a police car, light flashing, inching along and using blasts from its siren to clear the busy street. Behind us was another police car, with the grumpy detective riding shotgun. I had no doubt that behind that was a parade of news vans.

"The chief asked them not to broadcast anything at this point," Paul said to the rearview mirror. He was driving.

"Do you think they'll comply?" I asked, twisting my neck around to see if any cameras were pointed in our direction.

"Well, our timing was right," Paul said, checking his watch. "Too late, really, for the six o'clock news on a big news day like this one. They don't like to violate a direct request from the chief. Could shut down their sources in the future."

"Why do you think we're going to Arlington?" I said to Elvis.

"Because that is where there was a white van stolen this morning, and also a license plate," he said.

I looked at him. "I can see why you think they used a van, but surely more than one van and one license plate have been stolen in the metro area today," I said.

"We have the first two letters," Elvis said.

"How?" Paul asked.

When Elvis hesitated, I said, "From the *squirrel?*"

Elvis nodded, his eyes on the dogs. Larry made no comment, but he smiled to himself. Humans had so little imagination.

"Far out," Robbie said from the rear seat.

"The squirrel can read?" I pressed.

"No, he can only show Larry what he saw," Elvis said. "That's why we only have two letters. That's all he could see through the branches. And I think he was distracted by the smell of the food. But Hank, that doesn't mean that Jillian was taken to Arlington."

"We're headed in the right direction, though," Paul observed.

"Man, I wish I could talk to animals," Robbie said.

"But Robbie, you can," Elvis said. "You are also an animal, so of course you can talk to them. But if you want to hear them talking back to you, you have to be very still and listen. Humans are not very good at listening."

"You got that right," Robbie said.

"I cannot talk to animals because I am not an animal," Elvis said, a little sadly.

"Yeah, but dude, you can make stuff disappear," Robbie said. "Plus, you got a killer Elvis imitation."

From 21st Street, after a long pause while the dogs covered much of the intersection and then seemed to reach a consensus with regard to their findings, the procession turned right onto Constitution in the direction of the Arlington Memorial Bridge.

"So the bloodhound is really tracking Jillian's scent?" I said.

"Pretty fucking amazing," Robbie agreed.

"This dog has tracked people in cars before," Larry said. "As long as the air is relatively still, he can do it."

"His name is Rudy," Elvis put in, ever the social lubricator. "The other one's name is Pearl."

"I'm surprised not to hear more horns blaring," I said. "Washingtonians must be a really mellow breed."

"Nah," Paul said. "You just get used to it is all. Every time the president goes some place, or even the vice president or first lady, all the traffic stops for the whole entourage."

"Yeah," Robbie said. "The dogs are kind of a novelty. Most

people are probably sitting there thinking, 'At least it's not that asshole Cheney.'"

"Yeah," Paul added. "Plus the dogs are cuter than the veep. Nobody's going to cuss out a dog."

Ginger had been unusually quiet since she'd arrived with the sweatshirt, and I suddenly realized in the silence what I'd been missing.

I turned around to look at her, sitting next to Robbie. "Ginger," I said, "is your cell phone turned off?" When she nodded, I persisted, "As in, completely off? Not on vibrate?" She nodded again. "Maybe you should turn it back on, in case Jillian somehow manages to call," I said. I reached a hand over the backrest and gently touched her shoulder. "It'll be okay. It will. We'll find her." Her eyes teared up.

I hoped I was right. Man, did I hope I was right. I was working hard to repress images of Jillian, bound, gagged, and blindfolded, locked in a car trunk or an underground bunker somewhere.

"Elvis is very good at his job," Larry said. This was a new role for him: Larry the consoler.

"That is true," Elvis acknowledged, "but Ginger is still worried about what is happening to Jillian, Larry."

I tried focusing on the dogs again so I wouldn't catch Ginger's weepiness.

"Are they really going to walk all the way to Arlington or wherever?" I said, still conscious of my own physical limitations. "Even the beagle?"

"Oh, yeah," Paul said. "Joe says they'll walk to hell and back if they're following a scent. I guess it's what they train for."

"How come they're so quiet?" I said. "The dogs, I mean. Aren't they supposed to bay when they're tracking?"

"Dude, you're thinking of hunting dogs," Robbie said. "Or *Shawshank Redemption*."

"Yeah, I guess it would be hard to sneak up on a perp if you could hear the dogs coming a mile away," Paul said.

"Have they worked together before?" I said. "I mean, it doesn't seem like it'd be all that common to have a bloodhound and a beagle work together."

"These two have worked together once before," Larry said, "about five years ago."

But Elvis was grinning at me.

"What?" I said.

"Hank, you should be a reporter," he said. "You ask so many questions. And you are a good writer because you're writing a book. Maybe you would like to write about something besides old cereal boxes."

I was momentarily stunned, not by his suggestion but by this confirmation that he'd paid so much attention when I had described my dissertation that he could remember my topic. My own mother couldn't remember my topic.

"There must be other things that you can use semenotics on," Elvis said.

The rest of us contained ourselves, but I saw Paul's shoulders start to quake and even Ginger smiled. Robbie exploded in laughter.

"Robbie, what is so funny?" Elvis asked, looking a little hurt.

Robbie leaned forward and threw his arms around Elvis's shoulders, which cleared the backrest by a good foot. "I love ya, big guy," was all he said.

CHAPTER TWENTY NINE

"What if they ditched the van somewhere and moved her to a car that wasn't stolen?"

We had crossed the Memorial Bridge at beagle pace, and were passing the Arlington National Cemetery.

"I don't think they did that, Hank," Elvis said. "They kidnapped Jillian in broad daylight. They would be afraid that someone would see her or hear her if they moved her to another car, I think."

"Man, look at all these high rises!" Robbie said. "How're we ever going to find her if she's in one of those?"

"I do not think Jillian is in a high rise," Elvis said. "That would also be too risky. I think we will find her close by in a house with a car park, or maybe a carbage." He pronounced the last word to rhyme with "garage."

What none of us had yet wondered aloud was how the power outage might have affected the kidnappers' plans, or Jillian's ordeal. It was now seven o'clock, and dusk. I felt my own anxiety mounting with the fading light. I wondered how long the dogs and handlers could hold out.

Fifteen minutes later, Elvis leaned forward and said, "Paul, I think we need to stop and decide how to proceed."

We were inching along the Lee Highway into a residential neighborhood filled with the kind of houses that Elvis had described. Paul spoke into his walkie-talkie and pulled over. Joe and Cisco jogged to the car, and Larry and Elvis got out. They all walked over to confer with the handlers, and a couple of cops and the grumpy detective joined them. There was a certain amount of gesturing. Larry looked at the dogs. One of the handlers changed his company jacket for a plain beige windbreaker, and then two of the Spartan Security guys seemed to be rigging the two handlers with electronic devices of some kind. The detective went back to the police car behind us, and the two cops got back into their respective cars. One of the handlers exchanged a wave with Larry, and the two handlers and their dogs moved on.

Elvis climbed back into the van. "Now, we wait," he said. Paul got into the driver's seat again and set a boxy device on the dashboard. He pressed a few buttons and a screen on the dash lit up, showing a map of the neighborhood with a pinpoint of blinking light slowly moving away from our location. A plumber's van with "L & G Plumbing" on the side pulled up across the highway, and the four Spartan Security guys crossed the road and got into it. Paul turned his head and said, a little wistfully, "They've got all our best equipment in there. And our best geek."

Voices came from the box. One said quietly, "Can you hear us, Paul?"

"Loud and clear, buddy," Paul said.

Another voice said, "Yeah, well, here we are, a couple of average guys, out walking our pooches in this nice, quiet neighborhood."

Another car pulled up in front of us about half a block. A young couple got out, unfolded a stroller and a baby—or what looked like a baby but was probably a doll— from the back seat in record time, and began to walk in the same direction as the dogs.

"That's not really a baby, is it?" Ginger asked.

Nobody seemed to know. In any case, nobody wanted to speak for fear of missing something coming in from the handlers.

Two bikers, lean in their skintight cycling shorts, zipped past us on the left. A minute later, another dog walker in a short haircut and loud jacket, crossed the highway in front of us and headed up the same sidewalk with a German shepherd on a leash.

Paul snorted. "I don't know why the Fibbies think they can't be spotted if they change their clothes. At least we have the light in our favor."

The streetlights had come on, but they didn't provide much illumination in the dusky half-light.

"Good thing those dogs are trained for distance work," Robbie said at last, after a long silence.

"Let's hope the G-man is," Paul said.

Every now and then, one of the handlers would say irritably, "Come on, Pearl! Get out of the street." And then after a pause, "You know better than that."

"Does he say that every time somebody passes them on the sidewalk?" I asked.

"Well, the last thing we need at this point is a humane society agent on the scene, I guess," Paul said.

"I don't know why not," Robbie said. "We got every other kind of law enforcement officer in the metro area."

"But Pearl knows he's not really mad at her, right, Larry?" Elvis said.

"She knows," Larry said. "She's a professional."

"O-kay," said a handler. "We're turning onto North George Mason. Can you see us?"

"Yeah, we got you," Paul said.

"What we got here is a nice little street of brick Cape Cods. Two stories, dormers. A-a-and, bingo! For Sale sign out front, probably rented, no lock box on the front door." He read off the name and phone number of the realtor.

"You copy that, Teddy?" Paul said.

"Copy," a new voice, female, answered.

Paul flipped a switch and we were looking at a dark video of the house he was describing. There was one light on downstairs and one upstairs, visible through drawn curtains, but it was hard to make out anything else.

The voice continued. "Blacktop driveway and—yes, we got us a van in the back. You see that sucker, Tom?"

"Too dark," came the other voice. "It's a light-colored van, but I can't make out the tag. Whoops! There goes Pearl!"

The other voice was sharp. "Pearl! You come back here! Pearl!" There was a scrabbling sound, then a sharp voice. "Bad dog, Pearl!" The voice turned cranky. "I don't know why I have to walk her. She always minds Susie, she never minds me."

After a short pause, during which the only sounds were the sounds of footsteps, the voice returned. "Here's the license. You ready?" And after Paul had copied it down, we heard, "Good dog, Pearl! Good dog!"

Paul said, "John, you got a visual?"

"Yep. Looks pretty quiet," a voice said.

The woman named Teddy spoke again. "We're moving into position."

The plumber's van pulled out, and in another few seconds it passed us and continued on.

"Bikers, where are you?" Paul said.

"We're on the street behind," a voice said. "Greg's gone to look at the approach from the back, but there's a lot of green space, all private yards."

"And yards on both sides," another voice added.

Nobody spoke for a while.

"What's happening?" I said, impatient.

"Probably contacting the realtor," Paul said.

Several minutes dragged by.

"The floor plan's just coming through," Teddy said. "I'm sending you a copy."

I hadn't noticed the printer mounted under the dash until it whirred into action.

There was a lot I wanted to ask, like why Spartan Security people seemed at this point to be in charge of the operation, as far as anybody was. It was clear that there were several agencies involved. Why hadn't the Bureau cleared the area and taken over?

I finally leaned over and asked Ginger in a low voice.

"They—well, we—were first on the scene with the right equipment, I suppose," she said. "Every law enforcement agency is still dealing with the fallout from the power outage today. They're all up to their necks in crisis." Her voice faltered a little. "One abduction probably just doesn't seem all that important to them right now."

"Not even with the spacemen involved?" I asked.

She shrugged. "Spartan's reputation helps," she said. "And Teddy used to work for the Bureau before she went to work for Spartan. So they know she knows what she's doing."

She leaned forward to study the floor plan Paul was offering for her inspection.

"I'm betting on an upstairs closet," he said.

She nodded. "Ask Teddy what she can hear."

In response, Teddy said, "Television downstairs. *Deal or No Deal,* if you can believe it. We've only heard two voices, speaking Arabic and English. Hold on." We heard her speaking to someone else. "Hold on," she repeated. "We're getting Morse code from upstairs."

Nobody breathed.

"It's definitely our girl. She's upstairs in a closet in the room closest to the top of the stairs," Teddy said at last. "Do you see it on the plan?" She paused. "Two men—well, that's all she knows about, anyway. Weapons unknown." She paused. "Now she's repeating."

"What's the boss say?" Paul asked.

We heard conversation, then Teddy was back. "Okay, here's the scoop. These guys—there are probably two of them—are cousins of the owner's sister-in-law, staying there while the house is being sold. All the information we have on them suggests that they're terrorist wannabes, not the real thing. But even wannabes can learn everything they need to know about explosives just by surfing the web. So we can't guarantee that the house isn't wired to self-destruct if something goes wrong. Best case scenario, we go in quietly, grab Jillian and get her out of there before we start throwing the tear gas."

After a brief silence, Elvis said, "Dudes, when do we boogie?"

CHAPTER THIRTY

He was the obvious choice, of course, our secret weapon: seven feet of laser-eyed, ducktailed crimefighter in a bulletproof package. There was some debate about whether he'd be sufficiently light-footed, but those of us who'd seen him on the dance floor and the basketball court had no worries in this regard. And he was wearing his high-tops.

But the boss, whoever he was, wanted to wait until dark, so we sat. Somebody in a Spartan Security windbreaker brought us a bag of drive-through burgers, but nobody, not even Elvis, had much appetite.

"Are the press still back there?" I asked Robbie.

"I think some of them are," he said. "But I think most of them got called away to cover other stuff."

"I hope not angry mobs tearing the Wardman apart, looking for us," I said.

Ginger didn't say anything, but I knew what she was thinking. She was imagining, as I was, Jillian locked in a closet, sending out her Morse-code messages again and again, hoping that somebody could hear them, but not really knowing if they were being received or not. Had they threatened her? Had they hurt her? Whatever they'd done to her, they hadn't made her forget her Morse code, and this was a consolation.

Elvis and Paul studied the floor plan.

At 8:30, Teddy gave us the signal. Elvis got out of the van, and

Paul got out, and there was further conferring with the suits. Then Elvis leaned back in and said, "Okay, Hank, let's go."

"Me?" I said. I wasn't resistant, only astonished. My law enforcement experience consisted of one year as a fifth-grade crossing guard, and my training ran to *NYPD* re-runs.

"I might need a roost," he said. "And besides, you will only ask me questions about it later."

The notion that I could give Elvis a roost was laughable, but I got out of the car. Paul unzipped my tan jacket and helped me into a black Spartan Security jacket. He fitted me with an ear bud, and supplied me with a gas mask that made me look like a postnuclear mosquito.

"I can't see where I'm going," I said, trying to find my feet at the ends of my legs.

"Leave it off unless you need it. Here." He pulled it down and stashed it over my shoulder.

"Where's his?" I said, gesturing toward Elvis.

"He says he doesn't need one," Paul said.

"Oh."

He slipped something else over my head. "Night-vision goggles," he said, fitting them over my glasses. He picked up my hand and guided it to the scope. "Check it out," he said. "You're going to have a few extra inches here, so watch where you swing your head."

"Cool," I said. I didn't feel cool. I felt like an idiot, and way underprepared for this mission. And now I had a scope attached to my nose.

The next thing I knew he was smearing something black on my face. It felt greasy and had a faint waxy odor. He took hold of my wrists, one at a time, in a businesslike way and smeared the same stuff all over my hands.

He started to hand me a gun, a revolver—that much I knew— and without thinking, I raised my hands and stepped back. He thought I was helping and reached around me. I felt the cold steel brush the skin of my lower back.

"Look," I said, "I've never fired a gun before."

"That's why we're giving you a revolver," he said. "You ever play cowboys when you were a kid?"

"I was usually the Indian," I said. "I had a thing for bows and arrows."

He looked at me. Then he reached around me and removed the

gun to show it to me. He produced a flashlight from somewhere and shone it on the gun.

"This is the trigger," he said. "You put your trigger finger on the trigger, and wrap your other hand around that hand to steady it. Keep your fingers away from the cylinder, aim low, and squeeze the trigger to fire. This is double-action, so you don't cock it. Just keep firing till the sucker hits the floor. Don't worry about the hammer. Got it?"

When I didn't say anything, he said, "Don't worry. Elvis and I have your back. Just don't let it fall down your pants leg and blow a hole in your foot."

Relief flooded me. "You're coming too?"

He replaced the gun in my waistband and said, "You bet your ass."

He blackened his face, pulled night-vision goggles over his eyes, hoisted a coil of rope to his shoulder, and turned to Elvis. "We're ready to rock."

Elvis was wearing his dark-blue Hoyas sweatshirt, and although he wasn't sporting night-vision goggles or a gas mask, his face was also blackened. In the dim light from the flashlight, he looked a menacing giant, and his face was grave.

"We're approaching from the back," Paul said. He showed us a sketch of the site. "Two houses here, nobody home in this one, feds have talked to the folks on this side." He pointed. "We go through the fence here, walk along the fence line, go over the fence again here. We want to approach from this direction. Window here is a bedroom behind the living room, where our guys are watching television. This window is a bathroom off the kitchen, so pretty likely to be covered. Jillian is in a closet here, on the second floor, over the kitchen. Your access is through this window from the roof of the garage. Okay?"

We nodded.

I heard Teddy's voice in my ear. "Ground floor toilet just flushed," she said.

Paul grinned at us. "Timing is everything."

The van dropped us off on the street just past North George Mason, our target. The bicyclers, who had changed into dark jeans and pullovers, met us there. The neighborhood was quiet and the odors of fried meat and fabric softener hung in the still air. One or two porch lights were on and blue light glimmered from behind curtains in living-room windows, but the curtains were all closed. Both of the houses we stood in front of, two large white Cape Cods, were dark.

"There's your entry," one of the cyclists said, nodding at a gate in the fence to our left. "The homeowner will keep the lights off until we give her the all-clear. There are trees back there, which will give you some cover, but trees mean twigs so watch where you step."

We passed through the gate and began walking. The night-vision goggles gave everything a surreal quality. Elvis stepped softly for a big man. At the back fence, Elvis boosted Paul, and then me. I held on to the rough wooden tops of the slats and eased my body down. Paul caught me and slid me down until my feet touched the ground. Elvis landed quietly behind us. We skirted the yard and crossed under the dark bathroom window to the back of the garage.

"Roost me up, Hank," Elvis said, his eyes on the roof.

I swallowed, gritted my teeth, and bent down, locking my fingers to make a shelf. I was determined not to make a sound, and I tried to will all of my adrenaline to flow into my hands.

I didn't need it. He was surprisingly light. Before I realized it, I heard the soft scrape of his sneaker against the roof shingles. As I straightened, a hand appeared in my line of vision. I grasped it and felt myself levitating. Then I was on the roof. Paul stayed below, but I saw him give us a thumbs-up sign.

We crossed to the window. I was behind him when he burned a hole in it. There was hardly any sound at all, just a flash of light and a faint whiff of hot metal. I made a note to myself to take a robot along on any future missions of this kind.

We climbed into a carpeted room empty of furniture, with only ghostly indentations to show us where furniture had once stood. It had the musty scent of a long-uninhabited space. The crescent moon did little to illuminate the room. But to our right as we entered through the window was the rectangle of the closet door that was our goal—a door with the illusionary grain of hollow-core and a cheap faux-brass doorknob with a keyhole at its center.

The sound of amplified applause drifted up the stairs. The volume was quite loud, I was gratified to note. We weren't directly above the living room, but I still worried about creaking floorboards.

"Tell her we're here, Hank," Elvis whispered.

"How do I do that?" I said.

"Don't you know Moose Code?" he asked, obviously surprised.

I shook my head. "It's okay," I said. "I'll think of something. Don't panic."

Since the only one likely to panic under the circumstances was me, he didn't respond.

I put my ear to the closet door, but I couldn't hear anything. I raised a hand and drummed my fingers on the laminated wood. Silence. I tried again. This time I got a response, a faint tapping. I hoped she wasn't trying to give me an important message. But surely she could already tell from my drumming that I was not adept at code. Unless I'd sent her an inadvertent message—"your dry cleaning is ready" or "snakes for dinner" or something like that.

A key left in the lock was too much to hope for. I backed up and went to stand next to Elvis.

The success of this operation depended on Jillian's response. She didn't seem the hysterical type, but who knew what they'd put her through.

This time I was able to see the flash of light in his eyes—so bright that I had to turn my head. When I looked back at the closet, the doorknob was gone.

I crossed to the closet and gently pulled the door open. Jillian sat against a far corner, her feet bound, her arms tied in front of her and resting in her lap, duct tape across her mouth. She was dressed in a khaki skirt and an Oxford shirt. Her shoes and jacket lay near her on the floor. Her pantyhose were badly run. Her hair, which had apparently lost its clip, was down.

She blinked up at us. I felt a rush of tenderness so powerful that for an instant, I couldn't move. Elvis moved past me and hauled her to her feet.

I didn't see what he cut the ropes with, but he handed them to me and I set them softly on the carpeted floor. She grimaced as he peeled the duct tape away, but she didn't make a sound. He whispered something to her, and she nodded, tried to take a step, and stumbled against him. He caught her, and while he held her upright, I bent and vigorously massaged her legs. When she tapped me on the shoulder and gave me a thumbs-up, I took her by the other arm and we guided her toward the window. Elvis bent to retrieve the shoes and jacket, but Jillian caught his arm and shook her head.

I stepped out onto the garage roof, pulled the goggles down, and leaned back in to help Jillian. As I did this, my scope scraped the window frame and Jillian stepped back with a tiny yelp. We froze. I strained to hear any sign of a reaction from the room downstairs, but nothing happened.

Jillian crossed her hands on her chest in a gesture of penitence, but she was grinning and her eyes were crinkled in mirth. I waved her out, worried that her amused astonishment at the sight of me in night vision goggles would cost us our whole operation. She straddled the window ledge, then leaned against me as she stepped through. Elvis came last, walked ahead of us to the edge of the roof, then kneeling, took Jillian's wrists and lowered her to Paul. He did the same for me, and despite the pain in my shoulders, I descended in a fog of heady exhilaration. On the ground, I turned to help Paul lower Elvis, who was hanging from the edge by his fingers.

I heard Paul say softly but distinctly, "All clear. Everybody's out. It's all yours."

And we ran.

Nothing happened—at least, not at first. The van stood idling at the curb. As we reached it, Paul grabbed Jillian's wrist, and said, "Explosives, Jilly. Did you see or smell any explosives?"

She shook her head. "But I didn't *see* anything, Paul. And the garage just smelled like a garage to me."

The van door slid open. Joe was behind the wheel. Ginger pulled Jillian into a bear hug, whispering fiercely, "Thank god, thank god, thank god!" Elvis and I climbed in. From my vantage point, all I could see of Jillian in the dim interior was her shaking back.

"Jesus, Ginger, give the chick some oxygen," Robbie protested.

Ginger must have loosened her hold, because, with a sigh, Jillian disengaged and leaned back against the seat. Her eyes glinted, and I thought she was crying. I reached over the seat and patted her knee awkwardly.

Then I realized that she was laughing as well as crying. "What the hell was that you were playing on the closet door, Hank?" she said. "The theme music from *Bonanza?*"

"It was supposed to be the *William Tell Overture,*" I said.

This set off another fit of giggles— uncontrolled, but not hysterical. "There I am, sitting in the dark, bound and gagged, barely able to breathe from the closeness and the stench of sweat and Kung Pao chicken and hoisin sauce, and I hear this tapping. When I couldn't translate it, I knew it must be you, Hank. You can't imagine how comforting that was, to know that you were on the other side of the door, just madly tapping away. And I thought that if you were there, Elvis and Larry couldn't be far behind. So I just crawled into a corner to wait and see what would happen."

Ginger interrupted her. "But are you all right?"

Jillian sighed. "Yes, yes, Ginger, I'm fine, apart from the ribs you broke when I got into the car."

Joe handed back a bag from the front seat. "Here. Take your mind off your troubles, kid."

"Is this what I think it is?" She took the bag eagerly and looked inside. "Awww, you guys! A tomato and mozzarella Panini! You shouldn't have."

Joe eased the van away from the curb. "Larry's got the beer."

Larry handed her a bottle, smiling.

"You guys!" she said.

Joe drove around the corner and pulled in behind the plumbing truck. We were now parked a block away from the house we'd just left and, as he pointed out, upwind of it. It was visible through the front windshield. We pointed out the house to Jillian.

"Gee, it just looks like an ordinary house in an ordinary neighborhood, doesn't it?" she said through a mouthful of sandwich.

"They're evacuating the houses on either side," Paul said, "in case there are explosives."

Robbie was leaning over, his elbows resting on the back of Jillian's seat.

"So what happened to you?" he said to her. "Were you scared?"

The second question seemed gratuitous to me, but Jillian didn't seem to object. "Those guys were scary," she said, "but the scariest thing about them was that they didn't really seem to know what they were doing. They seemed to be flying by the seat of their pants. They chloroformed me, so I missed the first part of what happened. I woke up woozy and my head hurt but I couldn't feel it because my hands were tied behind my back. I could still smell the chloroform"—she made a face—"and I was just too tired to get up. They had blindfolded me. I knew I was in a moving car, but it wasn't dark enough for a trunk, and I was lying flat, so I assumed it was a van of some kind."

She took another bite and chewed. "I think this is the best sandwich I ever ate. But I may never eat Chinese food again."

"Then what happened?" Robbie prompted her.

"Well, then, the van broke down or something—it was really weird—and that made them edgy, and they started shouting at each other. They never said a word to me, except to order me around. And then one of them got in the back with me and put something against my head, which may have been a gun. It felt like a gun. And he said, 'No talk.' At first I was sure I was a goner. I could hear the other guy banging around in the engine. And then, for the longest time, nothing happened. This guy with the gun, or whatever it was, smelled like tobacco and sweat. Sometimes they'd trade places, and the other guy smelled exactly the same. And I smelled of Chinese food, of course. I couldn't hear any traffic sounds, or even ambulance sirens or anything. It was weird."

"Larry stopped the world today," I told her, "for more than an hour. No power. That's why you didn't hear anything."

Her eyes opened wide and she looked from Larry to Elvis. "You stopped the whole fucking world on my account?"

Larry smiled. "No, not on your account."

"We didn't even know you were missing, Jillian," Elvis said earnestly. "If we had known, we would have come sooner."

"Aww, thanks," she said, reaching out to touch him on the cheek. She took a swig of beer. "Man, I can't believe I missed it! The whole world came to a standstill, and I didn't even know it."

"Larry can do it again, if you want him to, Jillian," Elvis offered.

She grinned at him. "Let me think about it, big guy."

"So then what?" Robbie persisted.

"There's not much to tell. When they started the van up again, just like that, I figured maybe they'd fixed it after all," she said. "The guy who was on guard duty climbed out of the back and got into the front and we drove off. When they took me out, I could tell from the smell that we were in a garage, probably. They took me upstairs and locked me in the closet and that was it."

"Didn't they say anything about what they were up to?" Ginger asked with a worried frown.

"Not to me," she said.

"Ten o'clock," Paul said. "Time for *Heroes*."

A van pulled up ahead of us and about a dozen dark figures emerged. I could dimly make out the distorted profiles caused by gas masks, goggles, and weapons.

"Should I go open the door for them, Paul?" Elvis said.

"Better let them have their fun, big E," Paul said. "They love to break stuff."

We heard the sound of breaking glass as the tear gas canisters hit the front windows. We heard shouting, but couldn't make out the words, and then a faint crash that might have been the front door. More police cars and vans suddenly appeared, and the house was washed in artificial light from floodlights, as smoke billowed from the windows, reflecting the staccato red flashes of emergency lights.

It was over before the smoke had cleared. Two men, bent over, retching and rubbing their eyes, were escorted out onto the front lawn and made to lie face down while they were cuffed. Porch lights were flickering on up and down the street as curious neighbors came out to see what was going on.

"Show's over," Joe said, and started the van. "Score one for the good guys. Let's get Jillian home."

A large hand appeared before my eyes, silhouetted against the light.

"Give me six, Hank," said Elvis.

My hand burned for hours afterward.

CHAPTER THIRTY ONE

It was late. I sat on the couch between Robbie and Cisco. Larry sat in an armchair, and Elvis sat on the floor, play-wrestling with Getlo. There was only one lamp on in the living room, but the dining area, where Warren was studying, was brightly lit. Except for Warren, we were all drinking beer. But even though all of the major networks were broadcasting Larry's YouTube video, he didn't seem all that happy.

"But you pre-empted Leno and Letterman, man!" Cisco was saying, waving an arm in the direction of the television set. "Don't you know what that means? That's like—shit, I don't know. That just never happens!"

On the screen, a somber Larry sat behind something that could have been a conference table, patiently explaining what would happen if Earthlings continued to develop nuclear weapons for extraterrestrial deployment. The bogus flag of the intergalactic organization he represented was putting in another appearance on the wall behind him, its missing planet precariously reattached.

"Do you think Larry was right to sit behind the table, Hank?" Elvis asked. "They had an armchair for him, but Ginger said it looked too casual and friendly."

"Good call," I said. "He looks like a head of state."

"A head of what?" Elvis said, turning to look at me.

But I was sucking on the joint that Robbie had passed me. I'd had the impression that we were passing this joint around, and we were, but I was beginning to realize that the only people who were actually taking hits were Robbie and me.

"Hank, I hope that that drug is not bad for dogs," Elvis said, frowning.

"Tell her not to inhale," I said lazily, and passed the joint on to Cisco, who passed it to Elvis, who tried to pass it to Larry, who declined. Elvis held it suspended like a teacup in a bear's paw.

The camera zoomed in for a close-up of Larry's face, earnest and sad. He was talking about what a beautiful planet Earth was—one of the most beautiful he'd seen. A newscaster replaced him on the screen, and Cisco muted the television.

"That true, dude?" Robbie said, plucking the joint from Elvis's fingers and turning his head to look at Larry.

"It is a beautiful planet," Larry affirmed.

"Even though it only has one moon," Elvis said, "and not as many light shows as some planets."

"Yeah, but we got all that blue sky," Robbie said with an expansive gesture. "Blue oceans and green fields."

"Amber waves of grain," I put in.

"Mountains," Cisco added. "But I guess other planets have those."

"And rock and roll," Elvis said. "And dogs. Dogs are very beautiful." He stroked Getlo's ears. "But Larry's home planet is also beautiful," he said. "And it's time for us to go back."

Nobody said anything. We knew he was right.

"If he stays any longer, someone will shoot him," Elvis said.

"Or someone else will get hurt," Larry said. "We were very, very lucky with Jillian."

"We knew they might attack Larry again, but we did not expect to cause harm to innocent stand-byers," Elvis said.

"On this planet," I said, "they're usually the ones who get hurt."

Larry nodded. "I see that now. So we have to go."

"Hey, man, you did what you could," Robbie said. "The rest is up to us."

Elvis pushed his huge frame up from the floor, then bent to scoop up Getlo.

"Will you all come to see us off?" he said.

I woke up. "You mean now?"

"Yes, Hank," he said. "It's time." He held up his wrist, pointed to his watch, and grinned at me.

Larry stood as well, looking more rumpled and weary than I'd ever seen him look. He read my expression—well, probably he read my mind. "I'll rest once we're under way," he said. "And besides—," he said, and paused.

This time I read his mind. "You're going home."

CHAPTER THIRTY TWO

"Would you like us to drop you off in Indiana, Hank?" Elvis offered. "Or will you stay and help Jillian with the police?" He gave me a sly smile. It was lit by the ship's running lights, which reflected off the trees and gave the clearing a soft glow.

I crossed my arms over my chest and smiled back. "I guess I'll stay for a while."

"I told you that we would find a dolly for you in Washington, D.C.," he said.

Robbie threw his arms around Larry and said huskily, "Now, I don't ever want to see you back here, you old son of a gun," he said. "If we don't make it—well, just think of me as a million specks of space dust, floating through the galaxy."

"But Robbie," Elvis said, "you will not really be destroyed. We can only destroy your body, and—." Words failed him and he looked to Larry for help.

"We can only destroy physical things," Larry said. I could have sworn that his own eyes were glinting in the soft glow. "We can't destroy their essence."

"Good to know," Robbie said. "In that case, maybe some day my essence will pay a call on your essence, over there on the other side of the universe."

"I'd like that," Larry said.

Elvis held Getlo in the crook of his arm, stroking her ears. "Hank will be a very good friend to you, little Getlo," he said to her. With a sigh, he handed her to me. She seemed to grasp the solemnity of the occasion, and for once lay docile in my arms.

"Are you sure?" I said.

"Dogs are not made for space," he said. "She would miss the Earth."

He put his arms around both of us. I expected a crushing embrace to match the pressure on my heart, but instead, I felt enveloped in gentle, pulsating warmth that melted away every ache in my heart, my head, my body. My bones evaporated. I felt disembodied, as if, for just an instant, my soul expanded from a point of light in the middle of my chest and radiated until it filled the unimaginable vastness of the universe. Then it collapsed again, returning me to a physical body that felt wholly peaceful.

Elvis stepped back. "Later, gator," he said, and blinked.

Larry was already turning toward the descending ramp.

As I watched, a caterpillar shadow bobbed against the light-flooded incline, slowly making its way down. Larry bent to retrieve it, set it to one side, turned, smiled and waved.

Elvis didn't look back.

We watched while the ship swallowed the last of his silhouette, and then the ramp itself. We watched while it rose gracefully against the starry sky, its lights dimming until the stars glittered behind it. We watched it glide past the moon and grow smaller and fainter until it faded into the sky, leaving only the winking stars.

CHAPTER THIRTY THREE

I know you're not waiting for me to tell you whether Earth survived. It's still here. But as Robbie keeps reminding us, "Time works differently in outer space," which is his way of saying that we're not out of the woods yet.

I'm not optimistic myself, not about the future of the planet. Even under the threat of global annihilation, people continue to wage war, usually for no better reason than to secure the oil that will probably burn the planet to a cinder long before the extraterrestrial destroyers arrive. There are other reasons, of course, including the elevation of one peace-loving god above another. Christ, the revenge wars begin to seem like the most rational ones around. And meanwhile, in bunkered secret laboratories around the world, blinkered scientists and engineers are no doubt working hard on an extra-planetary deployment system for our deadliest weapons, the global freeze a memory insubstantial as vapor.

Contemplating all the ways in which we're trying to destroy our own planet kind of makes you root for extraterrestrial annihilation. It would probably cause less general misery in the short run, and in the long run—well, Robbie's image of space dust drifting off to find the boundaries of the Big Bang appeals to my imagination.

They were right, our space pals, to be worried about what would happen next. Larry would certainly have been shot dead again within the week. In fact, the morning after he left, a man armed with an assault rifle was arrested in the hotel lobby. He belonged to a neo-fascist organization that had raised $3,452. 27 to reward an assassin and hide him after the mission was accomplished.

"Twenty-seven fucking cents!" Robbie shook his head in wonderment when he heard the story. "What's that about? Some kid gave his milk money?"

And they were right, too, about the innocent bystanders. We Earthlings are not the kind of people to exempt innocents from our bloodlettings. Fifteen days after the spacemen departed, a deranged Korean immigrant, who happened to be an English major, gunned down thirty-two random victims on the campus at Virginia Tech. I was glad in a way that I wouldn't have to explain it to Elvis.

I'm not trying to depress you. I wouldn't do that. Like Robbie, I was changed by my alien encounter, and left with an inexplicable, irrational hopefulness about things—well, extraplanetary. The whole enchilada, as Robbie calls it. The whole grimtigrog.

I took a leave from grad school, but I doubt that I'll ever go back. For one thing, I can no longer think about my field of expertise as anything except "semenotics," and that has its down side.

Robbie found me a place to live—a house shared by two musicians, a law student, and an intern at GW Hospital. They all like Jillian, and she likes them. Getlo likes all of the resident creatures, including the dog, three cats, ferret and parrot. Eco likes his new fire escape and, to my surprise, Getlo, who worships him.

Jillian and I have a comfortable relationship. We spend a lot of time together. We eat out, go for walks, or just stay home and cook and watch old Elvis Presley movies.

I live off the advance I've been paid for this book—a staggering amount, if you ask me, that quadruples my annual income. And I didn't really want to write this book, not really, but Robbie talked me into it.

"People are curious, man," he'd said. "Nothing wrong with that. They should be curious. And you're the one to tell them all about Larry and Elvis and their mission, and how fucking *real* they were, you know?"

"What about you?" I'd said. "You've known them longer than I have."

He shook his head. "I'm no writer, dude. You are. You got to make things clear, man, and beautiful at the same time—the way it was with them. You're the one." After a minute, he said, "Besides, what these publishing guys are offering you ain't chump change, bro.

Take it, and use it as a down payment on your new life. What the hell?"

"Well, will you help?"

He looked surprised, even touched. Then he slapped me on the back. "Sure, I'll help."

"Then I'll pay you as a consultant," I said.

"A consultant," he'd echoed. "Far out. Never been one of those before."

As I said, it's not the book I wanted to write; I don't feel adequate to the task. But lately I've been thinking more about the books I do want to write, now that this one's almost finished. I feel like I've spent a lifetime staring at my shoelaces, and overlooked the rest of the universe.

It could happen to anybody, Robbie says. In fact, it happens to almost everybody.

Now, I sit at my desk late at night, looking out the window past the trees and the clouds, past the moon even, and I begin to get a glimmer of what Adam and Eve felt when they were forced from the narrow confines of Eden after all of those conversations with God, when *the world was all before them*—and the next world, and the next world, and the next.

ABOUT THE AUTHOR

D. B. Borton teaches English at a Midwestern liberal arts college. She has published eleven mystery novels in two series, the Cat Caliban series and the Gilda Liberty series. As an academic writer she has published work on film, women's ghost stories, and girl detectives. To join Borton's mailing list and receive notices about her new work, please visit her website at www.dbborton.com.

www.ingramcontent.com/pod-product-compliance
Lightning Source LLC
Chambersburg PA
CBHW050315110726
47899CB00007B/2248